Sara Anna Marsh

Maidenhood

Vol. 1

Sara Anna Marsh

Maidenhood
Vol. 1

ISBN/EAN: 9783337366520

Printed in Europe, USA, Canada, Australia, Japan

Cover: Foto ©Andreas Hilbeck / pixelio.de

More available books at **www.hansebooks.com**

MAIDENHOOD.

BY

MRS. SARA ANNA MARSH,

AUTHOR OF

"CHRONICLES OF DARTMOOR,"

&c., &c.

" Maidens should be mild and meek,
Swift to hear and slow to speak."

IN THREE VOLUMES.

VOL. I.

LONDON:
HURST AND BLACKETT, PUBLISHERS,
SUCCESSORS TO HENRY COLBURN,
13, GREAT MARLBOROUGH STREET.
1867.

LONDON:

PRINTED BY MACDONALD AND TUGWELL, BLENHEIM HOUSE,

BLENHEIM STREET, OXFORD STREET.

TO

MY DEAR NIECES—

CATHARINE JANE AND MARY GRACE CHRISTIAN ;

AND ALSO

TO MY DEAR GODCHILDREN—

AMY SOPHIA,

KATHARINE ALEXANDRA,

AND

MILDRED.

INTRODUCTORY.

"DO, my girl, try and give us a story without a villain. I assure you I never saw a villain. I am bound to believe such creatures exist, but I am as sure as I am that I hold this pen, that the greatest amount of real suffering in life is not produced by villainy. Life is made up of two elements—an element of will and an element of fatality. The misery which is struck out in the conflict, or rather the interaction of the two, has usually for its apparent and efficient excuse the misunderstandings of people of average —and sometimes more than average—goodness.

"Let me earnestly dissuade you from writing a novel of the *detective* order. A long sensation story, whose movement is carried forward stage by stage, puzzle after puzzle, in the manner of a detective officer playing the novelist, and to leave on the mind, even of any one who has been entertained by it, a strong emotion of disgust. It *must* do so if it makes its way for any length of time among the domesticities," &c.—*From Henry Holbeach, Student in Life and Philosophy.*

CHAPTER I.

WE will not write a chapter on bells, and the
impressions they make on susceptible or
even on passionless natures; we shall content
ourselves by saying that the bells rang merrily
from the old church-tower of Prellsthorpe, and
the listeners thereto were very variably influenced
thereby.

"Our time will be taken up with dinners, balls,
visitings here and there, and goodness only knows
for what!" murmured the learned Rector of Prellsthorpe, as he paced with his hands behind him,
backwards and forwards through the shrubberies.
"And I do not think those very sweet bells ever
sounded so wearisome or so discordant to mine
ear."

There were at the same time two fair girls in
the flower-garden, and they also made their remarks on the same subject.

"How glad and playful the bells are to-night,"
said Brenda Cheetham, the Rector's daughter.

"How merry and joyous!" said the Lady Grel Stuart. "I love bells, Brenda, they are almost like human beings, they seem to tell us so much— and they are indeed jocund and exultant now. Listen, Brenda, listen!"

The girls stood for a moment or two in motion-less silence, then the stillness was broken by the Lady Grel, who said :

" Yet sometimes, Brenda, these same bells weep —positively weep."

" That is pure nonsense, Grel. They are always glad, and happy-sounding, and mirthful to me," said Brenda Cheetham—" only excepting the lugubrious time of ' tolling, tolling.' "

" Hush, Brenda !—do not mingle a sorrowful omen with joy-bells."

Brenda Cheetham did not reply. She was oc-cupied in trying to bring into order the vigorous and lengthy trailing shoots of choice Ayrshire roses that grew in that part of the garden, and the Lady Grel walked on alone.

"I cannot quite restrain my delight at the knowledge that my relatives are indeed at Prells-thorpe Park—even in Brenda Cheetham's pre-sence this joyfulness on my part will peep out ; gladness—gladness and joy of heart make me an-ticipate a future happy career—that I shall now enter the world—that I shall not always live here in this quiet Rectory."

And, in spite of some reproach of conscience as

to her desire to leave a place that had always been a home and a haven of rest to her, she moved rapidly from one path to another, skipping now here now there, in a pleasurable state of excitement, now touching this flower, now that, gathering here one and there one, inhaling their combined sweetness, and still listening—listening to the bells pealing merrily on.

"I could dance—positively dance gleefully at the ever-recurring chime of those gay joy-bells! How glad they are, nay, how merrily clanging; there is not a single tear—no, not one!" and again the Lady Grel paused and listened.

Had she been as learned as ourselves who write her veracious history, perhaps she had not uttered the next sentence we have to record from her lips. We know that moisture in the atmosphere produces an effect upon the sound of bells, in some instances and in some low localities, so to lower the tone of each bell as to make the peal sound more of a minor than a major octave; and the unlearned, and, in this matter, superstitiously-minded Lady Grel Stuart, records this fact in the following speech:

"Why, the very last marriage-peal rung from that belfry was a weeping, weeping chime! And where is the bride now?"

In some counties the old crones in the villages say, " The bells are crying—the marriage will not be a happy one." We conclude the Lady Grel had been brought up in this lore.

"I have no remembrance of my uncle and aunt," resumed she, "and but little of Irene and Danby—it must be some nine or ten years since we met." Then, after a little pause, her thoughts again turned to the bells. "There again—there again," said she, "the joyously clamouring peal. Those sweet bells, those learned bells! They foretell happy meetings, heartfelt greetings, dancing and song, hearths and homes, hope and love— I know it and feel it—I feel it. Ye bells, oh! ye bells, ye sportive bells, ye make me glad and merrie-hearted! Ah! I am formed for companionship, not for isolation.

"If anyone could read my thoughts," continued she, musingly—"if they could see into my desires, and look upon me thus elated, they might wrongly interpret my character. I have been happy here in this peaceful Rectory—I love and reverence my kind and excellent tutor and guardian, Mr. Cheetham, and also I love and esteem Mrs. Cheetham. For Brenda, though I feel and know she and I are very different, yet while we have been together we have agreed well enough—or perhaps, I should say, we do not quarrel. It is rather change of companionship than actual distaste for my present position—rather a longing for novelty, and, also, rather a wish to enter that far-off world my cousin Irene describes so charmingly in her letters, than a desire to forget these, my kind friends, under whose hospitable roof I have lived so peaceably."

But the lady's further musings were interrupted by the appearance of Mrs. Cheetham, who said :

" How these bells do weary me ! "

" Then, indeed, I do wish they would stop," said Lady Grel, raising her eyes to the belfry ; and, to her amazement, suddenly, as she spoke, the clamour ceased.

" Now, if every wish of my dear ward's could be answered as quickly and as favourably as this," said the Rector, who now joined the ladies.

" You would consider it highly proper to counsel me always to wish for things good in themselves—ay, so good, that the attainment of them should neither do harm to me nor to others. Now, do not shake your head so mysteriously ; you know you consider it a duty to counsel me," said the Lady Grel, playfully.

" A privilege—indeed, a privilege which, I fear, will soon be taken from me. We shall lose our sweet ward ; she longs for the grand and the gay. Already she——"

" Hush !—hush !" said the Lady Grel, deprecatingly—" I know I wish to see the world—I know I rejoice that my own relatives will dwell so near to this Rectory, and I acknowledge my inward happiness, and my aspiring hopefulness. But if you, my dear sir, or, indeed, if any here think I shall leave my present pleasurable and tranquil home without regret, they are mistaken. Indeed, as you know, I still intend to make this residence my real home, though I admit I wish to know more of the world at large. I pray you, think not ill of me," and here the young lady stepped back a little from the group, which now consisted of Mr. and Mrs. Cheetham and Brenda, and her figure dilated, and her eye kindled, as she continued, in eager and hurried tones : " Here the very stones speak to me of the past—the past, that delights me to remember, and to dwell upon ; there," and she raised her arm, and pointed in the direction of Prellsthorpe Park, " the ground is untrodden ; it may—and I trust it will—bring companionship, peace, and love, but it has no enduring past. Here I have truth, nature, reality, kind friends, and affectionate hearts—these I have proved. There, I have relations and novelty, a new and unaccustomed routine of my daily life ; it is the untried freshness that brings the charm."

" The dews are heavy—we will not remain longer in the open air," said the good Rector, approaching his ward, taking her kindly by the hand, and drawing her arm through his own, as he left the garden, followed by Mrs. Cheetham and Brenda.

The Reverend Charles John Cheetham had been tutor to the late Earl of Prellsthorpe, who, on coming to the title, had taken the earliest opportunity of bestowing one of the many livings in his gift upon his friend, and who was all the better pleased that the living of Prellsthorpe fell so opportunely, since it would be the means of continuing to him the society of a gentleman for whom he had a strong personal regard.

The late Earl was a man of letters. Left a widower with an only child, and mourning the loss of his Countess deeply, he retired prematurely from the world, in which he had hitherto lived with so much honour to himself, and took refuge in a life of quiet study in the country, his only companions his baby daughter and Mr. Cheetham, then residing at the Rectory. If he ever felt a regret that this child was a girl, and, consequently, could never succeed him in his titles, and the wealth belonging to them, he, at least, never expressed so much. He was ardently attached to her in her babyhood, and saw more of her infantine doings, and heard more of her childish sayings, than most fathers. Delighting in the literature of the day as well as in that of past ages, enjoying the society of learned men, and yet, by his early loss in his Countess, debarred for a time from entering the world, his great and well-stored mind turned for relaxation to the pretty sayings and doings of his little daughter, Grel.

At about the age of five years the little lady was consigned to the care of the first Mrs. Cheetham for one hour each day, this lady undertaking her education jointly with that of her own daughter, Brenda.

Lord Prellsthorpe had never been of a vigorous constitution, and whether from his great love of, and devotion to, literature, or his rather unwise and lengthened seclusion, or his grief for the loss of his lady, or for all these causes together, or for any other cause, certain it is his health gradually declined, and he became aware he should not live to see his little child grow to womanhood.

He consigned her, in the event of his death—which happened shortly after—to the guardianship and protection of his friend, Mr. Cheetham, to be brought up by him in the bosom of his own family, with his own and only daughter. The Earl was not an ambitious man. He did not stipulate that at a given period his high-born child should enter the walks of fashion and take her place among her equals. She was under the entire control of Mr. Cheetham until her eighteenth year. The Earl had only a moderate personalty to bestow upon her, and if at the time of his death, as the daughter of a nobleman of high rank, the young lady's portion was not large, in the strict integrity of her guardian, and her own somewhat long minority, her wealth had nearly doubled; and on her coming of age at eighteen, she would not longer be regarded as a portionless, if those of her own rank did not consider her a rich young lady. At the opening of this chronicle the Lady Grel had passed her seventeenth birthday. Prellsthorpe Park had been uninhabited from the time of the death of the late Earl. His brother, the present peer, after consigning his relative to the family vault, made over the dwelling-house to the care of servants. His time since

that period had been spent for the most part in
occasional sojourns in the various capitals of
Europe, though this was not so much by his own
wish as by that of his lady, who was a great invalid, and dependent on a large circle of acquaint-
ance for her daily amusement, and who delighted
in the change from one place to another.

Early in the London season of the year 18—,
this lady had been recommended by her medical
attendant to try the bracing air of Prellsthorpe,
and to put herself under the care of a physician of
repute in that neighbourhood, a Dr. Quinn.   This
advice she had very reluctantly followed, but life
is dear to all, and, reassured by the promise that
Lord Prellsthorpe and her son and daughter would
leave London for her sake, and take up their residence in the country, she at length consented to
abide by the opinions of her physicians.

And thus it happened that the Lady Grel
Stuart was in expectation of meeting with her
nearest relatives, and of having a change in the
ordinary routine of her life.

Another death caused a great sorrow for the
time being at Prellsthorpe Rectory—Mrs. Cheetham died soon after Lord Prellsthorpe.   In the
course of a year or two her place was filled by the
present Mrs. Cheetham, already introduced to the
reader.

It is true, as we have recorded, that Lord Danby
and the Lady Irene Stuart had consented to accompany their invalid · mother to Prellsthorpe

Park, but their ideas of country life were widely at variance with such, as they very early discovered it to be at this season of the year. "The country" in their experience meant large baronial or ducal residences, filled with the nobility and gentry of the land, with a change in the usual routine of their amusements—riding to cover with a pleasant party instead of the Bois de Boulogne, &c.; but to retire to the country to hear the cuckoo, when London was fast filling, was almost too much for their patience. The lady mourned over London lost to her for this season, at least; and the gentleman wondered if the month of August would ever arrive, or if it could even be possible to live until grouse-shooting commenced, at which time he might hope to flee from the wearisomeness and tameness of Prellsthorpe to better employment and more congenial society.

"I yawn whenever I turn my eyes around this heavy saloon; do not you, D.?" said the lady.

"I do not so much care for the heavy and faded furniture as I do for faces—faces, Irene—human faces. If one had only some stupid girl to tease, or some pretty one to please, the house and its sombreness might do well enough. Heigho! Ren—Ren, I say, what on earth shall I do with myself?"

"What shall *I* do, D.? Wood says there is not a living creature within twenty miles, excepting only the stupid old Rector and his wife, who have had our cousin Grel all these years; and a Mr.

Hamilton, a recluse—a bookworm, a sort of dignified stolid old bachelor, who goes nowhere, sees nobody, and—I daresay does nothing."

"Then I will give him something to do. Where does he live, Ren? Tell me, and I will play off upon him a few practical jokes, that may serve for the time being to amuse me, and—and help to enliven him. Ha! ha!—ha! the very thought raises my spirits!"

"You remember Prellsthorpe Abbey?"

"Yes, Ren. The old sinner lives there, does he? But your information is not entirely to be relied upon. There is a wonderful old gentleman living at Heraldstowe; he is as old as the hills, and there are other marvellous human beings on that side of the Park. Let me explain to you, Ren. The village of Prellsthorpe and the Rectory are on one side of the Park; the Abbey, with its grounds, on the other. And on the same side as the Abbey, but some miles distant, dwell sundry neighbours of different degrees of rank.

"Then we shall not have much to do with that stupid and stony village, D.?"

"Only to drive through it when we wish to visit on that side of the county; but the best people live on the other side."

"And who are the best people?"

"The Barrymores of Heraldstowe; the Fortescues; and the great Catholic Maynooths of Wolfscraig. When I was here some six or seven years ago, I became intimate with several first-rate speci-

mens of dulness belonging to these families. We
will look them up in due time, Ren, amuse ourselves, and sharpen their wits somewhat."

"They must look us up, D.," said the lady
yawning.

"But now that I look into that past, say seven
years since, I recall my cousin Grel's sweet face.
Ren, suppose we go to the Rectory, and so take a
peep at Grel. She will turn out a queer little
countrified dot, no doubt. When I saw her last,
Ren, she was growing up after the pattern of the
Cheethams, round, and dumpy, nothing of the
Stuart in her; her sweet face soured by rustic
learning, her high birth lowered by consorting with
strange individuals. A smile would be a boon to
your features at this moment, Ren; but we shall
enjoy a hearty laugh if we only look up Grel:
come, Irene, come?"

"Nonsense, D., the Rectory ought to come to
the Park. And besides, 1 hate walking, and I
could not walk so far if I made the attempt."

"True, Ren, true. The Rectory ought to come
to the Park; but Rectories do not always as they
ought, and in this instance it is a little too early
to expect even a Rectory to make a call upon a
Park. Ah! ah! ah! do you not know, Ren, that
the Rectory sent to inquire after the Park? And
a long reply was concocted between the excellent
butler and the gracious housekeeper belonging to
this establishment here, to the purport, 'That my
lady was very ill with the effects of the journey,

that Dr. Quinn had desired her ladyship to keep her room ; that my young lord and my young lady were very tired, and quite unused to such trouble-some journeys,' &c., &c.—and upon these crumbs the Rectory will naturally subsist for a day or two longer, if we do not break in upon their dreams. And so, Ken, if the Park goes to the Rectory at so critical a time, only imagine the astonishment of the natives! How they will be taken aback! How very wide they will open their surpassingly ugly eyes! Do not say me nay, Irene ; I will drive you. It will be something to do."

"It will surely turn out stupid, D."

"It will surely release us from our present stupidity. Come, Irene, come, rouse yourself; you will die of the malady of yawns, if I do not rescue you by this drive. I shall ring for my horses."

CHAPTER II.

" FOLLY IS THE PRODUCT OF ALL COUNTRIES AND AGES."

"HAVE you seen Mr. Hamilton, mamma ? " said Brenda Cheetham. "He called about half an hour ago, and said if he did not meet with you in the village he would call again."

"No, love, I have not seen him. In all proba-bility he wanted to make some arrangement for the school-feast. Was that it ?"

"Oh! no! I ventured to hint as much, but he pooh-poohed me in his usual manner."

"Nonsense, Brenda. He is an ex——"

"My dear mother, Mr. Hamilton will not be without a supporter while you live, although he does pooh-pooh your daughter most abominably."

"Is that the Mr. Hamilton who has lately arrived in this neighbourhood?" said the lady Grel.

"Lately arrived, my dear," said Brenda mockingly.

"He is an excellent well-meaning and gentlemanly man, my dear," said Mrs. Cheetham, "and if he would only marry, there might be a nice lady companion at the Abbey for you and Brenda, as well as for our new comers at the Park."

"We must send again to inquire for your relatives, Grel," continued she; "I fear the journey has been very trying to the Countess."

"And he is not married," said the lady Grel, referring to Mr. Hamilton; "why, I really thought he was a staid father of a family."

"Looks staid, Grel," said Brenda again mockingly; "and is not married, at least to the best of our knowledge in these parts. Only think, dear Grel, that very dignified, very excellent, very handsome, and certainly 'staid' Mr. Hamilton has never loved!—proof, not married!"

"Never to love, and never to marry, are two things, Brenda; not married is no proof of not loving," said Grel.

Brenda elevated her eyebrows, and stooped her head in the attitude of listening.

"And yet it is true, a man may love without even intending to marry; and also marry without being in love," said Grel, replying to Brenda's attitude.

"Is it possible!—the base creature!" said Brenda, affecting to discredit Grel's remarks.

"But I, as a woman," resumed Grel, not at all seeing that Brenda was drawing out her opinions on this subject—"I, as a woman, determine——"

Now the expression of Brenda's face arrested her attention, and she suddenly ceased speaking.

"Determine what, Grel, dear?" said Brenda, in a more agreeable tone and manner, which together reassured Grel, and gave her courage to finish the sentence.

"I determine, Brenda, that I will not marry unless I love most devotedly. I cannot say I will not love unless I marry, because, you see, it might happen that——"

Grel again paused, and blushed, and Brenda resumed:

"Charmingly sentimental, my dear, and I only wish that 'staid' Mr. Hamilton heard you."

"Hush, Brenda!—hush!" said Grel, her brow and cheeks crimsoning with annoyance—"I was only talking a little nonsense with you, and was not thinking of Mr. Hamilton."

"My dear girls, do not quarrel on such foolish matters," said Mrs. Cheetham, "and more espe-

cially now, for is not that the Prellsthorpe livery?"
—she pointed to the open window.

The surprise and conjectures of the three ladies
at the sight of a carriage from the Park were
speedily put an end to by the announcement of
Lord Danby and the Lady Irene Stuart.

" My dear Irene!—how very kind!" said Grel,
approaching her cousin with *empressement*.

" Kind!—to be sure—very kind. Did we not
know Mrs. Cheetham's kindness was perennial?"
said Lord Danby, purposely perverting the meaning of his cousin's words. " Were we not sure
she would receive old friends at any hour?"
continued he, as he retained Mrs. Cheetham's
hand, and stooped to her in a friendly manner;
when she attempted to speak, he interrupted her
by saying, " Not a word, my dear madam—
your tongue is of no value to you," and he gently
pressed her hand in a kind manner, " for your
eyes are windows, by the means of which we read
your heart, and we there discover that we are
welcome. I see even more—I see that you not
only forgive the rashness of this unearthly-houred
intrusion; but more still—even that you have
forgotten and forgiven the boyish follies of your
very devoted friend, Danby."

" Indeed, I am truly glad to see you again,"
said Mrs. Cheetham.

" I know you are—say no more—say no more.
Here, Irene," continued he, as he transferred the
hand he had persisted in retaining to his sister—

" this is *the* Mistress Cheetham, the benevolent, of
whom you have so frequently heard me speak.
Take her to your heart—she is worthy thereof ;"
and then, turning to Mrs. Cheetham, and changing his mockingly-playful manner to one of mock
solemnity, he said : " This, madam, is my very
beautiful sister, the Lady Irene Stuart, commonly
called Ren."

Mrs. Cheetham turned to the Lady Irene, and
said all that was necessary on so auspicious an occasion.   When the two ladies had seated themselves,
Lord Danby turned to Brenda Cheetham, who
had been standing looking on, with an expression
of astonishment in her countenance, and said :

" I am Ren's brother, Danby—pray who are
you ?"

" Your long and eccentric speeches, and
unusual mode of proceeding, have so terrified me,
I shall have a difficulty in remembering my own
name, thus suddenly called upon," said Brenda,
mockingly.

" Then we will graciously allow your ladyship
time to recover your self-possession," said Lord
Danby, with a low bow, " and give our attention,
for the time being, to our very charming cousin,
Grel," continued he, as he approached Lady Grel,
and offered his hand.

" What a love Grel has grown !" said the Lady
Irene to Mrs. Cheetham.

" A love, Ren—a perfect love ! And now it is
all up with me !" said Lord Danby—" curious,

Ren, is it not?" continued he, as he retained the Lady Grel's hand, and turned to his sister. " I *would* come and see her. Bear witness, Ren, was I not eager to come?"

" Indeed you were," said Lady Irene, laughing. But she did not explain that Lord Danby's eagerness arose from the desire to have " some stupid girl to tease, or some pretty one to please."

" Yes, I insisted upon breaking through all rules of etiquette, and following the dictates of our hearts ; and it turns out I came to take note of the wondrous improvement these last few years have wrought," and Lord Danby seated himself by Grel's side, still retaining her hand.

" I am glad you came so kindly," said Grel, with a smile and a bright blush.

" To be sure you are. Always speak the truth, Grel, in spite of the example of fashion. Perhaps you do. And you surely perceive that I am the very quintessence of plain-speaking ?" And then he stooped, and said, in soft, low tones—" I love you, Grel."

Grel started and blushed, and turned away without speaking.

" I love you, and I shall take you for my own," said he again, in low tones, which were only heard by Grel.

Lord Danby was amusing himself with his cousin's simplicity.

" You must have my consent first," said Grel, with some spirit, blushing still more ; and yet, in spite of herself, feeling flattered by her cousin's attentions.

" That is very easily gained, for no lady would dream of refusing me—would she, my Lady Thorhilda ?"

Lord Danby had turned to Brenda Cheetham.

" I say my cousin Grel may go farther and fare worse. Now, what say you to that, my Lady Thorhilda ?" said he, again addressing Brenda Cheetham.

" I quite agree with you, my lord," said Brenda, mimicking so exactly Lord Danby's manner, as to cause the lookers-on to smile.

" You quite agree with me !" said Lord Danby in a tone of surprise, and fixing his eye on Brenda; " and I quite agree with myself, that I can bring back to your terrified-away memory the knowledge of your own name ! I thought *I* had some recollection of you, though you were unable to remember yourself," said he, laughing. " You are Brenda Cheetham. Oh ! Brenda, Brenda, short-memoried Brenda, recall the past !—recall those days, nay, *that* day—that very day ! Why, Brenda, you pulled the rosy-checked apple from between my very teeth, and said I had stolen it from the favourite tree in your favourite garden. And so I had. But, Miss Brenda, it is my turn now. I am come to make good my residence at Prellsthorpe Park. I shall henceforth be one of your nearest neighbours—will not I visit that bitter-sweet past upon you !" continued he, holding up his finger; while Brenda Cheetham, by her blushes, seemed to acknowledge the truth of the accusation, and, by her smiles, to take pleasure in Lord Danby's notice. She was sitting by the open window, and at this moment turned to reply to some one who had spoken to her from the lawn.

Then she said to Mrs. Cheetham,

"Mamma, Mr. Hamilton wishes to speak to you."

"Perhaps you will excuse me?" said Mrs. Cheetham, as she left the room.

"Is that the Mr. Hamilton of Prellsthorpe Abbey?" said Lady Irene.

"Yes; your nearest neighbour at the Park," said Brenda.

"Why, Grel, you blush as if Mr. Hamilton were somebody of consequence in your eyes," said Lord Danby in a whisper. "Tell me, is he a favourite?"

"I do not know him," said Grel; but she knew that the mention of his name had disturbed her, because it recalled the conversation she and Brenda had had before the arrival of her cousins. Grel had been so accustomed to hear Mr. Hamilton spoken highly of by both Mr. and Mrs. Cheetham, that she was quite prepared to think well of him herself when she did meet with him, and admire him as much as she durst admire a handsome man who had never once spoken to her. Lord Danby sat for a second or two scrutinizing his cousin with keen eyes, and then he said,

"What sort of creature is he?"

"One to excite your pity; for some foolish people make a great lion of him, because he has some ten or twenty thousand a year," said Brenda.

"Is it possible!" said Lord Danby. "Now, which do you wish me to pity, for I am not clear on the subject—the foolish people, or the great lion?"

"Mrs. Cheetham thinks most highly of him, and he is certainly a good man!" said the Lady Grel.

"Good according to the times, Grel," said Brenda; "and these are wonderful times. No one can be called good now-a-days who does not build schools, cram the poor children with knowledge they cannot understand, and the fathers and mothers on beef and beer on high-days and holidays; who does not give yearly doles of blankets to every cottage in the village, and loads of coal and faggots of wood to make each cottage-fire burn; and, after all this, even barrels of meal and bags of potatoes to keep life in the bodies of these our hard-worked and hardly-treated peasantry!"

"And Mr. Hamilton does all this with his twenty or thirty thousand a year?" said Lady Irene. "And what else, for a man who does so much must surely do more?"

"Restore the church, of course," said Brenda laughing; "and equally, of course, give two or three bells, by way of pulling down the old tower.

And then he builds soup kitchens, and fills them with soup; and baths and wash-houses, all for the poor; and—and I told mamma one day I half expected he would not finish until he had lodged them all in his grand old Abbey."

"Lodged all whom?" said Lord Danby in a voice of consternation. "Do you mean lodge the poor?"

"Yes, the poor. You need not be so astonished," said Brenda; "there are not more than two hundred in the whole parish, and the Abbey contains I cannot tell how many beds, but surely quite enough for our village."

"A very original idea: I commend you for it, Brenda the marvellous!" said Lord Danby.

"Now, if he would only lodge all the poor for a month or so in his grand old Abbey, there can be little doubt but that he would have done enough to make himself famous, and he might then quietly repose upon his laurels for the remainder of his charitable life!"

"Brenda!—Brenda! you are the most satirically amusing young lady it has ever been my good fortune to meet," said Lord Danby, laughing.

"He never goes to balls, or races, or any places of amusement, I suppose?" said the Lady Irene.

"Do not tell her, Brenda—do not tell her," said Lord Danby. "Ren is making up her mind to the best way of spreading her nets to catch the lion, and of course if he does not dance Ren will eschew balls; so do not tell her."

"I will tell you all I know," said Brenda, turn-

ing to the Lady Irene, "and give you my powerful
help.   He dances well, and at the last Prellsthorpe
ball——"

"Prellsthorpe ball!" said Lord Danby, starting
up.   "Do you mean sincerely that this horrible
Prellsthorpe village gets up a ball?"

"Indeed, yes, on especial occasions," said
Brenda laughing.   "The last was got up by the
Rifles, and Mr. Hamilton danced with all the old
maids in the room!—yes, all the well-known wall-
flowers—all the very, very old maids who had not
been asked——"

"Patience, patience, I can bear no more!" said
Lord Danby, affecting to stop his ears.

"Asked to dance," resumed Brenda, "within
the memory of man; and who were very much
puzzled what answer to make in the first place,
what steps to make in the second, and to know
what to do with the honour thus forced upon them
in the third."

"He did not dance with charming Brenda, the
satirical?" said Lord Danby.

"He anticipated my refusal, and did not ask
me," said Brenda, quietly.   "No, no, I confess it,
he did *not* ask me to dance; and he is often uncivil to me.   But the Rifles had got up a bazaar,
to be followed by a ball, to meet expenses of some
kind, and that was the real reason for a ball in
Prellsthorpe.   Yes, he is uncivil to me!"

"Uncivil to you!—what can he mean?" said
Lord Danby.

"He tells my mother I do not help her enough in visiting the poor; and he avers he often sees me enjoying a ride on my pony."

"Wicked little Brenda, the marvellous; why do not you ride over him?" said Lord Danby.

"He thinks me 'as full of faults as an egg is full of meat.' I differ from him on that point," said Brenda. "I think he has no business with my faults or my perfections; and I just toss my— as you, of course, would say—'very pretty head,' and do as I please."

"Excuse me, indeed you are wrong," said Lord Danby; "I should not call your head 'very pretty,' or even pretty."

"The greater the proof that it is so," said Brenda, demurely.

"Ah! you forget my talent for truth," said Lord Danby.

"It seems to me, Mr. Hamilton is certainly good and charitably disposed," said Lady Irene.

"He will do. Will he, Ren?" said Lord Danby. "Bashfulness is not one of Ren's faults. Now, it would not surprise me if Ren attracted this great lion from——"

"From lesser stars," said Brenda. "Ah! when you have seen as much of him as I, you will be glad to resign him."

"Irene thinks fifty thousand a year worth having," said Lord Danby, laughing.

"Ten thousand, D.," said Grel, correctively.

"Most modest cousin. Ren would spoil the

shape of her nose at the thought of so paltry a sum," said Lord Danby.

The lady Grel looked puzzled, but did not reply.

"Fifty thousand would be worth the consideration of most ladies," said Lady Irene.

"Well, then, Ren, what say you? Miss Brenda is willing to resign the lion—Grel must have nothing to do with him—that is on my account," added he, *sotto voce*, to Grel; "and you require amusement. Suppose, now, by way of attracting the notice of the lion, you commit yourself to a few absurdities, such as 'clothing' and 'firing' a few old women."

"Yes," said Lady Irene, now laughing heartily, "a few old women, D.; and so curry favour with this great lion, Miss Cheetham."

"You and Grel are not very likely to try to curry favour with anyone," said Brenda, mockingly; "and yet, as I gaze upon you, the fact seems to strike me that you will both interest this very fastidious Mr. Hamilton."

"Oh! Grel, Grel, do not smile and plume yourself on your attractions—you are mine," said Lord Danby.

"Mr. Hamilton has not condescended yet to notice Grel; he visits his old Abbey once or twice a year for about ten days or a fortnight; and, hitherto, something has happened to keep Grel out of the way," said Brenda.

"Quite right. The fates knew she was meant

for me," said Lord Danby. "You see, Brenda, Grel is not sufficiently wicked to attract his notice. She rides *her* pony too well to call down his censure. Is it not so, Grel, the very beautiful?"

"I have not seen Mr. Hamilton three times, D., nor spoken to him once," said Grel, blushing brightly.

"But, then, Brenda, knowing there was in this neighbourhood such a person as Mr. Hamilton," said Lord Danby, "who sees to everything, takes care of everybody, asks the old maids, poor things, soups, coals, meats, breads, potatoes, blankets, baths, and washes the poor; and that he does all this work in ten days or a fortnight, and then hies himself away to commit greater marvels in other places,—I say, knowing as you do of this gentleman's residence at Prellsthorpe for the time being, why do not you lay up your pony in clover, pull a very long face out of that very round, rosy-cheeked one, and allow the lion to catch you in a dirty cottage now and then?"

"Because I choose to make my visits to the poor when Mr. Hamilton is out of sight and out of hearing; and I also choose to ride my pony every day while he is at the Abbey, to give him the pleasure of seeing how entirely I abide by his opinion."

"You are the most amiable and original young lady I have had the pleasure of meeting for many a long year," said Lord Danby, rising, as he saw Lady Irene taking leave of Grel; "and that affair

of the rosy-cheeked apple, that you pulled from
between my very teeth, was the precursor of—of—
your present smile. Good morning, Brenda, the
wilful. Grel, dear Grel," continued he, in low
tones, as he held her hand, "we shall meet again."

And the brother and sister returned to the Park.

CHAPTER III.

" READ, TRY, JUDGE, AND SPEAK AS YOU FIND."

From the Diary of the Lady Grel Stuart.

"SURELY I never experienced so intense a
stillness! Not a sound, not a breath of air,
no moon—but myriads of glittering stars. The
sky clear, and blue, and bright, the stars numberless, gleaming and scintillating. I enjoy this
silence, and apparent loneliness at this late hour.
One seems to have more companionship with
heaven, when one has so little of the noise of earth,
of its worries and confusions !

"But now, I must record it is just one week since
that memorable day in which Irene and D. came
so kindly to see us. And in that one week I have
known more of earth's bustles, perplexities, and
chafings than in all my previous life beforetime !
I almost feel it necessary to ask myself—since I
wished so heartily for change—to ask myself what

sort of change I had set my heart upon ? Not
noise and clatter, that is certain ; because D.'s
attacks make me sad. Not eternally running between the Park and the Rectory, only to have a
light-tongued, somewhat foolish talk as the result.
Certainly not the fact that is every day making
itself more strongly felt ; not the feeling of dislike,
positive dislike of D., and something very like in-
difference towards Irene. A conviction that almost
makes me wish my cousins were not at the Park !

"I suppose it was foolish to be discontented with
my quiet life, and to long for change. Now that
I have had this one week of fusses, I turn to my
books and music with rapture, and I greatly solace
myself with them, as a relief to my disappointed
expectations.

"But books and music do not fill every corner of
my heart ; I have some longings that must still be
deferred ; since I do not satisfy them in the com
panionship of my two cousins.

"It is true I shall see more society ; perhaps in
time meet with others, more congenial to me and
my tastes than they are. We dine at the Park
soon ; there I shall meet Mr. Hamilton, and this I
desire very much, although to myself, I may confess, I stand in some little awe of him. I intend,
when I meet him, to be very silent myself, and to
listen to him, and watch him ; that I may form
my own opinion from my own observations, and so
not allow myself to be biassed by Brenda Cheetham's ill-nature.

" I am sorry to say it, even to myself, but I am
daily conscious of more and more dislike towards
Brenda. She is clever, but in some things vindictive.
Often meanly jealous of trifles; trifles that cannot be
altered, and for which no one is accountable, or to
blame. She wishes to be tall and slight, like me;
she is short and rather stout. I wish I could make
her tall and slight; I would to make her happy.
But as I cannot, then I wish she would not be
unamiable and spiteful to me, and dislike me because I am taller and slighter than herself.

" How she does admire D.! I wish he would
talk to her, instead of to me. Nothing seems to
go right. Soon I shall be longing for my old
quiet life to return upon me; for the Park to be
again shut up, and myself left in peace to pursue
such occupations as please me. Ah, me——!"—
End of extract from Diary.

" You find your cousins very much to your liking, Grel," said Mrs. Cheetham one morning, when
the two ladies were alone.

" Somewhat different from my preconceived
ideas," said Grel.

And then, fearing she had confessed, or was
on the verge of admitting too much, she added,

" Irene is very handsome; but then this she was
sure to be, or——"

" Or she would not be a Stuart," said Mrs.
Cheetham laughing, as the Lady Grel hesitated to
complete the sentence. " You and she are very

much alike. Oh! pray excuse me, you will think
I am following the lead of your flattering cousin
Danby! I rather meant to say you might easily
be taken for sisters. The black hair, the fair
complexion, the darkly fringed eyelids, even the
outline of the features and the movement of the
figure, are strikingly alike."

"Is D. redeeming himself in my uncle's good
graces?" said Grel abruptly. "There was something
sadly wrong a year or two since, was there
not?"

"I know no particulars. Lord Prellsthorpe has
had a good deal of anxiety; and we have been
told your cousin has occasionally met with strange
treatment; but we quiet people know very little of
the affairs of the fashionable world."

"Do you not remember, a few years ago there
were reports to D.'s disadvantage? These things
recur to me now, like old sorrows."

"I do not believe all I hear, my dear. People
unconsciously exaggerate the reports they carry
about, like the fable of the three black crows. The
worst I ever heard, and even that admitted of
doubt, was that Lord Danby was cut on the race-
course, by some very old friends of your uncle's
family. Mr. Cheatham and I agreed at the time,
that probably there was but little truth in the report; and as your cousin has continued to hold up
his head, I feel sure we were right. Have you
heard Lady Irene is already supposed to be a great
attraction to Mr. Hamilton?"

"Yes; Brenda told me. I think Irene will hardly condescend to marry a commoner. When ladies of her rank accept a lower, it is generally for—for——"

"Too often, my dear, for the sake of the wealth they do not themselves possess; but this, you think, could not be the case with Lady Irene. She has a private fortune of her own, sufficient to prevent the necessity of such a step. She was heiress to your aunt, the late Lady Clementina Stuart."

"Yes, Irene was Aunt Clem's heiress. And you think Mr. Hamilton has already—what shall I say?—fallen in love with her?"

"Ah, my dear, strange things are said, and odd remarks made even in this quiet part of the world. I am told—but, Grel, dear, I do not like to repeat such things—and yet I have been told the admiration is from her to him! And another thing, my dear, it is whispered that the Lady Irene is *not* so rich as she ought to be, after coming into possession of the great wealth of her aunt. She has lived much abroad, in Paris and Vienna, and, like Lord Danby, not been very prudent—of course, I only mean in money matters. It is said the Lady Irene has been accustomed to play for as high stakes even as Lord Danby."

"What a terrible thing to say of a lady!"

"Yes, my dear, very terrible; let us hope it is not entirely true. I think there must be some exaggeration. Indeed, I have only mentioned the subject to show that your cousin may even be in as much need to marry some rich commoner, as other ladies of her rank have been before now. But, my dear, we are letting time slip through our fingers. Lord Prellsthorpe dines at seven, and we have still to attend to our dress."

"I will not keep you waiting," said Grel, as both ladies left the room.

CHAPTER IV.

"ONE STORY IS GOOD TILL ANOTHER IS TOLD."

PRELLSTHORPE ABBEY was a place of some importance. The grounds were extensive and well kept up; the estate large, and under the surveillance of its owner.

The house was of a period some two or three hundred years preceding this chronicle, but well cared for by the constant residence of a house-keeper and major-domo, with a proper establishment of domestics. It was a show place, and only tenanted by its owner for a few days, or a week or two at a time; though, on certain days in the week, always accessible to visitors.

Mr. Hamilton had, for the last year or two, made the Abbey more of an abiding place than formerly—he had returned more frequently, and remained longer at a time. He was from this cause beginning to be better known in the county of Z——, and to mix himself up more with county matters. Indeed, for the last twelve or fifteen weeks he had been so constantly resident, as to take his place at the magisterial board, not only regularly, but with very much influence. He was found to be well-versed in our common English law, and in all business connected with courts of session and assize—that is to say, with the knowledge an influential magistrate ought to possess. Also, the judgments he gave, when on the bench, had the basis of justice in a remarkable degree; and the punishments he awarded were tempered by mercy. And thus, Mr. Hamilton, in the course of the last month or two, had risen to an importance in the county of Z—— he had not before enjoyed.

On the arrival at the Park of the Earl and Countess of Prellsthorpe, Mr. Hamilton soon became on more intimate terms there than he had been with any of the surrounding gentry. Not that he was not well known to the county gentlemen generally. But, we must add, that though Mr. Hamilton met the aristocracy of the neighbourhood on all public occasions, he had not hitherto condescended to visit them in private, beyond the formality of a morning call, alleging, as an excuse, "that he had no suitable establishment at the Abbey, and that, until he was better prepared to receive visitors, he must himself decline to visit."

For the *on dits* of the county of Z——, as to Mr. Hamilton's occupations, they were many. Some gave him credit for an ability equal to Glendower's, to

" Call spirits from the vasty deep."

Some even averred " the spirits" came when they were called ! Some said he gathered gold from the hills on his estate—they had seen him at work with a hammer, chipping off pieces of something here and there, and carrying away in his basket. Some said he made gods and goddesses of the stars, for that there was a room in the Abbey formerly used by the lordly abbots, fitted up with a telescope, always ready, pointed to the heavens; and, by means of which, Mr. Hamilton communed with the distant inhabitants of the starry spheres, and made himself able to tell of their doings. Some said he wrote learned treatises on all the difficult topics of the day, for he was never seen in his own " sanctum" without a pen in his hand; and had not unfrequently been caught in the very act of correcting a proof.

There was also a rumour that Mr. Hamilton was a married man, and that in some one of the houses on his distant possessions his wife was shut up in strict privacy. No one could tell how this strange report had arisen. Most people had heard of it. Some credited it, and these latter said that there was some foundation for the rumour, inasmuch as when his very ancient housekeeper,

Mistress Age, had been questioned by the curious among the many visitors to the Abbey, as to the probability of her master, Mr. Hamilton, changing the life of a bachelor for that of a married man, the elderly lady would shake her wise old head, and say :

"Not yet a bit—no, not yet. There was a reason why her master just did not change his condition then." The old lady added : "She could not exactly explain, but it was her opinion that Mr. Hamilton would wait until—until—why, in fact, she could not say more."

But garrulous age often forgets, like early youth, how much it admits by only telling a little, and Mistress Age, in her old age, was no exception to this rule.

It is true, the whole county of Z—— were open-mouthed at the fact that Mr. Hamilton had really become intimate at Prellsthorpe Park ! *Intimate !* It was even said he made excuses to call there often—that he never refused an invitation from the Park. All this was premature, and much of it absurd; but then we are penning a truthful chronicle, and must perforce note down the bad with the good, the absurd with the real, &c., &c.

CHAPTER V.

" HE WHO CONCEALS A USEFUL TRUTH, IS EQUALLY
GUILTY WITH THE PROPAGATOR OF AN INJURIOUS
FALSEHOOD."—*Augustine.*

" WELL, Grel, and what now do you think of
Mr. Hamilton, for I saw you observing
him ?" said Brenda Cheetham, when the two girls
were at length alone together, a day or two after
the dinner at Prellsthorpe Park.

" My opinion is unchanged : in the first place,
I think him handsome and dignified, but in the
second, I do *not* think him in love with Irene—I
hear most people have that opinion."

" And then, Grel, your cousin Danby; he is
certainly in love with you," Brenda sighed.

" Do not say so, Brenda ; you ought to know
better. I admit he chooses to profess love to me
in public. But, Brenda, think, think! Do we
not know that real love likes not lookers-on? And
D.'s love is always most visible when others are
present."

" Indeed, Grel, we ' lookers'-on,' as you call us,
can treasure up quite enough to understand many
things. You say Lord Danby's professions of
love to you are not real ?"—Brenda spoke
bitterly—" *I*, as a ' looker-on,' would wish no
brighter or more real to me," and now she spoke
enthusiastically.

"Brenda, are you serious?" said Grel, in astonishment—"I assure you he only talks nonsense."

"He does not look nonsense," said Brenda,
again bitterly. "I never saw a greater expression
of admiration in my life, from man to woman, than
from Lord Danby to you."

"Then, Brenda, I wish he would transfer it all
to you—all, Brenda!" and now Grel spoke
enthusiastically.

"I wish he would," said Brenda, fervently.

Whether Brenda's wish was written down by
the "Recording Angel," we, who chronicle, are
not able to say of our own absolute knowledge.
But Brenda had her wish—that much we may
chronicle for the advantage or satisfaction of our
readers. Brenda Cheetham eventually had Lord
Danby's love and admiration *exactly* as Grel had
it now. Brenda had heartily desired this—her
desire was granted. But to return to the conversation between the two girls :

"Admiration is not love," said Grel ; "and,
Brenda, how you do worry me about D.! He
does not love me. Do you not know love is silent
and secret?—it is love I should like, and, believe
me, admiration is only a bore."

"And do you mean to tell me, Grel, that you
do not like Lord Danby?" said Brenda.

"He is my cousin, remember that, otherwise I
should not like him," said Grel.

"Why, then, do you allow him to devote himself so entirely to you?" said Brenda.

"I have nothing to do with his 'devoting himself,' as you call it. He chooses to make a butt of me for his own amusement."

"How blind you are, Grel!—he adores you; and how often it happens that men love us whom we cannot love; while he, to whom we could give a heart, is caught by some other."

"Who is sentimental now, I wonder?" said Grel, with a smile—"and all this came to light by your asking me what I thought of Mr. Hamilton."

"Well, then, Grel, to return to the great lion, Mr. Hamilton," said Brenda. "He has told mamma he shall be present at the distribution of prizes in the school-room—he will even be present while the children are examined. In short, he will now begin to do just all those things he has omitted up to this time. And so, Grel, you are at fault in your judgment of Mr. Hamilton and Lady Irene; and if you are at fault there, you may also be at fault as to the 'love and admiration' of another, who shall be nameless," and Brenda sighed and paused. "It is the Lady Irene," resumed she, "who has prevailed upon Mr. Hamilton to step aside from his ordinary routine, and you think he is *not* in love with her! Grel, you are very blind."

The conversation was interrupted by Mrs. Cheetham and Lord Danby.

"We have been arranging for the drive to the Abbey grounds," said Mrs. Cheetham.

"I have ordered my phaeton for four o'clock, Grel. Will that suit you?" said Lord Danby.

"I do not understand you, D.," said Grel in a tone of surprise.

"Why, my dear Grel, I drive you to the *fête* in the Abbey grounds!" said Lord Danby.

"Not you—not you, D.!" said Grel impatiently; "indeed, I made no engagement with you!"

"I did not accuse you of engaging yourself—I merely state the fact. I drive you to the Abbey grounds—when shall you be ready?"

"I am obliged by your kindness," said Grel suavely, and trying not to offend her cousin, "but I wish to go with Mrs. Cheetham."

"My dear Grel," said Mrs. Cheetham, "what a mistake I have made! I sent to tell Miss Stone I had a place for her. Poor thing! it is so far for her to walk—nearly two miles—and I quite understood from Lord Danby he had arranged to take care of you. What can I do?" Mrs. Cheetham was evidently in great distress, and so also was the Lady Grel.

"What, flashing up again, Grel!" said Lord Danby. "Mrs. Cheetham, is she not handsome in her anger? I pride myself on your indignation, love," added he *sotto voce* to the Lady Grel; "it calls up your beauty marvellously—and when shall I come?" said he, again speaking aloud.

"I do not wish to go to the Abbey," said Grel, hoping, by the self-denial of remaining at home, to avoid the drive there with her cousin.

"Nonsense, Grel," said he, taking her hand and carrying it to his lips. "I shall drive you."

"You have no right to treat me so, D., and I will not go," Grel spoke more angrily than was usual with her; she turned away, as if to leave the room, and Lord Danby said in quiet tones,

"Grel, I said nothing about 'right.' You take things so strangely, like a half-educated girl. It is true I understand 'might.' However, to please you, I confess myself beaten. Addio!"

And, bowing and smiling, Lord Danby left the room, and eventually mounted his horse and rode away.

"Do not fret yourself, my dear," said Mrs. Cheetham, "we must manage to take you."

And Grel seated herself in an attitude of deep thought. She had looked forward to the enjoyment of this *fête* in the Abbey grounds, as a young girl who had seen but little of the world would naturally. But she had not calculated upon being tormented by her cousin, or upon being prevented by him from watching and observing in her own quiet way the different county people assembled there. Mr. Hamilton himself, the lord of the feast, she had, as it were, set her heart upon examining leisurely during those intervals which were sure to be at her own command; and now, as she sat quietly thinking over her disappointment, she felt she would rather stay at home than go *with* Lord Danby, and have him at her side for the evening.

Punctually at four o'clock, and just as Mr. Cheetham's horse and the Rectory carriage came round, Lord Danby arrived in his phaeton.

"Now, what shall I do?" said Lady Grel, clasping her hands together, and speaking in a tone of much annoyance. "Brenda, let him drive you." Brenda's reply was lost by Lord Danby's entrance.

"Now, Grel, love, will you allow Mr. Cheetham to drive you? You see," said he in a kind voice, "that will leave Mrs. Cheetham the power to take Miss Stone, and if you agree to my proposal, I can ride Mr. Cheetham's horse."

Now, could any one have been more kind or more considerate for the feelings and comfort of the entire party than Lord Danby had been, by this thoughtful conduct! Grel felt ashamed of her ill-temper, and impulsively made reparation.

"Thanks, dear D.; you are so courteous," and she offered him her hand, which he accepted, and retained during their conversation. "You will excuse my hastiness, D., I will behave better for the future."

"You are always charming, Grel," said he.

"And Mr. Cheetham will drive me, you say?" said Grel.

"I am sure papa will not attempt to drive those spirited horses," said Brenda; but Grel heard her not, and Lord Danby, as he continued to hold her hand, said,

"Come, then, darling; let me place you nicely."

They left the room together, Grel delighted with the turn affairs had taken, Brenda watching from the open window. Mr. Cheetham was in the hall, evidently preparing for the drive.

"So like your good-natured self, my dear sir," said Grel, stopping to speak to him. But Lord Danby hurried her on, as Mr. Cheetham said,

"Eh? What, my dear——"

Grel turned and nodded smilingly to her guardian, while Lord Danby pressed her hand gently, and said,

"Now, Grel, I will make you comfortable," as he handed her into the carriage, and affected to pull the carriage-rug into its place; this done, he seized the reins, and, without allowing a moment for remonstrance, jumped up by her side, and, lashing his horses, drove rapidly away.

Grel did not scream; but she had some difficulty in restraining the expression of her annoyance. She tried to speak quietly, for she had an instinctive dread, which was unusual, of giving offence.

"You said Mr. Cheetham should drive me, D.." said she at length, breaking the silence.

"I asked if you would allow him to drive you?"

"And I said I would—I said yes—do you hear me, D.?"

"I hear you, and I know what you said; but

if you would allow Mr. Cheetham to drive you in my carriage, Grel, I certainly would not. It pleasures me, Grel, to look upon you when you are angry, and I knew I should put you in a terrible rage. However, the longer you rage, the further I'll drive," said he, deliberately turning his horses from the road that led to the Abbey.

" Where are you going, D. ?"

Lord Danby put his horses on, and did not reply.

" I ask you why you drive this way ?" said Grel in her turn, putting her hand on the reins.

Lord Danby first removed her hand, and then turning to her, said,

" Let me caution you against touching my ribbons, neither myself nor my horses will stand it. But I have not replied to your query. I drive *from* instead of *to* the Abbey, to allow you time to cool. I do not choose to take you into society with such flaming red cheeks; a little colour is all very well, indeed rather becoming, with your dazzlingly fair complexion. But red, hot-looking cheeks, and proud, flashing, and defiant-looking eyes, with an angry and snappish tone of voice—these are not meet for the educated and the courtly. You must cool, Grel—and then——"

After a silence of a few seconds, Grel said,

" And what then, D. ?"

" Ah ! you *are* coming round, I can hear it in the tone of your voice. 'And what then,' did you say? —then you will be the better able, and probably the more willing, to listen to my love. You flout me heartily in public, pray take your fill of flouting now, while there are no witnesses. And when you have scoffed out all your spleen, you may perchance listen, not only with more patience, but with more politeness."

"But you are driving *from* the Abbey, D.— why should you do that?"

Grel tried hard to speak calmly.

"I have already told you," said he quietly.

"Take me to the Abbey, D.—I insist upon it, that you take me there!"

Alas! she felt very angry.

"Yes—insist as much as you please," said he, putting his horses on to a very fast pace.

"I will throw myself from the carriage," said she with a desperate start.

Lord Danby was tall, and rather spare than stout. He rapidly passed the reins from his left to his right hand, and then putting his arm round Grel's waist, said,

"And now, my beautiful Grel, what is your next move?"

She felt his hot breath upon her cheek, and shudderingly turned her excited countenance upon him, as she said,

"How dare you, D.! Let me go, you have no right to torment me so."

And she struggled to free herself.

"I dare anything, Grel; and I will soon make myself a right from which there shall be no appeal.

But you shudder, and fret, and fume, and storm, and rage, as if I were some highwayman of the last century, running off with your dainty lady-ship! Why, Grel, I am your cousin! I have had a cousin's privileges thousands and thousands of times! And I expected them; nay, looked forward to them again, on my return to the Park!"

Grel in her inmost heart acknowledged the truth of all this. And yet strangely enough "the cousin's privileges," that had been so agreeable to her in years gone by, were not agreeable now. Sometimes, when she was examining herself and her feelings, Grel wondered which was the most changed, Lord Danby or herself.

"I did indeed suppose," pursued Lord Danby, "that D. might have been treated with common civility by his own cousin Grel—the little Grel Stuart of former happy days. And you say you will throw yourself from his carriage! will you? Ah! ah!"

Lord Danby's laugh was not pleasant, Grel heard it and felt more dismayed still.

"You treat me scurvily in the presence of Brenda Cheetham, who is truly a kind-hearted and charming girl. You turn me adrift in this lady's presence, and think I shall keep my temper! You are mistaken; the Stuarts are all alike. I am as fiery as you, though, perhaps, I do not choose that every pretty girl shall know it; and I have as strong a will of my own as you, Grel! And you think because you are a beauty, a born beauty, as

are all the females of our house, that you will not
gratify your own cousin—also born handsome as
are all the men Stuarts—gratify your cousin with a
little play! I say you shall, Grel!"

The horses still trotted on, and Grel knew she
was in Lord Danby's power. If she did not
speak, it appeared to her as if he would still talk
on, through the long hours; and if she did speak,
she feared to anger him more.

"It seems to me an arbitrary game you are
playing now, D.—and why do you not set me free?"
for he still had his arm round her waist.

"You may play more strange games before the end
of your life; and if I have any insight into futurity,
I say you will. In reply to the latter part of your
question, I shall not set you free till—till you entreat me, love; ah! ah!—entreat me with dainty
words, and sweet smiles, and loving glances."

"That I shall never do!" said Grel, giving way
to her long restrained anger.

"Time is of no value to me," said he with much
nonchalance. "I can afford to drive you on, and
on, till nightfall, ay, and through the long night
also. If you can afford a like drive, we are in for
a like pleasure."

Grel turned away her head to hide the tear that
started into her eye, caused by her dismay at Lord
Danby's cruel speech. Drive her through the
whole long night! What would become of
her?

"There are some things I cannot afford. One

is, to be humbled by one woman in the presence of another. You have your answer, and know your fate ;" and then Lord Danby again put his horses into a fast trot, while he himself hummed the favourite air from the last new opera.

Poor Grel! she was in a sore strait.

***

CHAPTER VI.

" MANY HAVE COME TO A PORT AFTER A STORM."

" I TELL you to unhand me, D. ; you shall be made to repent your rude behaviour!" said Grel.

" I rather think *you* will be the first to repent, Grel!" .

" Do you, then, wish to offend me, D. ?"

" I care nothing either for your moodiness or your smiles here—*here*, while we are alone ; but in the presence of others I will not be treated ill ; and whenever in the future you dare so to treat me, you shall have the bitter repentance, my cousin !"

" I really did not at any time mean to displease you, D. Oh, do set me free!" said she, struggling in his grasp.

" Free ! I would as soon pitch you out of the carriage myself as set you free, until I have humbled you !"

"At least, be reasonable, D., and tell me what you wish? Pray do not drive so fast!—oh, pray do turn your horses!" Poor Grel! she was compelled to entreat.

"Ha! ha! we are coming round, are we?" said he in a mocking tone, and urging his horses until they seemed almost to fly along the road. "First, my sweet coz," resumed he, as he turned and gazed upon her, "you understand, I shall tell you I love whenever I please; next, I will say what I please to you, or to any one. I will speak when I please, and always do as I please, in the presence of any one, and you shall not say me nay."

"You have no business to say anything you please to me, either when you are alone, or in the presence of others!" said Grel, trying to keep up her courage.

"I am not saying I have 'business,' or I have 'no business' to do such and such things. I say I will *do* them, and no one shall say me nay!"

"Set me free, D.; indeed you hurt me keeping me so long in one position," said Grel.

"Have I not said I will humble you?—and I tell you again, I will."

"What is your will?—pray, oh, pray tell me!"

"I have already told you. I will not be dictated to—I will not be scorned; and I will be treated kindly and well in the presence of others, *always*."

"It is your ill-behaviour that has called forth

mine—if, indeed, I have ever behaved ill," said Grel meekly.

"That has nothing to do with the matter. I do not say 'I will behave well;' I say I will be treated well."

"And you call this play! D., I do not like such play."

"I have said," resumed he, "may I not play with my coz? And I say again I *will* play with her, and a charming game we will have together, Grel! But, to dare to put me down in the presence of Brenda Cheetham!"

"Oh! pray do not hold me so tight—I cannot breathe. And what of Brenda—Brenda Cheetham?" gasped Grel.

"She is a charming girl! I love her. I do not choose that the lady I love shall have a chance of thinking ill of me."

"Love her!" said Grel, now in much astonishment, and remembering his professions of love for herself. "How many do you, then, profess to love?"

"I never count hearts, nor ladies," said he.

"Why, there is another mile-stone!" said Grel. "Oh! do, pray, turn your horses round! What shall I do!" continued she struggling. "D., do tell me, what is this mighty will of yours that is so to humble me?"

"First, promise obedience to my wishes, and then seal the promise by a kiss Oh! yes, how full of wrath we are!" said he mockingly. "Why,

Grel Stuart has kissed her cousin D. some hundreds of times! But it matters not; my horses will run on, and if I keep to this pace we shall be in Landeswold by six o'clock."

"Do have some pity, D. What will the assembled world at the Abbey say?" said Grel, trying hard to restrain her tears.

"What do I care what people say of you! But if you wish me to set you free, humble your proud heart, express your sorrow for the past, promise obedience for the future whenever your cousin wishes for a little play, then kiss me, and I will turn my horses' heads towards the Abbey."

"Just heaven! D., what are you asking?"

"I ask you to kiss me."

"I will not, D."

"Will not what, Grel?"

"I will *not* kiss you—do as you will, or as you can, *I will not kiss you.*" Grel emphasised the last few words, but she spoke with more of dignity than of anger.

"Then, coz, you know you will lose cast by driving with me to Landeswold—with me alone—and at this late hour."

"I know I feel offended," said Grel; "I think your treatment of me deserves my indignant anger. But, D., I have not placed myself in this miserable position by any intentional wrongdoing of my own. I cannot prevent you driving me to Landeswold, and by that one cruel act of yours laying me at once at the feet of the hard-judging, as an erring and perhaps self-willed girl! But my faith saves me, and I trust in a Power greater and more abiding than yours, that shall over-rule all for my good. I will not kiss you. And I care no more for the expression of your will, nor for your artfulness in betraying me into this misery, probably than you do for my refusal. Murder me!—stifle me!—I am sufficiently humbled by being your prisoner. I will not willingly allow my own actions to lower me in my own opinion! I tell you, D., sooner or later your own base deeds will recoil upon yourself; and once again I tell you, D.—I will not kiss you!"

"By Jove, Grel! Why, you are worth hundreds and thousands of other women! You shall not kiss me; and I will set you free, and kiss you. But you will not throw yourself from the carriage?" said he, as he was about to withdraw his arm, which had hitherto been round Grel's waist.

"No, I will not," said Grel, and she felt herself free. "But still, D., you drive on and on," added Grel; "will you ever return to the Abbey?"

Lord Danby did not reply. He turned his horses' heads, and began to trot sharply back.

This was such a relief to Grel after the strain upon her nerves of the last few minutes, that she suddenly burst into tears.

"Why, Grel, darling, in tears! I expected thanks."

"Thanks, D.," said Grel meekly, and still weeping, for, in spite of her recent courage, she

did not wish to offend him by neglecting anything
he expected from her.

"Bless me, how grand we are! But do not
weep—do not weep, tears will not do any good.
Do you not know I am in play?—that, truth to
tell, I play a game?"

"Yes, you have told me so. But what is the
game?"

Lord Danby did not reply. They sat silent
some considerable time, and then suddenly, as it
seemed, came within sight of one of the entrances
to the Abbey grounds.

"What, home so soon!—how can it be?" said
Grel.

"I knew *you* wished it, Grel; now, if you do
think me 'base,' and 'artful,' and in full possession
of all the bad qualities you so unsparingly heaped
upon me in your grand speech a short time since—
if you do think so ill of me, at least never say I
cross *your will* when you agree to mine."

"But I do not, and did not agree to yours,"
said Grel, forgetting that she might offend Lord
Danby again.

"Hush—hush! When I allow myself van-
quished by your pluck—well, that is a term used
by men, and, to tell you the honest truth, I do not
know another so entirely expressive of my meaning—when I allow you have conquered by your
'pluck,' you should not chafe me by petty contra-
dictions. But, Grel, do not weep. I will trot
back again if you do not dry up your tears."

"I am quite recovered," said she.

" You will dance the first and last dances with me, Grel ?"

The lady did not reply.

" Do you hear me?—the first dance and the last ?"

" I shall not dance, D.—I am tired."

Lord Danby deliberately turned his horses round, and again trotted back on the road to Landeswold.

" What are you doing, D. ?" said Grel almost in despair. To be within sight of the Abbey gates, to see the assembled crowds on the lawns, or in the distance in the grounds, and then to be turned away, and again feel herself driving swiftly on the road to Landeswold, almost took away her courage, and certainly again excited her resentment.

" I am driving to Landeswold ; if you are tired, you can rest quietly in the carriage," said Lord Danby.

" Now, what can you mean, D. ?" said Grel.

"I mean what I say. I am going to Landeswold. It is only five o'clock," added he, consulting his watch. " What, weeping again, Grel ! Why, you are a man in your ' pluck,' but a very woman in your tears !"

" In my weakness, D. I am not strong as you are, and so perhaps, as you say, a very woman in my weakness, or in the expression of it. Do not take me to Landeswold !"

Unconsciously Grel spoke entreatingly, and Lord Danby smiled as he said,

"Then dance the first and last dances with me?"

"Yes, I will," said Grel, feeling it was wiser to yield than suffer herself to be longer detained from the party at the Abbey.

Lord Danby turned his horses immediately, and again drove towards the Abbey.

"Never mind, Grel—I will not teaze you; you yielded your will to mine in that last promise; but you are a 'brick' for all that."

"A brick!—what is a brick?"

"Here we are; now look around you."

The gates were standing wide open, and Lord Danby drove in.

"Did you think we were lost?" said Lord Danby to Mr. Hamilton, who, with Lady Irene and some others, was in the act of entering the conservatory at the south entrance of the Abbey grounds.

"Allow me, Lady Grel," said Mr. Hamilton, coming hastily forward, and handing her from the carriage. "Ah! I fear you are not well. Danby, do not drive away; there are men somewhere near to take your horses."

"Not well, love?—what is the matter?" said Lady Irene.

"I have put her out, Ren—teazed her; oh! Grel, do not betray me," said Lord Danby.

"You surely do not mind D.?—what nonsense

to fuss yourself for anything he says or does!"
said Lady Irene.

Meanwhile Mr. Hamilton had busied himself
with silent attentions to the Lady Grel. A
garden seat had been rolled forward, and in the
course of a few minutes wine and biscuits were
handed to her.

"Place the tray on the seat, and leave it," said
Mr. Hamilton to the man who brought refresh-
ment. "Now, Lady Grel, if you have had a
fright from Danby's fiery horses, let me advise
you to restore your nerves," said Mr. Hamilton, as
he poured out and presented wine to her.

CHAPTER VII.

"DEEP RIVERS MOVE IN SILENCE—SHALLOW BROOKS
ARE NOISY."

"BRENDA CHEETHAM, will you ever stop
carrying cake and tea to those dirty little
bumpkins?" said Lord Danby, who had left the
party at the conservatory, and walked on alone.

"Yes, when I see you employed in a like
manner," said Brenda.

"Thanks, Miss Repartee—my back is not made
to be broken for or by bumpkins, or my tongue to
waste its sweetness on absent young gad-a-ways!
And, Brenda, as we meet so seldom uncontrolled

by the watchful eyes of others, I should think you
might put down the tea and cake, and come and
stroll with me."

" There are others more worthy of companionship in your eyes—to such I recommend you at
this present time, and then I, poor Brenda Cheetham, can attend to my duties."

" Humph!—now she is imitating Grel. How
soon one woman spoils another! And Brenda
will attend to her duties, will she?" soliloquised
Lord Danby, " which duties Brenda would have
no scruple in setting aside for the time being, if—
if she were sure of her admirer!

" Oh! woman, woman!—arch little creatures;
but I consider such conduct forgiveable; and
Brenda Cheetham is a charming woman, and
simple, in spite of her wit; and, it seems to me,
unsuspicious of evil. She would credit a down-
right declaration of love at once. And there, as
she is at this moment, tripping along among the
rows of bumpkins, how prettily innocent she
looks! She is too short, and too stout, and too
black-haired, for my individual taste. But it
would be easy to persuade her to the contrary, and
very amusing to me.

" Ah! indeed, and so Hamilton has turned
guardian to Grel!—I see the large party coming
away from the conservatory. Ren will not like
that—indeed, it must not be. Ren must win
Hamilton, and let him marry her, while I make
Grel think she *must* marry me, even though she

should win others; but I shall not marry her—I
like Gwen better. Ren, Ren, where can your
foolish thoughts be gadding? And why are you
leaning on the arm of the handsome Maynooth,
and looking your very loveliest? Irene, this will
not do. Hamilton is a proud man; you will lose
him if you try to propitiate others; but the Maynooth is good, as a match for you—the Hamilton
better.

"'Oh! my prophetic soul!' and there is the
good boy, Almeric Barrymore—'oh! my prophetic
soul!' I said he would fall. I was sure he
would fall, because he was so determined to
become a pattern gentleman—one whose doings
should be an example to the world. He would
never do this and that—of course not!" and here
Lord Danby laughed, and shook his head con-
temptuously. "No, no, he would not, a valiant man
he was then! But now there is a cloud upon his
brow—a shadow on his heart! Well, well, this *is*
excellent. 'My prophetic soul!—my prophetic
soul!'" and when Almeric Barrymore passed out
of sight, Lord Danby made his remarks on others
who were near.

"Pretty girl that Thorn, but a—hum—malicious, or envious, or something. And there is the
other, Sarah—ah! I remember, there are *three*
Sarahs somewhere. Common and ugly name,
accounts for common and ugly people—but the
Thorn is pretty, she is a Sara. I see them all—
first the Barrymore, and she, by-the-bye, has at-

tained a queenly height and bearing; second the
Fortescue, and she is sadly too short; she will
grow into a hen partridge, or a dame partlet; and
third the Thorn—Sara Thorn—ugly name, ought
to have been ugly girl; is not—and yet I feel sure
she is rightly named Thorn. She will often be a
thorn to less handsome women. Some day I will
make love to her. She, I am sure, is vain enough
to believe anything; *all* pretty women are vain;
all handsome women are—but what fools they are
to hand tea and cake to such a set of village
bumpkins. What on earth shall I do? I am
abominably tired of looking on; I must do something to save my nerves from giving way—either
please Brenda, or teaze Grel, or look after the
Sarahs—" and Lord Danby yawned, and walked
slowly on—" Ah!" said he, " I am saved!—there is
the Rectory Mother Bountiful!"

"Mistress Cheetham! and *unoccupied,*" continued he, as he walked to meet her. "Now this
is something to talk about, and ' make mouths at,'
—and I am glad to see you alone, for I want your
private opinion of my Grel? Is she not a sweet
creature?"

" She is indeed a lovely creature; and quite
fulfils the promise of her childhood. I do not
wonder at your admiration; but I do at your treatment," said Mrs. Cheetham.

" What can you mean? What have I done to
my dear Grel, to cause a remark of that sort?
Tell me—pray tell me?"

"She is even now suffering from some alarm in her drive with you from the Rectory here," said Mrs. Cheetham. "I blame myself that I did not prevent you from running away with her, as we all know you did. Indeed, we were more or less uncomfortable at your prolonged absence from the Abbey grounds; and when we saw you enter by the South Gate we knew you must have driven considerably round. Grel does not tell us what has happened. Some mad freak or other of yours, I said to Mr. Cheetham."

"Did you, indeed!—that was very unkind!— Grel did not understand me," said Lord Danby.

"So Mr. Cheetham said. And Brenda said, Grel's nerves must be of the weakest, if she could not endure the spirit of your horses, when you held them."

"Brenda is a brave girl," said he.

"We all know your horses are mettlesome; but we also know the power and skill of their master."

"But Grel did not;—and besides, I teazed her," said Lord Danby, "yes, I did. Nay, do not shake your head and look almost as handsome, as your superlatively handsome daughter—or step-daughter—but the good looks are all the same; and in truth, I teazed Grel shamefully. I told her I would drive her to Landeswold! Ah! ah! ah!— and she thought I was in earnest! You would have been wiser;—well, the darling became ill, and I relented, turned my horses round, shortened my

charming tête-à-tête with my lovely coz, and
brought her to the Abbey."

" You really are very——"

" Hush, hush ! I have not told you half, and I
want you to help me; will you, Mistress Gentle-
heart? I am promised to Brenda for the first
dance—indeed, Brenda likes to dance with me, perhaps you already know that—yes, she likes to
dance with me, and I with her, and we are
mutually pleased to gratify each other ; and when
we run away with each other you will forgive us,
will you not? Ah ! I see you will by that quiet,
amused, and unaffected laugh ;—but to return,
Brenda and I made up our minds to show off to
the bumpkins in the——"

" The what ?—or the who ?" said Mrs. Cheetham.

" The rosy-cheeked bumpkins attended by
Houris ! Well—how you do laugh ! I shall never
finish if you interrupt me so frequently ! Now,
when Grel fell ill I was obliged to try to make
her happy, and tell her she should dance the first
quadrille with me ; you will allow Grel felt com-
forted? But you perceive Brenda's pleasure and
mine 'are delayed 'cause of Grel's illness ! We
cannot help that, we are the victims of circumstances. Will you tell Brenda ; give my love to
her—well then compliments, Mistress Cheetham,
Shake-the-head ! Ha ! ha ! However, do you blame
me for making it up with Grel when I had so
teazed her ?"

"Not at all. And whether Brenda dances the first dance or not, I will answer for her wish, that you should in this instance have resigned her for Grel."

"Remember you, Mistress Cheetham of the Smiling Countenance, remember you are Brenda's friend, and mine also when we run away together. Yes—you laugh—but never deny that you are in the secret!"

The lady's reply is not worth recording; she felt sure Lord Danby was only amusing himself by talking "nonsense," that he would forget in the next minute. But Mrs. Cheetham lived to be reminded by Lord Danby that he had told her of his intention to run away with Brenda; and that though she did not actually promise to assist the run-a-ways, she certainly approved of their plans. As soon, however, as Mrs. Cheetham and Lord Danby separated, he said,

"A restless old fool, who takes me for one of the same genus as herself; but, if I had not wit enough 'to fool her,' I should indeed be a fool."

Soon after this, Lord Danby saw Mr. Almeric Barrymore standing alone, apparently watching the children. He went up to him, and said, abruptly:

"And so the Ghosts of Heraldstowe have visited you since I saw you last? How do you do?"

This was certainly a strange greeting after many years of absence, and Mr. Barrymore seemed to think so. He started, and turned pale; mechanically and silently he accepted Lord Danby's offered hand.

"Come, tell me," said Lord Danby, laughing, "have the Ghosts of Heraldstowe caught their mediæval worshipper napping?"

"Are you, then, the originator of these practical jokes?" said Mr. Barrymore. "Let me advise you to stay your hand; I shall not show you—I mean it is——"

"You mean, if you catch me playing off practical jokes at Heraldstowe, that you will shoot me?"

"You have hit the truth so far, that any person intruding into our private grounds, who will not tell his name when spoken to, stands a good chance of being——"

"Shot dead as a door nail," said Lord Danby; "and since such is your intention, I may as well have a witness to the fact in our old friend and neighbour, Mr. Thorn. How do you do?" said he to a gentleman who came hastily up. "What do you think?—as a greeting to my return to the county of Z——, Almeric says he will shoot me dead as a door nail."

"Hush!—hush!" said Mr. Thorn, the Vicar of Stowe-in-the-Valley.

"I did not," said Mr. Barrymore, in an indignant tone.

"Of course not," said Mr. Thorn; "we all know our friend, Lord Danby, exaggerates a

little "—and the old gentleman laughed pleasantly, and seemed to take the accusation as a
joke.

Mr. Barrymore turned away, but Lord Danby
said :

" Do not go until you have explained to Mr.
Thorn——"

" I said I would shoot anyone found trespassing
in our grounds after dark who would not give his
name," and Mr. Barrymore made his escape, and
the Vicar said quietly,

" I knew you were wrong—Almeric never uses
such strong language."

" You knew I was wrong—I assure you *you* are
wrong; you have a wrong idea altogether of what
has been said."

And now that the children have had as much
plumcake and tea as they like—as they have
enjoyed their merry games, and sung their last
hymn, and been dismissed with their teachers
from the Abbey grounds—now the quadrilles
form, and dancing begins. And while some
continue to saunter hither and thither—some to
stand and gaze at the dancers, and some to rest
on the seats around—suppose we, as privileged
pryers into hearts, just take a peep at the state of
Mr. Hamilton's, and listen to his unexpressed
thoughts.

" These cousins are very handsome," thought
he, as he stood watching the quadrille—" Lady
Grel the handsomer—so much more character.

The unsophisticated cousin queens it over the brilliant woman of the world."

Mr. Hamilton was supposed to be in conversation with Lord Prellsthorpe, Mr. Thorn, and Captain Fortescue; this was the ostensible reason for not joining in the quadrille. But it happened the three gentlemen standing with him did all the talking, while Mr. Hamilton, wisely affecting to listen, allowed his own thoughts to run upon the two Ladies Stuart and their doings.

"What could Danby have done, during their drive, with the Lady Grel? She was nervous, timid, and ill on her arrival. I mistrust Danby, as well as that beautiful Lady Irene. I have seen her very haughty, and heard her very dictatorial; she is not so with me—that is one reason for my mistrust. But my mind dwells on that handsome cousin, the violet-eyed Grel—the weeping maiden of my feast this day. Tears from a woman, if called forth by a man, tell tales. One thing is clear—she and Danby have not quarrelled; it was not a stormy drive, for they are dancing together now; he does not hide either his love for her, or admiration of her beauty, and she looks shy and timid.

"Yes, I read it all. Danby has made love to her, and she, the simple maiden—the truthful girl—has credited him. But it is all wrong. Danby is a man without a heart; he has pulsation, which ministers to his selfishness, but no heart. And so you wept, Grel, at the first words of love!"

mentally apostrophised Mr. Hamilton—"so like a woman! I wish I had spoken those words. How I gazed upon you at dinner, when I met you at the Park, and, oddly enough, I thought then that Danby's attentions were *painful* to you. I was mistaken. You fulfil some of my ideas about women; you combine beauty, goodness, gracefulness, and innocence, and with all these perfections, you love Danby.

"Woman, in her goodness and beauty, given to her so bountifully by her Maker, queens it mightily over our hearts. But woman, in her helplessness, and, above all, her innocence—her want of the comprehension of evil—too often falls a prey to evil-disposed men."

Mr. Hamilton had many interruptions to these his sober day-dreams; but we have preferred to give them without "let or but," and to suffer them to close the long day's *fête* in the Abbey grounds.

CHAPTER VIII.

"A LIE, THOUGH IT PROMISE GOOD, WILL DO THEE HARM, AND TRUTH WILL DO THEE GOOD AT THE LAST."

AND now it is necessary to introduce more particularly the characters—incidentally mentioned or spoken to by Lord Danby—who were present at the Abbey *fête*.

First of Mr. Almeric Barry-Barrymore. He is the grandson of Sir Hildebrand Barry-Barrymore of Heraldstowe. This gentleman was advanced in years, and of somewhat delicate health, in consequence of which Almeric had not been sent to a public school, or, at a later period of his life, to college. The old gentleman liked to see young faces about him; he enjoyed the sound of their merry voices, their playfulness and unsophistication. It will be remembered Lord Danby made a somewhat strange quotation from Shakespeare when he first saw Almeric Barrymore in the Abbey grounds—"Oh! my prophetic soul!"

Almeric was a boy of some twelve or fourteen years of age when Lord Danby was last at Prellsthorpe. Almeric was as fond of fun and frolic as any other boy, in a reasonable way, but he could not be brought to join Lord Danby in scenes of dissipation, and in such other practices as would cause certain annoyance to his tutor and kind relatives. Almeric honoured his tutor, who was both a scholar and a gentleman, and whose excellent principles and highly-cultivated tastes had directed the energies of his pupil into somewhat different channels from those pursued by Lord Danby, who, on this account, felt no hesitation in calling Almeric "a muff." But Almeric, in spite of rude epithets, or slang terms, combined with a good deal of quiet badgering, stood his ground, and would not suffer himself to be tempted into scenes uncongenial to him. If the matter had

ended there, perhaps all might have been well;
but Almeric, not content with avoiding for, himself the dissipation into which Lord Danby so
recklessly plunged, made repeated attempts to
turn his friend from such disagreeable pursuits.
As may easily be understood, this excited Lord
Danby's anger, and he at length replied with a
bitterness of speech for which he had always been
more or less remarkable,

"That _he_ should not disgrace his noble name
and high lineage by following in the wake of such
a 'slow-coach' as Almeric B. Barrymore, who spent
his time in reading musty old chronicles of the
Middle Ages, descriptive of wonderful people, who
went about the world fighting for some one thing,
that all their opponents declared to be 'a lie!'"

A great war of words arose upon this, and Lord
Danby argued on his part with much sophistry,
and turning all mediæval worthies into ridicule.

Almeric, more sincere, and better read in these
subjects, contended that the days of chivalry were
also days of truth and honour.

"Your head is full of mediæval folly," said
Lord Danby. "You yourself are at this moment
doing battle for 'a lie,' when you talk of the
Middle Ages as the days of truth and honour."

But Almeric was not to be talked out of his
conviction. He contended that he did not do
battle for "a lie"—that a lie was the meanest
subterfuge that was known or practised—a lie
was the very death-blow of all chivalric feeling.

Lord Danby called Almeric "the preacher," and
Almeric thought Lord Danby a reprobate. From
time to time, as they met here and there, one became still more sneering and taunting, the other
more prosy and preaching, until at length—as it
seemed by tacit agreement—they seldom met.

But it is still necessary to record, that on several
occasions Lord Danby had tried the effects of
superstition on Almeric's nerves, and on one particular occasion he had taunted Almeric by saying,

"You are afraid of the ghosts in the old house
at home, for you know well enough that the
ghostly remains of your worthy ancestors tenant
the coats of armour that stand in the hall, or on
the stairs, or in the long galleries ; and you dare
not, for the life of you, confess the truth as to
those mediæval days, and swear the men were liars
and the women faithless, in the fear of the
watchers and warders dogging your footsteps and
doing you some ill."

"The old barons will never harm me!" said
Almeric with some pride.

"You cannot deny that you have a strong wish
to propitiate them ? I have even thought it possible that Sir Hildebrand follows the goodly example of 'Sir Brian of the fiery eyes,' and has
the old barons, as you call them, to dine with him
occasionally."*

"I do not seek to propitiate my ancestors," said
Almeric again proudly, and without replying to

* See Note 1.

the latter part of Lord Danby's speech. "If I
did ill, or acted in opposition to the dictates of a
good conscience, I might naturally have a certain
fear of the ghosts of the worthy barons. For the
ghosts of men so loyal and true would abominate
a descendant who would disgrace their name; and
therefore, if such beings are permitted to plague
living men, I might in that case expect to come in
for a goodly share of torment."

This was, of course, mere boy's talk. And yet of
the two, Almeric was sincere in all he said, Lord
Danby—to use his own words—"only chaffing the
Mediæval."

Almeric felt that, as far as he knew good from
evil, he would never lower himself by doing ill;
and though he had no actual belief in the appearance on earth of such myths as ghosts, he had
no objection to invite them to come and warn him
of the consequences if he should do wrong—
but then he felt himself so strong in his good intentions !

But now it is time that Almeric should himself
explain—what the astute Lord Danby has already
discovered—viz. :

That he has a troubled conscience; or that his
mind is full of care.

CHAPTER IX.

" NO ONE KNOWS WHAT WILL HAPPEN TO HIM BEFORE
SUNSET."

ON one occasion Almeric had entered the
library at Heraldstowe, through the conservatory. He had found the book he wanted,
and on turning to leave the room, inadvertently
came in contact with the open door of a cabinet.
A small bunch of keys was dangling in the lock.
As this was a very unusual circumstance, Almeric
stood hesitating as to what would be the best thing
to do. To lock the doors and take away the keys
might cause annoyance to Sir Hildebrand, when
he made his appearance; but to leave the keys in
the lock might, besides vexing him, be the cause
of a serious rebuke to his sister, who had the charge
of the cabinets.

While these thoughts were passing through his
mind he had listlessly opened and closed the tiny
drawers one by one, and allowed his eye to run over
a number of valuable coins as they lay in their
small recesses; and, he was about to close the doors
of the cabinet, lock them, and take the keys to his
sister, when he caught sight of a coin that riveted
his attention. He took it up, looked earnestly at
it for a second or two, and then said—at first inquiringly—

" Is it the six-angel piece?"* and afterwards en-

* See Note 2.

thusiastically—"It is—it is the very coin!" He
moved nearer to the open door of the conservatory the better to catch the light—for the library
was rather a dull than a cheerful apartment—and ·
after again examining it, he said, "It is, in positive truth, the 'six-angel piece of Edward VI.' and
my dear grandfather——"

But he heard footsteps approaching, and with a
a little start, yet still retaining the coin, he walked
through the conservatory and re-entered the lawn.
And once there without turning to ascertain by
whom he had been interrupted, in the full blaze
of the sun's light he stood and re-examined the
coin, convincing himself that he really held in his
hand that unique coin, "The six-angel piece of
Edward VI."

The interruption had been caused by a servant
who came to look for Miss Barrymore, and seeing
only Mr. Almeric retreating through the conservatory, he had immediately retired. But Almeric,
after, perhaps, a minute or two of study over the
coin, recollected himself. He perceived that he
was walking away from the house, and he had intended to go to his own room; but he had done
this unconsciously, and while still scrutinising the
coin; and besides, he had no intention of leaving
the precious contents of the cabinet exposed—as
he himself had found them—to any chance visitor
to the library. Not that he absolutely expected
either to find thieves in his grandfather's household, or that marauders who understood coins and

their value should accidentally enter the library
while the cabinet doors stood open! He knew
they ought not to be standing open, and this thought
pressed upon him as he stopped in his somewhat
hasty retreat, and said,

"But I have this coin in my hand, and it belongs to that cabinet. Now it was only the other
day, my dear old grandfather assured me, that he
never had had this coin in his collection; though I
even remembered the purchase of it! Poor dear
old man, his memory is very treacherous! I have
long known he is not aware of one-half of the
treasures he has in his possession. And then
again, sometimes he takes it into his dear old head
to give away a number of duplicates—duplicates!
Yes—when they are really so, all very well; but I
have known him give others—not duplicates—because in some lights he can scarcely distinguish
one coin from another—and—he does not like to
have his mistakes pointed out to him. Now—I
should wish to keep this piece in our cabinet, because it is unique."

Almeric stopped in his walk, stood hesitating
for a second or two, and then turned to retrace his
steps towards the house. As he walked on he
muttered to himself,

"It is of no use to restore this to the cabinet.
The dear old man may give it away any day, because he does not know that he has it. And then
again he cannot miss what he is quite sure he does
not posssess!"

And Almeric laughed, tossed up the coin, and caught it several times in succession; and then he seemed suddenly to recollect—for he again stood still as if thinking—that if he determined to keep the coin, he ought to do something about the cabinet; he ought, at least, to seek out his sister and tell her the cabinet was unlocked. He would do so. He quickened his pace, and walked on towards the windows of the drawing-room which opened upon the lawn.

" I wonder now if, strictly speaking, this would be called a theft ?" thought he. " I certainly do not wish to thieve," and he smiled, and once more tossed the coin into the air and caught it—"and I certainly do not hide my treasure, nor—nor run away, as a thief most certainly would," and Almeric laughed aloud. " But now I will just suppose, the grandson and heir of Sir Hildebrand Barry-Barrymore caught in the act of robbing the old man's cabinets of a gold coin ! Why, it would set the world in a blaze! Talk of a capital hit for a melodrama !—it would make the fortunes of newspaper proprietors, and of the editors of periodicals! I'll keep the coin against all comers," said he aloud, and purposely using the language of chivalry—" I'll keep it," added he, " just to see what will come of it."

And still he continued to toss up the coin, each time higher and higher, and to catch it, laughing, and as if enjoying the idea—"Of keeping it against all comers, just to see what would come of it !"

Almeric had walked on while these thoughts arose in his mind; but when he arrived at the open drawing-room windows he ceased to toss up the coin, put his hand to his waistcoat pocket with an intention of placing it there; but, instead of this, he held it tightly between his finger and thumb, and did not withdraw his hand from his pocket, while, on attempting to enter the room, he stood as if spell-bound, one foot in the room the other on the lawn, and his finger and thumb in his waistcoat-pocket.

"Almeric, what is the matter?" said Miss Barrymore, who stood at the piano apparently turning over the leaves of a music-book, but who, on seeing her brother, advanced to meet him.

Almeric's tongue was as silent as his figure was motionless. He said not a word, but continued to stand in an awkward position, one foot on the carpet, the other on the lawn—one hand in his waistcoat-pocket, a small book in the other, and staring at his sister in an earnest and serious manner.

"Almeric—dear Almeric!" said Miss Barry-more, as she still drew nearer to him, "what is the matter? Are you ill?"

"What do you mean?" said he in an uncourteous tone. "I am not ill," and he entered the drawing-room.

But, in explanation of Almeric's unusual behaviour, it must be told that Miss Barrymore's position in the drawing-room commanded—through the half-open door into the library—a view of that very cabinet from which he had just taken the coin. His conscience suddenly whispered to him, "Perhaps my sister *saw* me take it?" and hence the paralyzation of speech and motion.

"Something must be the matter," said she as she returned to the piano, "for you are out of temper, and this is unlike yourself."

Almeric became suddenly red in the face, when he admitted to himself "that he had behaved in an exceptional manner," and that that alone would account for the alteration in his appearance. He knitted his brows, and unwittingly nipped the coin the closer—for he had not taken his hand from his waistcoat pocket; but ere he could reply in the bitter words that again arose uppermost, a sound of a door shutting violently arrested their attention, and Miss Barrymore went into the library.

Almeric followed. She went direct from the drawing-room door to the door of the conservatory —which two doors were opposite to each other— while Almeric, unperceived by her, closed the small drawer in the cabinet from which he had taken the coin. Meanwhile Miss Barrymore had opened the door leading into the conservatory, to ascertain the cause of its having been closed with such violence.

"I beg your pardon," said a voice from the conservatory.

"Is it you, Johnson?" said Miss Barrymore; "no harm done, I hope?"

"Oh! no, ma'am; no harm."

Miss Barrymore re-closed the door of the conservatory, and, turning round, saw—the doors of the cabinet standing wide open!

Almeric had felt indignant with himself for the uncomfortable feeling he had had, under the supposition that Miss Barrymore had seen him take the coin. "I do not mean to steal," were the very words he said to himself when he closed the drawer while Miss Barrymore's attention was attracted elsewhere. "I do not mean to keep the coin," thought he, "if my grandfather wishes for it. And I only do not replace it in the cabinet, because I fear it may be given away in a moment of generosity, from a want of the knowledge of its real value."

We are not defending Mr. Almeric B. Barrymore's position—only chronicling facts!

CHAPTER X.

"THAT MISCHIEF COMES JUSTLY THAT IS OF YOUR 'OWN SEEKING."

"OH!" said Miss Barrymore, clasping her hands together as she turned, and saw the cabinet doors open—"I had forgotten!"

"The fact is, Zara, I went to the drawing-room on purpose to tell you I had seen the cabinet open," said Almeric. "I came here to fetch this book," showing her the one in his hand, "but, somehow, when I saw you at the piano I thought perhaps you knew all about it."

Almeric meant—"perhaps you *knew I had taken the coin*—perhaps you saw me take it." But Miss Barrymore, who thought Almeric meant that she *knew the cabinet doors were open*, said, in a tone of annoyance :

"Indeed, I did not know all about it; you might have felt sure, Almeric, that there was a mistake somewhere."

"I *am* sure of it," said he, with a smile, as he now, for the first time, dropped the coin into his waistcoat pocket, which, up to this time, he had retained between his finger and thumb, and he rapidly thought as he did so :

"There were three mistakes : dear old grandfather made the first ; he said he had not the 'six-angel piece.' I made the second ; I thought Zara had seen me take it. She made the third ; she left the cabinet doors open."

At this moment steps were heard in the drawing-room. Almeric re-entered it, and saw his grandfather, Sir Hildebrand Barry-Barrymore, leaning on the arm of his man Jasper.

"My dear grandfather, good morning," said Almeric, hastening to his assistance.

"Sir Hildebrand is not so well this morning," said Jasper.

"I am only fatigued with the effort of dressing —rest will revive me," said the old gentleman, as,

supported by Almeric on one side, and his attendant on the other, he entered the library.

Almeric saw at a glance that the cabinet doors
were closed and locked. Curiously enough, he
then wondered if his sister had opened the
drawers, and taken note of the missing coin!—
forgetting that the cabinet was not suspected of
enshrining so great a treasure. When Sir Hildebrand was at length seated, Miss Barrymore went
up to him, and putting her arm affectionately
on his shoulder, kissed his forehead, as she said :

" I need not open the cabinet yet—my dear
papa must rest a little. Am I right ?"

" Yes, darling; I will sit quiet for half an hour,
and then if I do not ring come to me."

After ascertaining that the light was tempered
to Sir Hildebrand's liking, he was left to the
repose he seemed so much to need, and Almeric
and his sister entered the drawing-room.

" Almeric—dear Almeric, what an escape I
have had!" said Miss Barrymore.

Almeric raised his eyebrows, as if expressive of
surprise, but he did not speak. He had silently
made up his mind to let Miss Barrymore talk, that
he might the more easily find out how much or
how little she really knew on the subject of the
six-angel piece.

" What a sin I have committed!" said she,
raising her arms, and standing in an attitude of
consternation.

" A sin ?" said he, in a doubtful tone.

He was not thinking of her, but of himself. The desire to keep the coin was gaining upon him, and he had again asked himself if he could lawfully do so.

"Yes—a sin," resumed she. "But I will tell you all about it, for things happen so strangely."

"They do indeed," said he, as he thought of the coin in his pocket.

"Dear grandpapa is so particular about the keys of his cabinets——"

"Of course," said Almeric, "and so he ought to be—indeed, he cannot be too careful, if he would keep his valuables."

Almeric said this with a strong feeling of regret that one of these "valuables" was at that moment in his own pocket; he felt a great temptation to pull it from its hiding-place, and throw it on the carpet, but he did not.

"Ah! I have so sincerely promised him, dear old man, never to allow these keys to be lying about——"

"Or in the door of the cabinet," said he, reproachfully; for, with a foolish inconsistence, as it seemed to him, he wished he had not been tempted by the open door; but then he scouted the idea that he had any wish to steal, and yet he felt a sort of, what appeared to him, an unworthy alarm at the thought of retaining the coin.

"You are right," said she, "or in the door. You will not betray me, Almeric, for grandpapa would not trust me to be the keeper of his keys if he suspected me of the carelessness of this morning."

"Betray you?" said he, with some dignity; and then he added, in a quiet tone: "Do you think I would betray myself?"

He was replying to the thought in his own mind, that to reveal Miss Barrymore's negligence to Sir Hildebrand would also, in all probability, expose the fact that *he* had taken the coin. She did not understand him in this sense, and said:

"Ah! dear Almeric—I know you are the very soul of honour!"

Even that speech from his sister grated upon Almeric's nerves, as if, somehow or other, he did not deserve it!

"But you shall hear how it happened. Jasper came from grandpapa, rather early this morning, with a message to the purport, that he wished me to be in readiness to open the cabinet as soon as he came down. He wished to begin immediately to re-arrange certain drawers."

"The British Series of Gold," said Almeric hastily, and in a slight tone of alarm—for he felt at once that the drawer from which he had taken the coin would be the very one his grandfather had fixed his attention upon, and probably that he had seen the " six-angel piece!"

"No, Almeric, no; how excited you are! Grandpapa has had so many recent additions to his collection of the 'silver coins of the Romans,' that they will certainly be the better for a careful readjustment. But the British gold arc so nearly perfect, and so beautifully arranged, I should think he will not waste his time over them. However, I was to be ready in the library to unlock the cabinet and take out the trays he might ask for. I went, therefore, in good time, and placed his chair and table; opened the window, and tried to fill the room with fresh air before he came down. I unlocked the cabinet, leaving the keys in the lock, and then sat down with my crochet in my hand, patiently to wait——"

"You were actually in the room?" said Almeric in an agitated manner, and for the moment feeling as if his sister had seen him take the coin!

"Of course," said she; "I never unlock the cabinet and leave the room unless dear grandpapa is there."

Now Almeric knew she had seen him; impulsively, with a humbled and unusual feeling of shame, he buried his face in his hands; and then in a second or two recollecting himself, he raised his head, and with a flush of pride on his handsome features, drew the coin from his pocket, opened his lips to tell her how and why he had taken it, when she prevented him by saying, without having noticed his action or altered manner,

"I sat at my crochet, I cannot say how long, a few minutes, perhaps, and then Mrs. Palmer came to me for work for the school. Forgetting I had placed the cabinet doors wide open, I hurried off with her, and——"

"Then you were *not* in the room," said Almeric in low tones of content.

And now he again placed his fingers in his waistcoat-pocket, and again nipped the coin with a feeling of desire.

"I tell you I went with Mrs. Palmer," said Miss Barrymore, in some natural surprise at Almeric's peculiar manner, "and on my return I went to the piano in the drawing-room, thinking no more, for the time being, of dear grandpapa and his curious cabinets of wonderful coins than I did of the man in the moon! You found me there, dear Almeric, and when the conservatory door closed with a bang, fortunately *I* went to see what was the matter! Matter enough! Not with the conservatory, but with the cabinet of coins! I had just time to re-lock the doors, and take out the keys, before dear grandfather entered the room!"

"And yet, Zara, why lock them at that particular minute? You say grandpapa sent to desire you to have them open ready for him."

"He sent to ask me to be in the library, ready to open them. But you see I was in a fright, and so I closed them. We do such eccentric things when we are fussed, do we not, Almeric? I really meant to open the doors, instead of which I closed them."

"We do eccentric things, indeed," said he, "sometimes in a very cool manner,"—he was thinking of himself.

"Yes, we do. It was very foolish to lock the doors at that particular minute; my terror made me do exactly the thing I ought not to have done," said she.

"Suppose, during your absence, any one had surreptitiously entered the library, and stolen—"

Almeric paused, he was again thinking of himself.

"Lots of valuable coins!" said she, jingling the keys and laughing.

"I went to the library for the 'Eikon Basilike,' and after seeing the cabinet open, I determined to seek you, and know the reason of so unusual an occurrence."

"Why did you not come into this room, instead of going all round by the lawn, and entering through the window?"

"I went to the conservatory for the sake of light, and——"

"For the sake of light! oh, to examine the book in your hand."

Almeric blushed up to the very roots of his hair, and stood silent! Was it come to this!—had he then stolen the coin, and was he at that moment acting a lie!—for he remembered it was *the coin* for which he required light.

"The library is always dark," said Miss Barrymore. "Well, go on, dear."

"I fancied I heard footsteps approaching," said he with a sigh.

"Well, Almeric, do, pray, go on," said Miss Barrymore, impatiently.

And Almeric recovered himself, for he laughed as he said, " Why, my dear, I was like you—I did exactly the contrary to my own intention. First, I walked away from the library; then, I remember, I intended to seek you——"

"How strange and odd! But what had alarmed you? It was my fright made me act oddly—what had for the moment unnerved you?"

"The footsteps. I had gone to the door of the conservatory to catch the light—" again Almeric stopped as he remembered the sun's rays on the coin in his hand.

"To catch the light?" said Miss Barrymore; "ah, yes, on the book in your hand. And so you walked away reading, as you often do, dear Almeric; and then suddenly found—found——"

"Found I had walked wrong. Because, though I did not know you were in the drawing-room, it is certain I should not have gone to seek you on the lawn at this hour."

"And that accounts for your extraordinary stare of surprise when you saw me at the piano," said she.

"Does it?" said he listlessly.

"Yes; because you did not expect to see me there."

"Certainly I did not; and I cannot even now understand why you did not see me, or hear me in the library?"

"I had only that moment returned; indeed, I had not had time to know or hear anything."

CHAPTER XI.

"CONSIDERATION GETS AS MANY VICTORIES AS RASH-
NESS LOSES."

THE conversation between the brother and sister
was interrupted by the sound of a "silver
call" or whistle that Sir Hildebrand was in the
habit of using.

"I must go," said Miss Barrymore. And Almeric took up his hat and walked out of the open
window on to the lawn. When there, he recollected he meant to go to his own room, and he
went slowly round the house to the hall-door,
where he stood for a few seconds again attentively scrutinizing "the six-angel piece," in the
full glare of the sun. He held the coin between
his finger and thumb, as he musingly crossed to
the large staircase—opposite the great entrance
doors of the hall—and which branched to the
right and left on either side. Just as he placed
his foot on the first stair, he accidentally touched
the outstretched arm of one of the many coats of
armour standing there.

"I always said that arm was in an unsafe position, and so it is," said he, stopping to look at it.
He tried to bend the arm of the statue more to his
satisfaction, but failed. He would not allow himself to be conquered; he made another attempt,
which was more successful, only that in gaining

one point he lost another, for the coin slipped from between his finger and thumb. "Humph!" said Almeric, as he saw it caught in the hollow of the arm at the elbow joint. He continued to alter the position of the arm without observing that, by this movement, the coin was gradually sucked out of sight between the padding and the metal. Eventually he placed the statue in a position that satisfied him, and then he put his finger in at the elbow joint to poke out the coin; unfortunately he only touched the edge of it, and pushed it lower down. "Now, this *is* careless of me," said he, "but I do not mean to be beaten, even by 'six angels.'" He laughed at his own wit, and went more carefully to work. He had no better success; by some means or other it always happened that, instead of drawing the coin back to the edge, where it had been so accidentally drawn in, he pushed it lower down. He distinctly heard it rub or grate against the metal of that part of the arm called the "rere-brace," as with his long finger he tried to recover it. He desisted, and stood for a few seconds considering what would be the best thing to do. "Perhaps I might draw it forth with a small pair of pincers, otherwise I must take off the gauntlet, and push the coin out at the wrist." With this thought he ceased from his labours.

As he went up the stairs and through the long corridors, a feeling of annoyance at this new trouble took possession of him. Almeric was by nature good-tempered—by disposition thoughtful; but within this last hour or so he had felt more inclined to irritability than in all his former life.

In his own room, he seated himself in his cozy armchair at the open window, and fell into a train of thought.

" If it had been a shilling, or even a sovereign, I should have told one of the men-servants to see to it, and bring it to me. But—and it seems strange—I cannot like to ask anyone to look for the ' six-angel piece.' "

Insensibly he began to enjoy the scene from the window, which opened upon an extensive view of Heraldstowe Park. Almeric was fond of natural history, and Sir Hildebrand was one of the few gentlemen in England who would not allow a shot to be fired in his grounds, except for the necessary destruction of rabbits. The consequence of which was, that many rare birds were found at Heraldstowe, and all birds were tame. At a great distance from the house, and in the valley, lay a lake of some considerable size ; waterfowl were plentiful there. Almeric took a field glass, and sat watching a pair of herons, perched on the topmost boughs of one of the tall trees on the margin of the lake. Yet every now and then, and in spite of the home-scene, his thoughts went back to the coin. " I have been very foolish to let it slip into the arm of the Sieur Almeric Marmaduke Barry-Barrymore," said he—for the suits of armour standing in the long galleries, and in the hall at Heraldstowe, were named after the wearers of them in the days of chivalry.

The Barrymores, from generation to generation, religiously believed that these *very* suits of armour had been worn by the barons in the Crusades, and these suits stood in such excellent preservation in the hall and galleries, as to excite the surprise and veneration of those who had the privilege of examining them. If there were any doubt in the minds of the " privileged " as to whether these suits of armour were used at this period of time, or that, no one ventured to hint so much to Sir Hildebrand.

There is indeed excellent authority to prove —in spite of the faith of the Barrymores in their relics of the olden time—that there is no complete suit of armour in England of a date anterior to Henry VII., 1485—1509.* Nevertheless, the armoury in the Tower shows the effigy of Edward I., 1272, and of many others previous to the reign of Henry VII. How, then, did this extraordinary mystification, with regard to suits of armour, arise? Let the sins of the Barrymores, and of the Tower of London, in this respect lie upon the conscience of the Emperor Charles V.†

But to return to Almeric. He stretched out his legs, crossed one over the other, and fell, apparently, into profound thought. He went back to the time when, as a boy, he had talked to these

* See Note 3.   † See Note 4.

very suits of armour, and told them "that if he ever did an evil deed, he hoped they would come in all their panoply and punish him."

"Curious," said he aloud, "that I should think of this nonsense now. This is not an evil deed."

He remembered that in the olden time, and even down to a late period in the present century, Heraldstowe was said to be well tenanted by ghosts. He had read the legends connected with the house, which explained that every evil-doing Barrymore was always tormented by these beings from another world! He himself had no belief in ghosts, and he had laughed heartily at some of the legends; but assuredly at this moment he did not feel inclined either to laugh at what he had read, or to dispute the truth thereof.

"I believe it to be in the power of the imagination to fancy objects are present when there is, in fact, only empty space," said he, musingly.

And now, partly as an experiment, and partly with a feeling of defiance against the doctrine of "ghosts," he set his inventive faculty and his will to work to conjure up some unsightly sprite whom he might expect to meet in the dark, or on any unprecedented and unlooked-for occasion—that is to say, that he might expect to meet *if he had committed a sin by taking the coin!*

"Black, of course," said he, with a smile— "humpbacked, glaring fiery eyes, lame, malicious-looking, grinning, and showing its huge and hideous teeth."

He again fell into a reverie, chiefly upon the gallant deeds of his ancestors, who, by their suits of armour, were so well represented at Herald-stowe. Presently he closed his eyes, and withdrew from the glare of the sun; only a moment were they closed, but when he opened them, turning his head, at the same time, away from the open window, he started, and arose from his chair, eagerly gazing on some object in the distant part of the room.

"I really thought," said he, knitting his brows, and shading his eyes with his hand—"I really thought I saw the venerable Baron Almeric, whose panoply stands in the hall."

He reseated himself, but pushed his chair out of the reach of the sun's rays, as he said, with a genial smile:

"If the worthy Baron supposes I shall take him for a hobgoblin, he is mistaken. Nevertheless, I will keep him in my mind, for that was one of the most curious deceits I ever saw. Certainly, when I opened my eyes, there stood the Baron; but the longer I looked, and the harder I stared, the quicker the good gentleman vanished. No! I have not defined his movements—he did not *vanish*, which is to go suddenly; he *melted* away gradually, until at length I could see the objects in the room, at first hidden by his burly figure. I declare positively I have seen this sight!"*

Almeric remained seated a few minutes longer,

---

* See Note 5.

every now and then gazing round the room, half expecting—indeed, half hoping to see the Baron again.

"I wonder, now, if the old Baron is uneasy with those 'six angels' in his sleeve! If I were to see him again, and if he were to point to his arm that I had handled so roughly this morning— and, by-the-bye, the legends say that the barons do not like to have their panoplies disturbed—I should understand he was mutely imploring me to take away the thing that was useless to him! If he himself were only as clever as the greater number of these old barons are said to be, he would find the coin without troubling me to go to work, and offer it to me when next I pass through the hall."

And then Almeric sat wondering how such a posture would suit. In his mind's eye he altered the attitude of the Baron, as he was known to be then standing in the hall, and placed him in another, with the golden coin held between the finger and the thumb. At this moment the gong sounded through the house, and Almeric went to luncheon.

CHAPTER XII.

"NAETHING FREER THAN A GIFT."

IT is recorded somewhere in this chronicle that Sir Hildebrand Barry-Barrymore is an old man, and that Almeric is his grandson and heir. Of the Barrymores who lie dead and buried under their grand marble tombs in the church of St. Mary-on-the-Knoll, no account will be given. Almeric's father and mother and elder brothers lie there, but they and their lives have had no influence on him. He and his sister Zara were left orphans at an early age, and Sir Hildebrand brought them up. Almeric was approaching his twenty-first birthday, Zara her nineteenth. They both possessed in no small degree the gifts hereditary in the Barrymores. Like most in their position in the world, they were well bred, and well educated. The shades of character that invariably distinguish one human being from another will be duly chronicled. Nevertheless, it may be admitted even now that they were pleasant-spoken and agreeable young people, and general favourites throughout the county of Z——.

There are three "Sarahs" to be introduced to the reader in this chapter. Sarah Fortescue is the only child of Captain and Mrs. Fortescue. They reside in a handsome house called "The Pynes," at the south entrance of the town of Stowe-in-the-Valley; which town by the high road is fully four miles distant from Heraldstowe; but through the woods and fields, from the "Pynes" to Heraldstowe only about two. Captain and Mrs. Fortescue have no grand relations in this part of the county of Z——, and no grand marble tombs to be mentioned in this chronicle; but they are very excellent people, and visit with all the neighbouring gentry.

Of Sarah, their only child, it is necessary to say something. It will be remembered that she had the honour of being noticed by Lord Danby at the Abbey *fête*, who prophesied she would eventually become, by the appearance of her figure, a " Dame Partlet."

Sarah was neither tall nor short; nor fair nor dark ; nor thin nor stout. She was a creature of negatives. She was not ungraceful, for she had the elegant easy movements of a harmonious whole. Lord Danby might not agree with the expression, " a harmonious whole," and particularly as applied to Sarah Fortescue; but the mind is indicated by the motion of the body, and we do not admit Lord Danby as any great authority in such matters.

Sarah Fortescue's complexion would not bear the light of day ; and yet, strange to say, it looked clear and well at night. Her face was freckled, and her skin had a smudged and shady look by day ; but at night the unsightly freckles vanished, and Sarah's face—comparatively speaking—looked white. Her hair was brown, not too plentiful, and yet it was far from being scant. Her eyes were grey and her features small. She was on an introduction a plain-looking, well-dressed young lady, with just enough of fashion in her toilette to shew her standing in the county ; and just enough of shyness, to make clear to observing people that she had no personal friend; for companionship usually gives support, and promotes confidence in one's self. Sarah was an industrious, moderately accomplished, and useful girl; but as truthful chroniclers we cannot place her on a high pedestal.

The next of the three "Sarahs" is Sara Thorn.

She, too, was pointed out by Lord Danby at the Abbey *fête.* His opinion of her was also unfavourable. And here, in justice to ourselves, we must state it is our duty to chronicle Lord Danby's sayings and doings, but we do not vouch for the truth of any one single word he may utter!

In our judgment, Sara Thorn was tall and slender, and fair and fresh and blooming; we feel we can make something of her; perhaps even a heroine; who shall say?

Sara Thorn was the daughter of the Reverend Ulric Thorn, Vicar of Stowe-in-the-Valley. He came from a distant county to take the living of Stowe, some ten years prior to the opening of this chronicle. Stowe Church, sometimes called "St. Mary's," is the same as that previously mentioned as "St. Mary's-on-the-Knoll."

There were three remarkable "knolls" on the Heraldstowe estate. "The Cedar knoll," standing in the cedar grove in a distant part of the Park; and the two knolls near to the Vicarage, upon one of which the church was built, and hence the name " St. Mary-on-the-Knoll." The other was in the precincts of the Park itself, and crowned by a splendid group of forest trees. These two last-mentioned knolls were divided by the high road, which skirted one side of the churchyard, and which was within a stone's throw of " St. Mary's;" but the " knoll" in the Park was nearly half a mile distant from the road.

The handsome Vicarage, standing in its own grounds just outside the Park Gates, and near to the church, was the link between the town of Stowe-in-the-Valley, and the county of Z——. " County people" visited at the Vicarage, and the humbler gentry living in the town of Stowe were also received there. Mr. Thorn was a widower. He had a family of three—Sara about nineteen, Gerald about fourteen, and Rosa twelve. They were all good-looking; but Sara was a beauty, a belle, an accomplished, well-read, and clever young woman—perhaps not free from faults of character; but these, when they appear, will certainly be entered in this chronicle—but yet a very general favourite in the large and aristocratic county of Z——"

The third Sarah is partly known to the reader.

Zara Barry-Barrymore was tall, even taller than Sara Thorn. Her complexion was dark, toned by the clear rich blood mantling in her cheeks. Her hair was of a glossy dark brown, her eyes also were dark and large. It is right to record that Zara Barrymore was very handsome. She had a fine figure, a courtly manner, and the clearly chiselled features possessed by the Barrymores from generation to generation. She, too, was clever and accomplished.

There were reasons why the simple name of Sarah was spelt by these ladies in three different ways.

With the Barrymores it was a family name, and always written "Zara." In days of old—that is, in the times of the crusading Barons, whose panoplies peopled the halls and galleries of Heraldstowe— the name had not unfrequently belonged to ladies of great beauty and of high degree in their own far-off countries; who had married into the house of Barrymore, and whose sayings and doings had been recorded by the minstrelsy of that age. Hence the name *Zara* as a family name. When Miss Thorn grew up into young-ladyhood, and found that "Zara" was identical with her own name in its meaning, she, too, made as near an approach to that orthography as she reasonably could, and ever after signed herself "Sara."

Miss Fortescue, on the contrary, saw no poetry in "Zara," no improvement in "Sara;" she continued to be the old-fashioned "Sarah."

The meaning of the name is "Princess."

Now, Sir Hildebrand Barrymore said they were all three "Princesses"—ay, "Princesses" upon whose names and doings fairy tales ought to be written. Indeed, he was prone to say a great deal both to the young ladies themselves, and also on the subject of their names.

He called Miss Fortescue his "gracious Princess," because her name was "Sarah Anna." Now, "Anna," by some authors, means "grace," but Sir Hildebrand averred it meant "gracious." Miss Thorn he called his "winsome Princess," because she had been christened "Emily Sara," but the first name was dropped, for it was Mrs. Thorn's, and might have created confusion. "Emily" meant, according to some translators, "of winning speech," but Sir Hildebrand said "winsome" was a just meaning.

"Zara" meant "Princess," but we have no means of recording truthfully that Sir Hildebrand thought Miss Barrymore more of a "Princess" than the two other ladies; if he did think so, he was too courteous to express his thoughts.

Now, there were occasions in which Sir Hildebrand would talk very learnedly to these three young ladies; and on one of these he told them that

"All the Sarahs who inhabited this world were in the possession of three gifts. He had lived a long life, but he had never known a Zara, Sara, or Sarah without these three gifts."

Charming "Sara" Thorne ventured to dispute with him, upon the principle that "there was no rule without exception." Sir Hildebrand said, "She, Miss Thorn, ought to be that exception in her own proper person, for having dared to suggest such a thing. But pray," continued he, "do you know what these three gifts are that pre-eminently grace the Sarahs?"

Miss Thorn confessed her ignorance; Miss Barrymore and Miss Fortescue each pleaded utter unconsciousness of any superior gift belonging to herself. And yet Miss Barrymore was handsome, and knew it. But Miss Fortescue had the grace of modesty as regarded any high opinion of herself.

"Listen," said Sir Hildebrand, holding up his finger. "All Sarahs are 'handsome, clever, and good;' here and there you see an instance of one gift outshining the other two, but, as a rule, all Sarahs are 'handsome,'" and he bowed to Miss Barrymore; 'clever,' and he bowed to Miss Thorn: "and 'good,' like my 'gracious Princess' here," continued he, as he patted Miss Fortescue on the back.

Miss Thorn and Miss Barrymore began to dispute the position that Sir Hildebrand had taken up; and if anyone had heard how gallantly the old gentleman defended himself, no doubt his courage would have been admired, even though exercised on so unstable a cause.

Now, Miss Barrymore, who was herself so handsome, positively averred that "all Sarahs" were *not* handsome; and the 'clever' Miss Thorn said that "all Sarahs" were *not* clever,—and this, too, in the very presence of Sir Hildebrand! Miss Fortescue said not a word. The epithet "good" had been distinctly given to her. Perhaps then she thought that all the Sarahs in the world were "good" in right of their Christian name; it is certain she did not attempt to dispute the matter.

Will it be credited that a little harmless nonsense of this sort, uttered playfully by an elderly
gentleman, created bickerings, jealousies, quarrel-
ings, heartburnings, and such like? It did.

Miss Barrymore, as we have said, was very
handsome. And because she was so pre-eminently handsome herself, she contended that Miss
Fortescue was *not* handsome—never had been—
never could be!

Miss Thorn made just as great an outcry after
the gift of "cleverness" as Miss Barrymore had
done after that of beauty. She averred Miss
Fortescue was *not* talented; it was absurd of Sir
Hildebrand to so puff her up with the idea of pos-
sessing "three gifts." It was clear to all people of
sense and judgment that of beauty she had none, of
talent she had less, and of goodness she had it all to
grow! Surely here, then, was the "exception"
that proved the rule of the "three gifts to the
Sarahs!"

Sometimes "Maidenhood" is a little spiteful
to its sisters. We regret the necessity to chronicle
this.

The "three Sarahs" living in the neighbourhood of Prellsthorpe, and mentioned by Lord
Danby at the Abbey *fête*, are now all introduced.

CHAPTER XIII.

"ALL IS NOT LOST THAT IS IN DANGER."

OF the library at Heraldstowe we may say that, as regards velvet pile carpets, rich velvet chairs and sofas, carved oak furniture, stone mullioned windows filled with richly-coloured glass, through which the sun's rays glimmer and glitter now and then upon golden inkstands, carved ivory paper-knives, jewelled pen trays, charming statuettes in bronze and silver, elegant chandeliers, numerous books in dainty bindings— we say again that, as regards all these, and many more articles of use and luxury to be seen in the well-stocked libraries of wealthy, old gentlemen, we leave them, one and all, to the imagination of the reader. It is, however, necessary to make clear the geography of the room. First, then, there was but one window, and that a large, capacious oriel. This window was at that end of the library that looked upon the lawn. At the other end of the room was the fireplace, and the magnificently-carved oaken chimney-piece reaching to the ceiling. Midway in the length of the room was a door, opening from the conservatory ; precisely opposite to this was the door from the drawing-room. When these doors were closed, they presented huge mirrors, and exactly filled up the space between the bookcases. These bookcases reached to the ceiling, and filled the entire length of the room, if we except here and there a recess for a cabinet of costly workmanship. There was a small door at the right hand of the fireplace, used by the domestics in passing to and fro; this was masked by fictitious bookshelves, apparently filled with books, painted on the side next the library, and preventing, when closed, any blot or want of unity in the appearance of the room.

And now we will return to Almeric Barrymore, whom we left descending the stairs to luncheon. The three Sarahs were present, but not Sir Hildebrand; a tray was carried to him in the library.

" Grandpapa wants us all as soon as we have finished luncheon," said Miss Barrymore.

" What for?" said Almeric; " you must do without me—I am going to Stowe."

" Oh! nothing particular," said Miss Barrymore, " only Miss Fortescue has called with a message from her father, and as it is on the subject of coins, grandpapa is proportionately impatient."

" Are they, then, so very wonderful?" said Miss Thorn.

" I do not know," said Miss Fortescue.

" Did Captain Fortescue get them from one of the Jews who come this way sometimes?" said Almeric.

" I do not know," said Miss Fortescue.

" H., you are certainly one of the class of ' don't

knows' and 'can't tells,'" said Miss Thorn, laughing.

" Yes," said Miss Barrrymore to Miss Fortescue —" you are always careful of committing yourself : but perhaps that is rather worthy of praise than blame."

" Why do you call Miss Fortescue II. ?" said Almeric—" I have noticed this before to-day."

The two ladies who had transgressed laughed, while Miss Fortescue turned away to hide the pain she felt at being the subject of so many remarks.

" We call her II. because it is her ' gift,' " said Miss Thorn.

" No, Almeric ; we call her II. because she spells Sarah with an II.," said Miss Barrymore.

" She is quite right," said Almeric, " to spell her own name as she pleases ; she ought to retort, and call you Z.," said he, rather brusquely.

" Excuse me," said Miss Barrymore to Miss Fortescue—" I only spoke in play."

She had followed Miss Thorn's lead, and felt ashamed of herself. Sir Hildebrand's " call " was heard at this moment.

" There," said Miss Barrymore—" grandpapa is impatient. Shall we go ? Almeric, do come in just for a few minutes," and the three ladies left the room.

" And so your papa wants to see me, my dear ?" said Sir Hildebrand to Miss Fortescue, as soon as the usual greetings were over.

"Yes; he wants to show you his additions to his collection of coins."

"And I want to see your papa, my dear; for yesterday, amid a heap of gold and silver stowed away as duplicates, or coins, perhaps, of small value, I discovered two that I did not know I possessed. Will you tell him, my dear, I have the 'six-angel piece' of Edward VI., and the 'first gold sovereign of Henry VII.?' The six-angel piece was never in circulation."

"Never put into circulation!" said Miss Fortescue, in a tone of surprise; and she was going to add, "then how did it come into your possession?" for she was not aware that collectors of coins often purchase from the Mint for the sake of rare and perfect specimens; but Sir Hildebrand prevented this, for he said:

"Never in circulation, my dear. It is a pattern piece—would you like to see it?"

Miss Fortescue at once expressed a wish to see the coin.

"And then you can tell Captain Fortescue the show will not be all on his side," said Sir Hildebrand laughing.

Almeric entered the library at this moment. He intended to ride to Stowe—indeed, he had ordered his horse—but, to oblige his sister, he joined the party for a few minutes, meaning to retire as soon as he conveniently could.

"Ah! Almeric, you are come at the right moment," said Sir Hildebrand. "Just open the

cabinet and give me the third tray from the top.
I want to shew the ladies my 'six-angel piece,' and
'first gold sovereign.'"

Almeric stood silent from astonishment. He
could scarcely credit that he heard aright.

"Reach down the third drawer, my dear boy,"
said Sir Hildebrand.

"Did you ask me to do something?" said Almeric. "I beg your pardon," added he, recovering himself a little, and scarcely knowing what to
do in this sudden dilemma.

Meanwhile Miss Barrymore was in the act of
unlocking the cabinet, and he remained standing
by his grandfather's chair. Instinctively he
turned away his eyes with a sickening feeling of
dread at he knew not what; then he wondered
what he should say or do as soon as the discovery
was made that the coin had been taken from the
drawer. He looked furtively at the two young
ladies, Miss Fortescue and Miss Thorn, and wished
they were not present. He felt that he would at
once declare to his grandfather and sister the
actual facts, but somehow he could not do this in
the presence of visitors. These thoughts passed
through his mind much more rapidly than the
pen can jot them down ; and just as he saw Miss
Barrymore take the drawer from the cabinet, he
turned, with the double hope of escaping from his
uncomfortable position, and of going to the hall
to set the coin at liberty, and restore it, when a
loud exclamation, followed by a continued clatter

as of something falling, recalled him to himself, and he comprehended in a moment that Miss Barrymore had let the tray fall and that the coins were rolling over the carpet! Thought is rapid, and Almeric instantaneously felt that this mishap would assist him for the time being in concealing the absence of the coin, and probably give him time to liberate and restore it.

" They will fancy it is lying somewhere on the carpet hidden from their researches; and meanwhile I will go to work and—" and he turned to leave the room.

" Almeric, where are you going?" said Miss Barrymore. " Do, pray, help us."

Thus recalled to the actual scene before him, he saw the three ladies on their knees, searching for and picking up the coins. He imitated the ladies, and employed himself in searching for those specimens still missing, and congratulating himself on the fortunate fall of the tray, that would give him time to act, and to replace, or to restore the coin to his grandfather. The coins were carried to Sir Hildebrand as soon as they were found, and he occupied himself by re-arranging them. At length he said joyfully,

" All found !"

" All found !" said Almeric in a tone of very genuine surprise.

" Yes, my dear boy, all found! What is there remarkable in that ?"

Almeric did not reply. His mind was trying

to fathom the mystery of "the six-angel piece" having been restored to the cabinet without his assistance!

"You have given me the wrong drawer, my dear," said Sir Hildebrand quietly. "Replace this, which is the fourth drawer, and give me the third."

Did Almeric hear aright? Then his position was unaltered, and the coin would be missed! Again he turned to the door with the desire of escaping, if possible, from this second dilemma. Almeric's steps were arrested by a sharp cry from several voices, followed by the same clatter, clatter he had so recently heard. On the first alarm Almeric turned, and raised his eyes to the cabinet. Yes, he could confidently assure himself now that the right tray had been taken out, and that the coins were scattered over the carpet.

"What on earth is the matter with you, Almeric?" said Sir Hildebrand.

"Matter with me!—nothing," said Almeric, quite unaware that there was anything unusual in his manner or appearance.

"Almeric is fussing himself about the coins," said Miss Barrymore laughing. "I think, dear grandpapa, he is even more tenacious than yourself of the possession of rare and beautiful coins! He is vexed at our clumsiness in upsetting the trays."

"Is that it, my dear boy?" said Sir Hildebrand kindly. "I am glad and proud to find in you a

taste similar to my own. It is rare in one so
young. You shall have *carte-blanche* in the
matter of coins, Almeric, in addition to your own
income."

" I shall restore it, of course," said Almeric to
himself, a feeling of shame dyeing his cheeks for
the moment. "It is unfortunate, it is, for the
time being, in the clutches of the Sieur Almeric,
otherwise I would fetch it ! "

So thought Almeric, as he assisted the ladies to
pick up and restore the coins to Sir Hildebrand ;
but he soon found that he would not have had
the power to leave the room unless he had first
stated his reason ; for Sir Hildebrand was always
calling to him, to look here, and look there, to
stoop down and put his long arm under this
cabinet, and then under that, &c., &c.

And strange, indeed, did it seem to the whole
party so eagerly searching over the carpet, that
the only coins they could not find were—" the first
gold sovereign of Henry VII.," and "the six-
angel piece of Edward VI."

" I wonder where that gold sovereign can have
hidden itself ?" said Almeric, growing impatient at
the time he lost in crawling over the carpet.

" Exactly where the 'the six angels' have
hidden themselves, to be sure," said Miss Barrymore laughing.

" No, no, I deny that," said Almeric, eagerly
and truthfully, and forgetting that he might thereby betray himself.

"My dear boy, how anxious you are!" said Sir Hildebrand, unsuspiciously.

"But they may be found lying close together, for all your positive denial," said Miss Thorn ; "'birds of a feather flock together,' and these are rare and valuable birds."

"Where can they have rolled?" said Sir Hildebrand.

The young ladies crushed and rumpled their pretty "French organdies" by kneeling on the carpet, and creeping hither and thither ; and Almeric's head grew dizzy with stooping about, and affecting to look for a coin which he knew was in a very different place.

Sir Hildebrand himself joined in the search at length—for he, too, felt impatient with the delay, and tired of looking on. He even kneeled down in the oriel window, to examine closely the inlaid work; for the floor of the oriel was the only part of the room uncarpeted, and it was tricked out in beautiful patterns with different kinds of real woods, polished, and arranged in mosaic.

"Dear grandpapa, we cannot allow you to fatigue yourself!" said Miss Barrymore ; "surely we are able to look about until we find the missing treasures."

"They must be in the room," said Miss Thorn, "that is one comfort."

Sir Hildebrand re-seated himself in his easychair, and said,

"True, my 'winsome Princess,' they must, as

you say, be in the room. Almeric, lock the door near the fireplace and bring me the key."

Almeric obeyed.

"And now lock also the conservatory and drawing-room doors, and bring me the keys."

Almeric stood staring with astonishment at this new request from Sir Hildebrand. At that moment he was thinking over in his own mind the quietest and easiest means of making his escape, and of trying to coax that avaricious old Baron Almeric to restore to him the "six angels." But if his grandfather insisted upon locking the doors this chance would be lost. At this moment his eye fell upon Miss Barrymore, standing in a distant part of the room, pale and irresolute; then she put her hand to her brow as a spasm of alarm crossed her features; he saw that the possibility of these coins having been stolen while the cabinet doors were left open, had now pressed itself upon her mind.

"Now," said Sir Hildebrand, "bring me the keys, Almeric, and then we five are made prisoners here until the coins are found."

This was rather arbitrary on the part of Sir Hildebrand, and rather uncourteous. It appeared more than usually so from him, who was remarkable for his polished manners and high-breeding, Almeric slowly obeyed this disagreeable command. And then it became evident that this refined old gentleman of the old school had for the moment laid aside his dignity; for he took the keys from

Almeric, and put them into his pocket! This act seemed to have a curious effect on the three ladies—they ceased their search over the carpet, and stood silent and inactive. An exceptional occurrence almost always arrests the flow of our thoughts and actions ; it was unusual to find themselves " locked in," and, for the time being, that one subject took possession of their thoughts. But Sir Hildebrand had observed Almeric's attempts to escape—and had taken this means of preventing him from leaving the room.

" Are you sure the coins were actually in the tray?" said Almeric to his sister.

He asked this question because the " first gold sovereign of Henry VII." was missing, as well as the " six-angel piece," and he had *not* taken both !

" Ah ! my dear Almeric !" said Miss Barrymore, who fancied he was hinting at her neglect of the morning, in leaving the cabinet doors open. She was mistaken, he had no such thought—but now she felt almost overpowered with the nervous dread of what, perhaps, had happened through her own carelessness !

Almeric read his sister's thoughts, and moreover knew that one coin had been taken : for the moment an unworthy idea tenaciously pressed itself upon him—even that he might keep the coin and remain unsuspected !

" Deliver me from temptation" is one petition of our daily prayer. Only a minute or two previously, Almeric's most earnest wish had been to leave the room for the purpose of liberating the coin and restoring it; and now, tempted by the sight of his sister's inward acknowledgement of her fault, and certainty that the loss had been occasioned by her neglect, he resigned himself to his present position with less anxiety as to the result.

But all this time we are leaving Sir Hildebrand under the ban of acting uncourteously to his guests. After a short pause he turned to Miss Fortescue, and said,

"I am very much grieved, my dear 'gracious princess,' at this little *contretemps*. The coins must eventually be found, because they have not feet wherewith to walk away, neither have they wings——"

"You forget the invisible 'angel's wings,' my dear sir," said Miss Thorn, playfully interrupting him, "and also the immense power in the hands of the first sovereign in the land!"

She alluded to the fact that this was the *first sovereign* coined in England.*

"It seems almost incredible," said Sir Hildebrand, "that 'angels' should have the power to ruffle my temper; but I am afraid I shall not like the 'invisible wings' you speak of to cause my 'six angels' to become invisible to me."

"Why, my dear sir, they are only playing at hide-and-seek," said Miss Thorn; "'the sovereign' trying to capture 'the six angels,' or 'the six

* See Note 6.

angels' to fly away with the 'sovereign.'"

"True, true, my winsome lady—very well put," said Sir Hildebrand laughing; "therefore I shall keep up my spirits, bide my time, and *not* have the floor of the oriel taken up just yet."

"But I do not see that the coins are more likely to be lost in the bay-window than on the carpet," said Miss Fortescue in her simplicity. She did not know the difference between a bow, a bay, or an oriel-window.

"The floor of the 'oriel,'" said Miss Thorn in her wisdom, and attempting to shew that she knew an oriel from an aureole, "is a sort of par-quetage, so to speak, and if any small piece should by chance be displaced, the coin or coins might roll into the hole thus made, and there remain con-cealed. That is Sir Hildebrand's meaning, I think."

"True, true again, my 'princesses,'" said Sir Hildebrand, evidently trying, by his gracious speeches now, to make up for his want of courtesy only a few minutes previously.

"I wish the coins could be found," said Miss Fortescue once again in her simplicity, "because I know papa wishes to ride to Thorny-dyke, and he will not leave dear mamma until I return."

This was, of course, a hint to Sir Hildebrand that he was detaining her an unwilling prisoner. Miss Thorn turned away with a smile; but Sir Hildebrand, with much urbanity of manner, came forward to redeem himself in the opinion of his visitors, as he said,

"Tell Captain Fortescue I have no particular engagement on my list at present. I hope he will come soon; I am impatient to behold the recent additions to his collection. And also tell him he will have the advantage of me, and be able to shew much better trays than I, unless, indeed, I can recover my lost treasures."

Almeric and Zara had never given up the search. They were still feeling under, and behind cabinets, and conversing in low tones on the annoyances of the morning.

"Now, Almeric, take the key and let out the Princesses. They disdain to bestow their sweet smiles any longer on an old worn-out knight like myself. Set them free—set them free!"

"I am afraid I must go," said Miss Fortescue deferentially.

"Yes; papa waits for his morning's ride. And my 'winsome princess' is longing to shake out her flounces and furbelows, that have been so sadly crushed by her kind search over my carpet. Good morning, I bow you both out," and Sir Hildebrand arose and bowed in an old-fashioned, stately manner. "You may well wish to get out of this hot and close room!" continued he to Miss Fortescue. "Tell me, have I not been unmerciful?"

By this time Almeric had unlocked the door.

"Good morning," said Miss Thorn, as she shook hands with her friends. "I do hope you will soon find the coins."

"Good morning," said Miss Fortescue. "I wish
I could stay longer and help you."

And the two young ladies walked away together.

CHAPTER XIV.

"ANGER BEGINS WITH FOLLY, AND ENDS WITH REPENT-
ANCE."

THE two friends walked through the lawns and
shrubberies of Heraldstowe, and across a
corner of the Park, on the way to their homes,
when they at length arrived at a stile that separated the Park from a wood through which their
path lay. This was a large, old-fashioned stone
stile, consisting of two deep steps of stone, and
two upright stones at the top, through which very
obese people might find some difficulty in passing.
Miss Thorn went first; unfortunately as she
passed through the narrow opening at the top, she
entangled her dress. On setting it at liberty, and
shaking it, something dropped with a ringing
sound, and rolled to the edge of the stone step,
bumping down upon the second, and again rolling
along, eventually to drop upon the ground. By
this time Miss Fortescue was at the top of the
stile, pressing through the niche, and Miss Thorn
had descended on the other side, and, turning,
said to her companion,

I 2

"What have you dropped?"

"Not anything. It was you when you shook out your dress," said Miss Fortescue. "I distinctly heard something fall."

"I!" said Miss Thorn in a tone of astonishment; "no, indeed, it was you," and she began to look about eagerly; but as she could not see anything, she turned to her companion, and said, "I cannot see anything."

"When you shook out your dress, I heard something fall upon the stone step."

Miss Thorn's countenance was expressive of annoyance, but she remained silent.

"It had quite a metallic sound, and rolled——"

"I heard that metallic sound," said Miss Thorn, interrupting, "but I am sure I have no purse, nor money of any kind about me."

There was, perhaps, more vexation expressed in Miss Thorn's voice than in her countenance, but Miss Fortescue had no clue to either. Miss Thorn, for her part, felt sure she had not dropped anything, and this very positive feeling made her mistrust her friend's statement.

"Let us, at least, try to find it," said Miss Fortescue—"if yours or mine, it will be a pity to leave it here."

The two ladies searched for some little time unsuccessfully.

"I am weary with stooping, and trying to discover invisible articles," said Miss Thorn, in rather an unamiable tone, but she recrossed the stile, and continued her investigation there.

After only a few seconds, she picked up something, as she said, in joyful tones,

"I am right—I knew I was right—look, look, look here!" and she held up something between her finger and thumb.

Miss Fortescue now recrossed the stile, and saw in Miss Thorn's hand the "first gold sovereign of Henry VII."

"The first gold sovereign!—ah, then, it fell from your dress," said Miss Fortescue.

"Now, what will you say next against the positive proof in my hand?" said Miss Thorn, in rather an irritable tone.

"It fell from your dress when you shook it at the top of the stile," said Miss Fortescue, as thoroughly convinced of the truth of the words she uttered as her friend of the contrary, but she was less angry than Miss Thorn.

"It fell from yours, if, indeed, it fell from a dress, as you began to mount the stile," said Miss Thorn, growing more impatient of contradiction; "you see it is on this side, not on that. I was there—you were here."

"I had not put my foot upon the first step when I distinctly heard it fall."

"True, most 'gracious princess,'" said Miss Thorn, in tones of irony, "and here it is, just where you were standing."

"But I heard it roll from one step to another. I tell you I heard it fall as you shook out your dress; it must have lodged in some part of the trimmings as it fell from the tray."

"You are really very clever, so easily to understand what the sovereign has been doing with himself while we have so anxiously made our search," said Miss Thorn, the very pertinacity of her companion only adding to her own displeasure; "and now, since you can so coolly account for his hiding-place, perhaps you will inform me what has become of the 'six angels?'"

It is to be understood here that Miss Thorn had no belief in the coin having fallen from her own dress. The fact that it was found lying exactly where Miss Fortescue had been standing, seemed to her sufficiently to prove this. Miss Thorn was not habitually unladylike in manner, or harsh in her judgment of others. But on this occasion she was both, from the conviction in her own mind that she had not let the coin fall. Even when Miss Fortescue pointed out to her that she had heard the ring of the metal on the stone step—had also heard the coin roll, and drop upon the second step—Miss Thorn was unconvinced. But to return.

Miss Fortescue stood gazing on Miss Thorn in mute astonishment. First wondering why she should object to declare the actual truth—that it had been accidentally caught and retained in the trimmings of her dress; and secondly, paralysed into silence and consternation by being almost accused of knowing where to find the 'six-angel' piece. At length she gasped out, " What can you mean ?"

" I mean, you have just dropped this gold sovereign !—perhaps, if you shake yourself again——"

Miss Thorn was now much excited in manner.

" It was *you* who shook your robe !" said Miss Fortescue, interrupting her friend in a tone of indignation.

" If you shake yourself again, and with a hearty good-will," resumed Miss Thorn, " perhaps you may then drop the ' six angels.' "

This was unpardonable ; even under the influ·ence of anger, it was a very unwarrantable accusation, and the only excuse that can be made for Miss Thorn is that she was not at the time conscious of the full power of her own words ; her mind was warped from its customary rectitude by the pertinacity, and as it even appeared to her, the unjustifiable charge of Miss Fortescue against herself.

" I did not drop that gold sovereign," said Miss Fortescue, " and I know no more of the ' six angels' than you do, nor perhaps even so much."

These last were unlucky words, because they only increased Miss Thorn's anger. And we must again record the fact that, as a rule, she was courteous in manner, and scrupulous in the use of proper expressions ; but in this instance her displeasure overcame both her politeness and her language.

"O—o—h! 'nor perhaps even so much!' Then you deliberately mean to accuse me of carrying away Sir Hildebrand's coins? But you shall return with me, if you please, to Heraldstowe, and speak of me in my own presence."

And now she took hold of her adversary, as if she would compel her to do as she had said.

"Do let me alone! How can you be so rude?" said Miss Fortescue, disengaging herself.

"Let us go together—let us restore both the coins at one time," said Miss Thorn.

Rapidly it had flashed through her mind that where one had been caught up, and retained when it fell, so, also, might the other have been, and this idea, properly explained, could not have given offence to anyone; but unfortunately, independent of her excited countenance, her cold, sneering manner, coupled with the hint that Miss Fortescue had also in her possession the other lost coin, was more than enough to arouse so gentle a person even as Miss Fortescue. She almost shouted an indignant denial of any knowledge of the "six-angel piece," for her companion's ungracious demeanour had made even her lose temporary control over herself. But, at the sight of Miss Fortescue's aroused wrath, Miss Thorn cooled, and took immediate advantage of her own improved position.

"Then I may tell Sir Hiledbrand—since you refuse to return with me—that you have not the other coin?" said she in a subdued and ladylike manner, and as if she were saying the most trifling thing in the world.

"You may tell him what you like. I have not the coin, you know I have not. I cannot return, you know I cannot. And you will not tell the truth, you know you will not!"

Here Miss Fortescue's temper overbalanced her judgment—it is the case sometimes with "Maidenhood." She, in seeking to defend herself, really accused her friend! It was unpardonable to say, "You will not tell the truth, you *know* you will not." It may seem strange that this recrimination did not chafe Miss Thorn still more. It did not. On the contrary, she enjoyed the fact that Miss Fortescue had forgotten her customary propriety of manner. The two stood on the same pedestal now, and could not, therefore, the one accuse the other! And so Miss Thorn replied,

"Hoity toity! here is a tragedy queen! Bene, bene, bene, bene!" and she playfully danced a few steps backward as she spoke. Then she paused and took breath, and said coolly and deliberately, "I do not know that you have not 'the six angels,' I should think, yes, you have, because as they fell together, peradventure they might have been caught up together. I do not know that you cannot return with me to Heraldstowe. I should think on an occasion of such importance, yes, you can. And as for whether I will or will not tell the truth, judge what I shall say at Heraldstowe, by my cour-

age in replying so fully to you now." She turned
as she spoke, and with the first gold sovereign in her
hand, retraced her steps to Heraldstowe.

For a moment or two Miss Fortescue stood spell-
bound. She felt conscious she had given up all
power to her adversary. She had been unguarded
in speech, unrestrained in temper, and now she
was left unable to act for herself—at least, to act
in the matter of the coins, for she knew she was
nearly an hour later on her return home than she
had intended to be. As she walked on, she felt
she ought to have propitiated Miss Thorn, and
made a friend of her, or she ought to have returned to Heraldstowe. Not that she, or even
that Miss Thorn, had been in fault in the matter
of the coins, for clearly it was an accidental carrying off—unknown even to the lady who had been
so unfortunate as to purloin, for the time being,
so great a treasure. But these facts did not add
to her comfort, and she hurried to "The Pines"
in an unhappy mood.

Captain Fortescue's handsome grey stood impatiently pawing the earth when Miss Fortescue at
length arrived.

"I am so sorry to be late," said she apologeti-
cally, and looking heated and uncomfortable with
her hasty walk; and, indeed, almost unable to restrain her tears, as she thought over the vexatious
events of the morning.

"Is anything the matter?—has anything happened?" said Captain Fortescue, scrutinizing her
attentively.

"I have hurried home—dear papa, that makes me look so hot, and unlike my natural self." Sarah did not say this evasively, or with any wish to turn aside Captain Fortescue's query. Miss Fortescue deserved the epithet " good " bestowed upon her by Sir Hildebrand, and had no conceal- ments from her parents. She knew Captain For- tescue's ride had been delayed for fully an hour by her unavoidable detention at Heraldstowe, and therefore she tried now to delay explanation until a more convenient opportunity.

Captain Fortescue was an affectionate husband and kind father; he patted Sarah on the head as he said,

" Never mind, my dear; Grey Bessie must make up for the time you have lost." And Sarah was left with her mother and her perplexed thoughts.

Meanwhile Miss Thorn made the best of her way back to Heraldstowe. She found Almeric and Zara greatly fatigued by their continued and unsuccessful search for the missing coins.

" You are surprised to see me return?" said she.

" We are proud to receive you," said Sir Hilde- brand with his accustomed courtesy.

" Look here!" said she, and she held up the coin.

" Good heavens!" said Sir Hildebrand, startled out of his politeness, " the first gold sovereign! Where did you find it ?—and how could it escape from this room ?" He took her hand as he spoke, and led her up to the window, examining the coin as they went up the room.

"You see, dear sir," said she, as she cast her eyes on the rich mozaic-work of the floor—"you see, dear sir, I shall save you from the sin of destroying this exquisite marquetry."

"But how and where did you find this, my missing 'first gold sovereign?'" said Sir Hildebrand in much astonishment; and then he added before she could reply, "Have you also the six-angel piece?"

Miss Thorn shook her head, but did not speak.

"My dear young lady," said he caressingly, "I implore you not to keep me in suspense. This is too serious a subject to be turned into tricks and legerdemain!"

"I have only this one coin, dear sir, and perhaps you will allow me to tell you how it came into my possession."

Sir Hildebrand graciously nodded assent. And with faces in which curiosity and surprise were blended, Almeric and Zara stood listening to Miss Thorn.

"You may remember H. and I went off together?"

"Miss Fortescue and you," said Sir Hildebrand correctively.

"Yes; we walked on, talking of the mischances of the morning, through the shrubberies and Park, until we came to the stile at the bottom of the hill. I went over first, for we all know H. is none of the quickest," added she with a little playful laugh, and something fell, with a ringing metallic sound. Miss Fortescue thought 1 had dropped something. I thought she had dropped her purse, and we stood for a second or two each accusing the other. We examined the spot where we then were; there was nothing to be seen—no purse, no money, no anything. At length I re-crossed the stile, and searched on that side; and there, where Miss Fortescue was standing when we heard the sound, there lay the coin!"

"Wonderful!" said Almeric, "how fortunate she should drop it where it could so easily be seen and recovered."

" It seems surprising she should even have walked so far before dropping it," said Miss Barrymore.

"Very much so," said Sir Hildebrand, as he stooped to re-examine the coin, and stood turning it over and over—"but now about the 'six-angel piece'?" said he, looking up interrogatively.

"She did not let that fall," said Miss Thorn; "at least, not while we walked together, or to be known to either of us."

For the thought crossed her mind that it might have fallen, and so have been lost in some part of their walk.

"It does not follow because she accidentally carried away one coin," said Almeric, "that she also carried off the other!"

He said this because he knew where the "six-angel piece" lay hid.

"Then you think perhaps——"

But Miss Thorn was interrupted by Miss Barry-more, who said,

"They both fell at the same time, and from the same tray."

"Yes!" said Miss Thorn; "and if one became entangled in her dress, as I conclude was the case with the sovereign, it is quite fair to infer so also did the other."

"It is really unfair," said Almeric in a positive tone; "I am sure it was not caught up by her trimmings."

He spoke thus decisively, from his own certain knowledge that the coin was in the possession of Baron Almeric!

"Almeric!" said Sir Hildebrand in a tone of astonishment. "Why, I can see nothing more probable! You cannot find the coin on the carpet, and as one has by chance been carried away, pray why not the other?"

Almeric at once felt he had spoken imprudently, and trying to recover his false move, he said in a deferential tone,

"You are right, my dear grandfather; it may have been—indeed, it has been carried away, by one means or another."

He turned away as he spoke, devoutly wishing he could get the coin from the clutches of Baron Almeric, that he might restore it to Sir Hildebrand without more ado.

"I really think, Zara, we had better go to the

stile, and make a good search for the 'six angels.'
It is so naturally to be expected that if the coins
were caught and retained in the same trimming,
that they should fall at the same moment!"

Sir Hildebrand spoke eagerly and hopefully, but
Almeric said,

"What nonsense!"

And then remembering he ought not to involve
himself in the discussion, he turned away.

"I do not see any 'nonsense' in my proposal,"
said Sir Hildebrand.

Miss Barrymore and Almeric were walking down
the room together.

"I am quite sure it could not have been taken
from the cabinet," said she to her brother, *sotto
voce.*

"And I am quite sure that it could," said he,
impatiently.

Miss Barrymore spoke from a conviction of the
improbability—that any thief could enter the
library, and commit such a depredation unknown
to any member of the family; but Almeric replied
from the certainty of his own knowledge.

The discussion went on for some time longer;
but no satisfactory arrangement could be made.
Almeric objected to the waste of time; and Sir
Hildebrand thought time of no value in comparison
with the coin. He feared, if he did not make immediate search, that it would be lost to him for
ever; but Almeric had no such fear—he knew the
coin was safe.

"Any one might pick it up, pocket it, spend it, and know nothing of its real value," said Sir Hildebrand.

"That is impossible," said Almeric.

"What is impossible, my dear boy? I say very few would understand the value of that unique coin, because so few have any knowledge of numismatics—and, indeed, an uneducated man might find it, and fancy it was one of the old guineas!"

"Nothing of the sort!" said Almeric, "and, my dear father, I am quite sorry to see you so grieved for the temporary loss of the——"

"Temporary!" interrupted Sir Hildebrand. "How can we expect it to be only a temporary loss, if we neglect to search? I could have the patience of Job if I felt sure it would be restored to me; but the very fact of one coin having been found at so great a distance from the house, proves——"

"Proves nothing at all," said Almeric. "I am sanguine that we shall find the coin, if we only have a little patience."

But now that the excitement had been so great with the loss of the two coins, and the recovery of one, he felt still more averse to explain the real circumstances, and especially in the presence of Miss Thorn.

"My dear boy, the very fact speaks for itself," said Sir Hildebrand. "Our young friend dropped one coin, fortunately, where it could be seen and found. But as the other was not seen at that time, a good search ought to be made over that locality to prevent the terrible misfortune of any stranger finding and keeping the coin !"

" No stranger will have the chance of that," said Almeric, with a smile. " I feel sure the coin will be restored to you."

Miss Thorn now left Heraldstowe, promising to look well at the stile as she passed it on her way home, and Miss Barrymore said,

" Thanks ; you are very kind. As one coin has been found in the accidental possession of a visitor, I feel sure that, by some great good chance, the other may ' drop down,' or ' turn up,' and eventually be found."

Sir Hildebrand cast his eyes wistfully on the carpet, and did not seem willing that the search should be discontinued even in the library.

" The doors shall all be locked," said he to Almeric.

And then the hours were allowed to roll on in their customary fashion. The carriage came round at the usual time, and Sir Hildebrand left Heraldstowe with the keys of the three doors that communicated with the library in his pocket.

CHAPTER XV.

"FEAR CAN KEEP A MAN OUT OF DANGER, BUT COURAGE
ONLY CAN SUPPORT HIM IN IT."

SIR HILDEBRAND, on his return from his
drive, told Almeric and Zara that he had
thought the matter well over, and he now felt
convinced the " six-angel piece " had been carried
off unconsciously by Miss Fortescue, and that he
should never see it again. Almeric was uncomfortable, because he feared he could not recover
the coin from the statue without assistance, and
until he could produce it he was unwilling to
mention that he had had any hand in its disap-
pearance. He was doubly cautious, and unwilling
to state the real circumstances, because of the fuss
that had been created when the trays fell, and of
the presence at that time of Miss Fortescue and
Miss Thorn. If these two ladies had been absent
when the coins were scattered over the carpet, and
afterwards all recovered, excepting the two valuable coins, Almeric felt that then he should immediately have told his grandfather and sister exactly
where the six angels lay hidden ! But then, if
these ladies had not called, the trays would not
have been taken from the cabinet—the coins
would not have been scattered over the floor, and
the six-angel piece, in all probability, would not
have been missed. Under existing circumstances,

Almeric decided to let things take their course, and not trouble himself more than he could help. In fact, at this time his mind was more occupied by the curious appearance of his ancestor to him in his own room, than by the supposed loss of the "six-angel piece."

"I wonder if, by the power of my imagination, I had painted the figure of my ancestor on the retina! Would he, or ought he, in that case, to appear to me inverted?—I cannot say. I am not learned in this branch of science."

Thus thought Almeric as he renewed his toilette for dinner. After dinner Sir Hildebrand missed his snuff-box.

"I will fetch it," said Almeric, for it was in the library, the doors of which were still locked.

"No, no, Almeric; there is always a box in the sideboard," said Miss Barrymore.

This was given to Sir Hildebrand, and then he turned to Almeric, and said:

"Here are the keys of the library; when you go that way, unlock all the doors—I feel sure the coin is not there."

"So do I," said Almeric.

"Do not go on purpose, but in the course of the evening; when you unlock the doors, just look on the little table for my snuff-box, and bring it."

For it was now late, and they were sitting cosily together, a family party, over their wine and fruit—for Miss Barrymore had not left the

K 2

room—watching the moon's beams light up the tops of the trees, and flash here and there between this shrub and that—even making the jets from the fountain sparkle like silver ; for no lamp or artificial light was permitted to break the spell of the gradual decline of a hot summer's day into the silence and repose of a cool evening. Almeric promised to remember the snuff-box, and after a little more talk, he said :

" I think I will have a stroll in the shrubberies."

He wanted to be alone, to think on the singular appearance of his ancestor, and to make out in his mind a list of books he thought likely to help him to the solution of the wonder. He took up the keys and left the room, going to the library before taking his walk, that he might unlock the doors, and give the domestics access there, according to custom, and also take his grandfather's box at once. But the room was then quite dark, for, be it remembered, that as there was but one window in the library, and that filled with stained glass, it was at all times a dark room ; and as the beautiful oriel window, from its nature, did not open with doors upon the flowering lawn, as did those in the dining-room, and as the moonbeams could neither have such free entrance, nor gleam so brilliantly, it followed, as a matter of course, that even in searching for a snuff-box set with diamonds, and said to have been left on a particular table, it would be necessary to have a light.

He rang the drawing-room bell, and on the appearance of a domestic, asked for a taper. Then, while waiting, he sauntered out of the open windows of the drawing-room, and amused himself by recalling the figure of Baron Almeric, now standing here, now there, but always with the coin between his finger and thumb, and not in the position in which the suit of armour was known to be standing in the hall.

Presently he was attracted by the sight of a number of peacocks. Eight or ten of these beautiful creatures, with their many-coloured elegant trains and brilliant colours, were perched, some on the edges of the fountains, here and there one on a marble statue, some two or three flying up to the branches of the trees on which they meant to roost.

Almeric knew that a small number of these birds often came up to roost near the house, but in the cedar grove, which skirted the edge of the lake, they were in large numbers, and very tame. They seemed to his contemplative mind at this moment to have more than their usual elegance and beauty, amongst the statues and fountains, and in the lustrous light of the moon. The perfume of the night flowers wafted on the breeze, combined with the magic of light and shadow to attract him still further from the house. With his hands in his pockets, no hat on, watching the peacocks as one by one they at length retired to roost, he forgot his mediæval ancestor, and the loss of the "six-angel piece," and gave himself up to the enjoyment of the present scene.

The last bird had put its head under its wing, and seated itself securely for the night, when Almeric, now at a considerable distance from the house, turned to retrace his steps. Soon he caught sight of what appeared to him to be something unusual.

"What star is that?" said he, keeping his eye upon it. "Ah! I see, it is the taper I sent for before I stepped out upon the lawn. I had forgotten all about unlocking the doors and getting the snuff-box. What a long time I must have been strolling here!—and just catching the light glimmering like a star, I did not for a moment or two perceive that it was only a candle burning in the drawing-room."

On reaching the house, Almeric saw that the taper would die out in a few minutes.

"Perhaps it will last while I unlock the doors and get the box." He entered the library hastily, placed the taper on a table, and crossed the room, to place the key in the lock of the conservatory door, when the light suddenly went out.

"This is tiresome," said he, turning to cross the room and ring. As he turned, his attention was attracted by the moon's rays streaming faintly through the coloured glass in the oriel, and falling more especially on the snuff-box. "Ah! that is well," said he; "I see the glistening box—I will not ring." He tried to grope his way to the table, but stumbled over a chair, and hurt his ankle; he sat down and rubbed his foot to relieve the pain. When he raised his eyes the room had become dark—a cloud was passing over the moon. He still saw the box, even in the darkness, but it was like an *ignus fatuus*—if he moved his head the box seemed to move; and, besides, his foot still pained him. "I will wait till the clouds have sailed away," said he, "and then I shall see better, and perhaps not stumble over more furniture." He leaned back in his chair, and his thoughts reverted to his mediæval ancestor. The moon returned, or rather the clouds were gone, and Almeric half raised himself with an intention of finding the box, but—he stood, as it were, spell-bound!

There, in his grandfather's easy armchair, sat the Sieur Almeric Barry-Barrymore! Almeric stood spell-bound for a few seconds, and during this time he wondered if the Baron's armour was still standing in the hall, or if it had really managed to escape and seat itself thus cozily in the library! With some small feeling of alarm, he tried to rush hastily to the door, but before he could re-cross the room, the Baron had hurriedly left his chair, anticipating Almeric's intention, and placed himself in such a position as to prevent him leaving the room.

The Baron now tapped the snuff-box—Sir Hildebrand's snuff-box studded with diamonds, which he held in his hand—and solaced himself with a pinch of snuff, after the fashion of Sir Hildebrand;

then, with a courteous bow, he presented the open
box to Almeric, that he, too, might follow so good
an example.

Almeric's anger and consternation got the better
of his good behaviour; he hit the box a thump,
with an intention of dashing it to the ground.
It fell from the Baron's hand, turned over and
over, emptied its contents on the carpet, and was
then recovered by the Sieur Almeric, who carefully closed it, and placed it in a breast-pocket.
Almeric thought within himself, " I never knew
until now that these suits of armour were furnished
with pockets!" But he said in loud tones of dismay,

"Good heavens! put down the box," for he
now feared that the snuff-box might share the
fate of the "six-angel piece," and be hidden in
some part of the armour, that might make it difficult to him to recover; therefore, with a view of
preventing such a catastrophe, he said, now in
tones of entreaty,

"Give it me back—it is my grandfather's!"

The Baron apparently took no notice of this
request, but stretched out his mailed hand, and in
the open palm exhibited the "six-angel piece,"
now glittering in the moonlight. Almeric joyfully
struck the hand, that he might thereby recover
the coin. He succeeded in his intention—it fell
to the ground, and rolled to Almeric's feet. He
stooped to take it up, and started at the opening
of the door. He made an exclamation, half in

terror, half in surprise, as Miss Barrymore said,
" What, in the dark, Almeric! We thought
you would have ordered the lamp in the drawing-
room; and grandpapa wonders what you are about."

" Do fetch a light, Zara; here is the coin—I
saw it lying on the carpet."

" Really, Almeric! I am glad, indeed!" said
she, as she retreated into the drawing-room and
rang the bell for assistance.

The moon's light streamed in—faintly and my-
stically through the oriel window—brilliantly
through the open door of the drawing-room, and
Almeric saw that his revered ancestor had left the
apartment. When Miss Barrymore returned,
Almeric was kneeling on the carpet feeling about
for the coin he had so plainly seen.

" Mind the snuff, Zara," said he.

" The snuff!—why, my dear?"

A servant brought a light; but after searching
for a length of time *the* *coin* was not to be found.
Almeric looked up in wonder and annoyance.

" I must take grandpapa his snuff," said Miss
Barrymore.

" You need not look for the box, Zara, he put it
in his pocket," said Almeric.

He was thinking of the intrusive Baron, whom
he had so lately seen. But Miss Barrymore thought
he meant Sir Hildebrand.

" No, dear Almeric!—if he had it in his pocket
he would not ask us to fetch it for him. See—
here it is!"

And she took the box from the table where Sir Hildebrand had left it.

"Is it there?" said Almeric in astonishment; "then he must have thought better of it, for I saw him pocket it!"

"What nonsense are you talking?" said Miss Barrymore, as she moved towards the door with the box in her hand.

"Nonsense! I tell you the truth. Probably he thought better of it, and replaced it. It is empty; I saw the snuff fall on the carpet," said Almeric.

Miss Barrymore turned and said,

"I know it, Almeric; but I re-filled it after luncheon."

She still thought he alluded to Sir Hildebrand, who had spilt the snuff on the carpet during the search for the " six-angel piece."

"I tell you it is empty now," said Almeric, trying to take the box from her.

Miss Barrymore successfully resisted this attempt, and opening the box, said,

"Now, will you be convinced?"

Almeric looked—and, lo! the box was quite full!

On this same evening, when they met in the drawing-room, Sir Hildebrand challenged Almeric to a game of chess. Almeric assented; but it was evident to the watchful eye of Miss Barrymore that he played without having much interest in the game. He looked pale, seemed restless, and nervous. He started at the smallest sound, and

often gazed around as if expecting to see some unusual sight. Sir Hildebrand, on the contrary, did
not appear to notice his altered manner. At times
his mind was pre-occupied with the events of the
morning, and occasionally, even during their game,
he referred to them. He again expressed his extreme astonishment that the "first gold sovereign"
should have travelled so far as the stile at the foot
of the hill; while still clinging to Miss Fortescue's
dress, the marvel seemed to be, that it had not
fallen long before, and been buried in the grass.
As for "the six-angel piece," the best beloved, and
in that sense the most valuable of his coins, he felt
sure in his own mind that he should never see it
again; nevertheless, just for the sake of doing all
that could be done, he thought it might be wise to
have the carpet in the library taken up, and the
most careful search made.

Almeric restrained himself from expressing any
objection to this plan—he tried quietly to acquiesce
in all his grandfather said, while he made up his
mind what would be the best to do on the morrow,
so as to prevent all unnecessary disarrangement.

"I must take off the gauntlet, and push the
coin until it comes out at the wrist," thought he.

But now, he began to feel uncomfortable at the
repeated appearance of the Sieur Almeric! True,
in this last instance he had *not* carried off the
snuff-box, though Almeric had seen him pocket it!
Neither was the snuff lying on the carpet, though
Almeric had so certainly seen it in a little heap!

These things were bewildering, and he felt unable to account for them. All through the evening, though apparently playing at chess with his grandfather, his mind was pre-occupied with these vexatious thoughts. Not for one moment did he suppose that the Heraldstowe ghosts were sufficiently awake to take an interest in valuable coins, or snuff-boxes set with diamonds. That he might be the victim of a pratical joke he thought possible ; but he would think the matter well over when he was again alone.

The real fact was, that while Almeric sat waiting in the easy-chair, and watching, as well as he was able, the passing of the clouds between himself and the moon, he had fallen asleep ! Miss Barrymore had opened the door rather hastily, as she at the same time said, " Almeric, Almeric," to ascertain if he were there or on the lawn ; and he, starting with a sudden noise, was unconscious that he had even closed his eyes ! His waking thoughts had been carried on in his dream, with much exaggeration, as is common in dreams; but the locality and the hour were the same as when he was actually awake, and these had combined to stamp his dream with a feeling of undeniable reality.*

But, as we have said, between the positive *presence of the real* in the library, and his own conviction of the *positive presence* of a shadow, he turned his thoughts to the subject of " practical jokes," and

* See Note 8.

tried to solve the mystery by that means. It is
true, he felt very highly indignant at the thought
that any one should dare to take so great a
liberty with Heraldstowe, and play tricks, and
perhaps stand invisible to him—that is, so concealed
as to see him without himself being seen—looking
upon his pale cheek, the better to laugh at him on
the morrow. All the time that he sat mutely
attending to the game of chess, and apparently
calculating the chance of this move or that, he was,
in fact, turning over the future in his own mind, as
to the best means of discovering the trick.

"Yes, the trick!" said he aloud, unconsciously
giving utterance to his troubled thoughts.

"No, my dear boy; indeed it is a fair move,"
said Sir Hildebrand, wonderingly.

"Oh! quite fair, my dear father. Excuse me,
you see——"

"Checkmate," said Sir Hildebrand joyously.

"Pooh, pooh, nonsense! Can you mean it?—
am I really beaten?" said Almeric, bending over
the board.

"To be sure—to be sure you are, in spite of all
your deep thought and your slow moves. To tell
you the truth, Almeric, I felt quite up to the
mark to-night—quite equal to the conquering of
the best of players."

But the fact was, Almeric had been careless and
inattentive; and this loss of power in his adversary
had given to Sir Hildebrand a consciousness of
superiority in the game not always present with him.

Sir Hildebrand retired for the night, and Zara and Almeric were left together.

"I am weary—weary," said Almeric despondingly; "the fuss of the day has knocked me up."

"I am sure you look sufficiently weary," said Zara; "indeed, you have looked ill all day—from the moment you stepped in at the window this morning until now you have been quite unlike your real or your former self."

"Well, Zara, the fuss about this coin worries me."

"Ay, so it does me. But there had not been a fuss when you came in this morning, and you looked pale and careworn then," said Zara.

"Did I?" said Almeric. And then he recollected the annoyance he had felt on seeing his sister at the piano, and his dread that she had seen him take the coin through the half-open door. "But perhaps the coin was gone even then," continued he defiantly, and speaking from his own truthful knowledge of the fact. And then, feeling that somehow this seemed to criminate himself, he added, "or it was intended to be lost, set down in the annals of futurity; and so it was the evil presentiment of this tiresome loss that worried me then," and Almeric sighed heavily. "But let us change the subject; and let me tell you I do not like Miss Thorn——"

"Not like Miss Thorn! She is a lovely creature, Almeric, and all the world admires her!"

"She is unamiable; I did not think so until

to-day. She is jealous of that little Fortescue.
I almost think she would be glad to cover her with
opprobrium! She hates her; I saw it in her eye
when she gave us the scene at the stile."

"Your zeal misleads you, Almeric; you were
always partial to that stupid Miss Fortescue. I
do not wish to blame her for the accident of carrying off the coins, but I must say, when you depreciate Sara Thorn for the purpose of exalting
Sarah Fortescue, you do them both injustice!"

"Ah! well," said he, "I like straightforward,
well-meaning people. I think the Thorn is neither—the Fortescue both."

"Almeric, how uncourteous you are!" Almeric
rarely used slang terms, or spoke of a lady without
using her proper title, hence Miss Barrymore's
surprise.

"I cannot imagine how the coins could be
caught up in her plain, simple muslin," continued
Miss Barrymore. "If you would solve that pro-
blem, you would do something clever."

"I am not clever to-night; but I promise you
that in the future it shall be proved Miss Fortescue
did not carry off the *coins*."

Almeric used the word in the plural, because
he, in common with others, thought Miss Fortescue
had accidentally taken away the first gold sovereign; but he knew she had not had the "six-
angel piece," and this he intended to liberate and
produce. Miss Barrymore, as she had no key to
the whereabouts of the latter coin, thought her

brother was only trying to exalt Miss Fortescue undeservedly; and she replied, with more satire in her tone than was usual,

"I am sure Miss Fortescue ought to be very grateful to her champion!"

"Good night—good night," said Almeric, as he hurried out of the room.

"There, now I have vexed him! I wish I had not," said she. She opened the drawing-room door, and followed him.

"Kiss me, dear Almeric," said she, as she put her hand on his arm.

"Good night, my dear sisse," said he, as he stooped and complied with her request.

CHAPTER XVI.

"MORE THINGS AFFRIGHT THAN HURT US."

AS soon as Almeric reached his own room, he lighted a large moderator lamp, which he was accustomed to use when he intended to study before retiring to rest. On this occasion the lamp alone did not content him. He lighted the tapers at the dressing-glasses, those in the lustres on the mantel-piece, and two others standing on a side-table.

He then put back the drapery, drew up the blinds, and opened both windows wide. We have said it was summer, and the moon still shed her bright light over the beautiful shrubs and many-coloured flowers—over the handsome groups of trees in the park, marking distinctly on the green sward their dark shadows, as they stood picturesquely placed here and there, and tipping the topmost boughs with a hue of silver.

This scene did not seem to give any pleasure to Almeric. He seemed nervous and restless—we might almost say anxious. He did not attempt to undress, neither did he sit down to read as he had beforetime frequently done at night. He opened a drawer, took out a revolver, examined it carefully, and saw that it was loaded, and ready for use. He placed a table close to the window, put the revolver upon it, and then began to pace the room backwards and forwards, occasionally stopping, now at one window, now at the other, and gazing well round the lawns, as they lay flooded with the moonlight; but the more distant parts of the Park did not seem to attract his attention. The stillness would to most watchers have appeared profound, but Almeric detected the slight whisper of the grasshopper lark; he heard its " chirp, chirp," from the moment he opened the windows, and he knew that this tiny creature " sings through the whole summer night."*

" *Alauda minima voce locustæ*," said he, " the ventriloquist of birds. It seems so near often when it is so far off. When we are close to it, its song is no louder; when it is far, far away, we

* White of Selbourne.

fancy it near. It is the quality of the note, no doubt, as we say of the human voice. It is not the loudest that can be heard the most clearly, but the voice of the best quality of tone, whose lightest whisper can——"

"Bome, bome, bome!" went the huge clock in the stable court, and Almeric started from his reverie.

"Twelve o'clock only," said he, with a deep sigh. "I wish the man would come, if he means to come, for I will certainly try if he be mortal!"

He had hastily snatched up the revolver at the first stroke of the hour; he now put it on the window-sill, and sat for some little time watching the changing shadows caused by the moon's nearer approach to the horizon.

"She will soon be gone," said he, impatiently, and alluding to the moon, "and then the whole landscape will be in darkness."

He crossed the room to a book-shelf at the other end, from which he took an almanac, and, rapidly turning over its pages, found that the moon did not set till one thirty A.M. He replaced the book, and resumed his walk up and down the room.

"So far good," said he, in a voice of satisfaction.

And then he occupied his time alternately in gazing through the open window, and walking up and down the room.

"Ti, dum," said the great clock, giving the first quarter past twelve.

Almeric again started, and again seized the revolver. And so he did from quarter to quarter of each hour, never prepared for the sudden sound of the clock, though, as it seemed to himself, always in expectation of hearing the stroke, noting down carefully in his mind every lengthening shadow caused by the moon's decline, and counting the minutes till the sun would rise. Light—the broad light of day—that he might see the approach, if possible, of the Sieur Almeric, was what Almeric most desired.

"Total eclipse—no sun, no moon," would have made him still more excitable and nervous.

He heard the woodlark, "*Alauda arborea,*" join her song to the chirp of her connection, the grasshopper lark. He heard the loud song of the thrush, and he saw the blackbirds pick up those incautious worms that are fond of late hours, of the dew just tempered by the sun's rays, and of a good sniff of fine fresh morning air, before they retire to their subterranean dwellings.

Almeric paced his room up and down, and watched through the open windows, until he had seen all this, and much more. And when "the early birds" had made an excellent breakfast, and the singing-birds had tried to vie with each other in the melody and charm of their strains; when the lowing of cattle came upon the breeze in the awakening morning; when rural sounds were joined to the sounds of living creatures; when the moon was gone fairly to bed, and the sun shining high above the ground—then **Almeric** threw himself on the bed, the revolver placed on a table by his side.

Of Miss Barrymore, we may say she was nót kept awake in the expectation of a visit from some one of her ancestors, as Almeric had been. She did not expect to see, at any unknown minute, a strange, unearthly visitor, who came when he pleased, and retired in like manner. She was disturbed and anxious in mind from the loss of the " six-angel piece ;" and though she blamed herself for the negligence of the morning in having left the cabinet doors open, the more she reflected, the more she felt satisfied that the coin could not have been stolen—that is to say, that it would have been next to an impossibility for the sort of person who understood coins, and their value, and who would probably know where to look for them, to enter the library through the conservatory unknown to anyone of the establishment, and commit his depredations, and leave the grounds unseen. No ; this was impossible, in spite of her conviction that Almeric believed in it. The coin had been carried away—unintentionally, of course—by one of the ladies, and, in all probability, lost in the grass during their walk through the Park.

" And yet," said Miss Barrymore to herself, " it puzzles me to think that Sarah Fortescue's dress caught up the coins, because her muslin was so

slight, and so plain, and so simple—not a frill, nor
a flounce!"

And- so, though the same sounds might have
been heard by any listener from Miss Barrymore's
windows, and the same sights—or nearly so—seen,
she neither saw the one, nor heard the other.
Even the loud striking of the stable-clock did not
arrest her attention, nor make her start. She was
grieved, for her grandpapa's sake, at the loss of
the coin, and slightly put out of temper by the
fusses of the day, as well as by Almeric's cham-
pionship of the merits of Miss Fortescue, and
arbitrary depreciation of the charms of Sara
Thorn ; these, combined with the anticipated worry
of the morrow, had ruffled her customary well-
regulated temper. But she lay down to sleep
quietly. She did not require the light of half a
dozen candles and a moderator-lamp to dispel the
darkness of the night, nor was she wishful to de-
tain the moon, nor anxious for the rising of the sun.
If she had contemplated a visit from her restless
ancestor, we are not prepared to say what she might
have required. As it was, Miss Barrymore slept!

She awoke at her usual hour, 6 A.M. She
rang, and her maid brought tea. By half-past six
she was so sufficiently dressed as to be able, in
dressing-gown and slippers, to go and inquire after
Almeric.

"Poor fellow!" said she, "he was so unlike
himself yesterday, I am sure he is not well. I will
take him a cup of tea."

She tapped gently at his door. He did not speak. She tapped again. Still no reply.

"Ah! I knew he was ill," said she to herself. "He was so pale and restless yesterday—so unlike himself. I hope he has not locked the door." She tried the handle; to her great joy the door opened easily. She entered, but she was not prepared for the sight that greeted her.

The windows were wide open; there was a blight in the air, and that in addition to the other things made the scent in the room disagreeable. The light of the six wax candles still cast their dim glare over the room and through the broad light of day. The lamp was out, but the large black wick and the eddies of smoke on the ceiling told that it had not been turned off—of the perfume of its expiring agonies Miss Barrymore very uncomfortably became aware. A revolver was on the table, and on the bed, extended at his full length, and in evening costume, lay her brother— fast asleep!

To note down these particulars takes a little time. Miss Barrymore saw them at a glance. She silently placed the cup of tea on the table, and removed the revolver. She extinguished the flickering candles, and closed the windows. Then she turned to gaze upon her brother, and wonder what could have changed him so! He was restless even in his sleep. He looked haggard and pale. And then what could be the meaning of this strange arrangement of his room? Of the candles burning throughout the night?—of the lamp having been left burning?—of the open windows, and the revolver on the table, and Almeric stretched on the bed in evening dress?

This sleep was not dispelled immediately by her intrusion into his room. As she stood watching him, restlessly turning and muttering indistinctly, her thoughts recurred to the extraordinary change in his conduct throughout the preceding day. An incipient dread began to creep over her; she feared that this unusual manner, and this present disquiet, might herald the approach of fever, or—or even insanity!

"Fever would be a terrible infliction!" said she to herself. "I have never heard of any case of dementation in our family! Poor fellow!" added she with a deep sigh; "I will send for advice. I seem to love him the more, the more I see him helpless, and know him to be wayward."

The revolver she put into its case. She placed the case in a drawer, and locked it and took away the key, as she said to herself,

"This is better both out of his sight and out of his power."

She left the room, taking with her the cup of tea, and leaving no trace of her intrusion. She thought very seriously of the sad change in the appearance and bearing of her brother, and determined to have Dr. Quinn's opinion as soon as she could manage it, without exciting any undue alarm in the mind of her grandfather, Sir Hildebrand.

Meanwhile Almeric awoke. He was not a little surprised to see himself still in evening costume. That part of the adventures of the preceding night he had quite forgotten—that is to say, the fact that he had thrown himself on the bed for the sake of momentary rest to his aching limbs, and, from very weariness of mind and body, had fallen asleep!

He looked round for his revolver—he felt sure he had placed it on the table by his side. It was not to be found!

"Perhaps I replaced it in its case when daylight came," said he to himself, as he walked across the room to the drawer in which it was usually put. The drawer was locked, the key gone. Almeric was puzzled.

"I had it last night," said he whisperingly, as he pushed the hair from his brow. "Has *he* been here while I slept, and so disarmed me?—taken away the weapon by which I would have saved myself from his torturing surveillance by—by—" thought is rapid, and supplied the unspoken word, "murder." "Yes," resumed he, speaking aloud, "if it be a practical joke, I might actually kill a man! But if, on the contrary, this extraordinary appearance is not produced by some abominable human person, it would not be murder to kill a—a——" He stopped and seated himself.

"Now this is absurd," resumed he, as he leaned his head upon his hand. "I know that supernatural beings do not return to this earth. I know,

that the being whom we call 'Satan,' has no
palpable form by which to be seen by us; nor do I
believe that he is permitted to visit this world—that
is to say, in an absolute form—why, therefore, does
my mind run on to such thoughts, and mingle the
idea of supernatural beings with the tricks of—"

But then these words arose unbidden in his
mind—

"Our adversary goeth about like a roaring lion,
seeking whom he may devour."

"But not to be actually seen by our eyes, and
in the garb of one of our own ancestors!" said he.

A loud knock at the door of his room startled
him from his very agreeable reverie.

"Come in," said he, impulsively.

And then he regretted his hospitality, for he
expected to see his unwelcome visitor; but no,
it was only his attendant with hot water for
his toilette. The man, however much he saw,
took no notice of his master's perplexed manner.
He was a well-trained domestic, who simply attended to his duties, and then left the room.

"I am sure I had my revolver last night," said
Almeric. "Let me think—let me think." During
the process of dressing, his mind gradually recalled
the events of the preceding night. "Ah! yes; I
had it on the table by the bed; I can remember
ascertaining that it was conveniently within my
reach!"

Clang, clang, clang, went the gong, the summons to breakfast; and before Almeric had com-

pleted his toilette, Miss Barrymore had again knocked at his door.

"Who is there?" said he, in a peremptory tone.

"Almeric, dear, shall you come down soon?" said she.

"My dear Sisse," said he, rushing to open the door, "I am just ready—in one or two minutes I will come."

"Ah! that is right—there are several letters," said she, as she turned and retraced her steps to the breakfast-room.

Almeric's spirits rose at the sound of his sister's voice.

"I really did not think of dear Zara—though, in truth, her tap at my door is no unusual thing. But then my thoughts are so full of him. And yet I wonder that I feel this sort of dismay. It is true I tried hard to conjure up an ugly sprite; but this is *not* the sort of sprite I meant to will to see! This looks so like absolute reality as to excite in me much wonder.

If it at all resembled the sprite I—by my imagination—had tried to call up, I should feel satisfied that it was a shadow, born of my own will, to come and go when I pleased. This is the reverse—for it comes when I least expect it; commits actions that annoy me, and goes away at its own time."

It seemed to Almeric that a low chuckling laugh resounded through the room; he started, and half feared to raise his eyes or gaze around; he did

not relish these inopportune and intrusive visits
from his great ancestor. The Sieur Almeric was
not to be seen ; and his descendant walked hastily
to the window and opened it. The same sound
again smote upon his ear, but this time he knew it
came from the garden. He looked out,—there was
Williamson the head gardener in conversation with
some one whose features were hidden from him.
He watched the two men for some little time, but
they continued to walk further from the house.

"I wonder if they made that queer chuckling
noise ?" said he to himself with a deep sigh, and
not liking to gaze round the room, while he completed his toilette ; "and yet, after all, I feel sure
it is some trick—some practical joke. I am vexed
that I feel unnerved, for I am sure I am very indignant !"

On leaving his room, Almeric purposely passed
through the hall. He had a great curiosity to see
if his renowned ancestor remained standing on his
pedestal ; or if he had decamped, carrying off the
valuable "six-angel piece" in his sleeve ! In spite of
Almeric's repeated assertions to himself, " that he
was not nervous ;" that he had no fear of, nor belief
in, the presence of beings from another world ; that
ghosts were myths, and he had to deal with realities,
—in spite of all this, it was with a sensation of awe
creeping over him that he entered the hall, and
turned to gaze on the well-remembered statue !

But there he stood : " The Sieur Almeric Marmaduke Barry-Barrymore of Heraldstowe, in the

County of Z——" &c., &c. as he was mentioned
in all chronicles connected with the House of
Barrymore. And he remained standing in the
self-same position in which Almeric recollected to
have left him; with his left arm, that retained the
coin, placed by his side; and the right pressed to
his chest! Almeric's awe fled, and his courage
returned when he saw the old gentleman had not
changed his attitude; he even went boldly up to
him and took hold of his mailed hand. His satisfaction was so great he forgot his sister was
waiting breakfast, and again made many unsuccessful attempts for the recovery of the coin;
and only unwillingly desisted upon calling to
mind the breast-pocket in which he had seen the
Sieur thrust the snuff-box on the preceding evening. He gazed now with great astonishment;
there was no appearance of anything of the kind!
At this moment a servant came with a message
from Miss Barrymore.

More than ever, now, he felt that the appearance
of the Baron to him, in such unexpected places,
and at such exceptional times, must be the work of
some inveterate practical joker—skilful in optical
delusions.

"I must find out who this clever person is," said
he to himself; "and yet though he has added a
pocket to the armour which is not there, why does
he fix upon this particular Baron? Why not
Baron Guy? Why not Anselmo?"

Meanwhile, Miss Barrymore had writtten to Dr.

Quinn, who was the usual medical attendant at Heraldstowe, and entreated him to make an early call. And when the brother and sister met at breakfast, and discussed their letters, and made arrangements for the day, Miss Barrymore still watched Almeric with a scrutinizing eye, noting in her mind his pallid, careworn face, his want of repose of manner, and his hurried and desultory conversation.

"The Baron Almeric Marmaduke" was never absent from the thoughts of "the Mr. Almeric Barrymore" of the present day. Voices were heard on the lawn, near to the windows.

"Who is with Williamson?" said Almeric, jumping up hastily, and rushing to the open glass doors.

"Veitch, from Landeswold," said Miss Barrymore; "he has some new idea about the treatment of orchids that Williamson wishes to introduce here; he came yesterday morning, and they have——"

"Came yesterday!" said Almeric, returning to the breakfast table—"why, I asked you most particularly if there were any strange workmen about the house, and you said 'no.'"

He thought now he had some clue to the means that had been taken to disturb him. "A practical joker," and especially in "optical delusions," must have an assistant.

"Veitch is not a workman," said Miss Barrymore; "indeed, my dear Almeric, he is a highly respectable tradesman, quite above doing a mean action, and most certainly above theft."

Almeric raised his eyes with a hard stare at his sister's intelligent countenance; he almost wondered she should explain to him that this tradesman was "above theft," because he, in his own mind, had never thought of accusing him; he knew exactly where the coin lay hid.

"She is thinking of the lost 'six-angel piece,'" thought he; "but it is not for the loss of the coin, but for the appearance of the Baron, that I wish to find some exciting cause."

It is true, Miss Barrymore was thinking of the lost coin. She concluded Almeric meant to imply to her that some strange workman had carried off the "six-angel piece." And acting still upon this supposition, and wishful to show to her brother its utter fallacy, she said:

"And, Almeric, I must tell you I cannot for one moment suppose that any person could have the power to extract that coin from the cabinet. It is, in fact, an utterly impossible thing that anyone could enter the library through the conservatory, go to the very tray containing that unique coin, and purloin it in that instant of time, and unknown to us all, and still leave the grounds without being seen."

Miss Barrymore spoke in a more decided tone than was habitual, the result of her strong feeling on the subject. Almeric noticed this change, and because he knew the real hiding-place of the coin, said, with a smile :

"You argue thus to save yourself from the consequences of your own neglect, Zara." And then, feeling mischievously inclined to mystify his sister, he added : " *I am sure* that the coin could be *stolen* in that small moment of time, and the thief get clear off with his booty. Ill deeds do not take long to do, and when done, they cannot be undone—that is the worst of it. You would think the thief a pattern thief if he first stole the coin, and then restored it to its owner, would you not ?" And then, perceiving he had said what was very painful to Miss Barrymore, and that she, to some extent, relied upon his words, he added : " But, indeed, Zara, I only argue for the sake of overturning your theory. You said it could not have been stolen in that short time—I say that it certainly could."

At this instant the conversation was interrupted by the entrance of a domestic to ask if Miss Barrymore had any further commands for Veitch, who was on the point of returning to Landeswold.

" Yes, yes," said Almeric to the man ; and then, turning to his sister, he added : " I should like to have a little talk with him, not only about the orchids, but as to the rearrangement of the paths from the shrubberies to the lawns—will you meet him with me ?"

Miss Barrymore at once agreed to accompany

her brother—the more because she saw him so
unusually excited, and hoped that her presence
would have power to restrain him, or, at least, to
put such a check upon him, as to prevent any
untoward act, rather than from any wish on her
part to see Veitch again.

But Almeric thought of the Baron, his ancestor,
and fancied Veitch might be an accomplice, and
an agent employed by some one fond of "practical
jokes."

CHAPTER XVII.

"CALUMNY AND CONJECTURE MAY INJURE INNOCENCY
ITSELF."

BUT to return to Miss Fortescue. On her
arrival at the "Pines," Captain Fortescue
set off for his ride to Thorney Dyke, unknowing
of the loss of the coins at Heraldstowe, or of the
misunderstanding between Miss Thorn and his
own daughter. He had no presentiment of evil,
and eventually returned home, but too late for
Sarah to unburden her mind. On the morrow
the same thing occurred—Sarah had no opportunity of speaking to her father alone. Mrs. Fortescue was a great invalid, very dependant on her
husband and daughter. She was a nervous and
very sensitive person, and easily made uncomfortable by any unprecedented occurrence.

Sarah, therefore, though she told her of the loss of the two coins, and that she had necessarily been detained at Heraldstowe during the search that ensued, and yet obliged to come away before they were found, did not tell her that she had been disturbed by Miss Thorn's loss of temper. Miss Fortescue felt that Miss Thorn had been more angry than the occasion seemed to call forth, even if she herself had happened accidentally to have carried off the coin. She knew she had not, because she distinctly heard the coin fall when Miss Thorn shook her dress. If it had only rolled to, the other side of the stile, it seemed that there could have been no doubt of the matter. But as it was, Miss Thorn had used intemperate language —she had been satirical and accusatory, and Miss Fortescue felt proportionately aggrieved. All this she would have explained to Captain Fortescue, but she had not had the chance.

On this day—the day after the fall of the trays in the library at Heraldstowe—Captain Fortescue had promised Mr. Thorn, the Vicar of Stowe-in-the-Valley, to support him at a vestry meeting which was announced for ten o'clock that morning. Putting, therefore, his fresh purchase of coins in his pocket, with the intention of walking to Heraldstowe after the meeting, he left home immediately after breakfast, without having heard one word of all the fuss that had so upset the Barrymores on the day before.

And the vestry met, and came to an end; and

then Captain Fortescue walked to Heraldstowe. He arrived as Sir Hildebrand was in the act of entering his library—that is to say, he had just made his appearance from his dressing-room, when Captain Fortescue was announced.

They were very old friends, though Sir Hildebrand was very much the senior, and their meetings were always very cordial and enjoyable to both. But on this morning Sir Hildebrand had not his customary agreeable manner. In point of fact, he was under the nervous dread that Captain Fortescue would make some allusion to the untoward events of the preceding day; and as the " six-angel piece" had not been restored to him, the subject was distasteful.

Miss Barrymore had not hesitated to point out, both to Sir Hildebrand and to Almeric, the startling anomaly that had so forcibly struck herself— when she recalled the scene of the falling coins, and remembered that *one* at least had travelled to the stone stile—for she had not failed to point out to them the fact that Miss Fortescue wore a very thin muslin, without trimming or flounce of any kind, as also a plain jacket of the same, without pockets! How could heavy gold coins be carried away unknown to the wearer in such slight material? Miss Barrymore had no suspicion inimical to the integrity of Miss Fortescue, but she could not shut her eyes to this extraordinary fact, that somehow *one* coin had reached the stile and been found there.

Of Sir Hildebrand, we may say, he was a gentleman of the "old school!" that school that had precedence of "the people's this," and "the people's that." And though we give our hearty and cordial support to the rights of "the people," and wish them all health, and peace, and plenty, we cannot but be aware that when barriers are once removed, and the high tide of any fresh state of things sets in, old manners and customs blend with the new, or die a natural death by becoming obsolete. Sir Hildebrand had not marched with the times, as many gentlemen of equal rank had; and in Sir Hildebrand's day there was perhaps a greater worship, even of the trappings of rank, to say nothing of the position for itself, than in our own. There was, too, a conviction on the minds of most country gentlemen, that the only really wicked people on the face of the earth were "trespassers on their lands," "poachers," and such like. And if "the divine right of kings" was a little on the wane in their belief, the supposition that any one of "gentle blood" could commit a crime, was still a special unbelief. Sir Hildebrand, therefore, even if Miss Barrymore had wished to cast a slur on the uprightness of Miss Fortescue—which she did not—would not have supported her. But he had been made sensitive and uncomfortable from the fact of these very remarks, and hence his nervousness on the arrival of Captain Fortescue. This gentleman did not notice Sir Hildebrand's reserve; he thought him looking ill, as he really was from the anxieties and troubles of the previous day. With great good-nature, therefore, and a sincere desire to draw him from dwelling upon himself and his indisposition—as the best method of being of service to an invalid—Captain Fortescue gave him the news of the day, and for the space of an hour sat talking on all the topics he thought would be interesting, until at length Sir Hildebrand quite forgot his annoyances, and became hearty in manner, and to all appearance his customary self. He had been thoroughly talked away from the thoughts that had oppressed him, and Captain Fortescue saw, with a feeling of satisfaction, that his old friend flourished under the treatment to which he had been subjected. Then, and then only, he drew forth his case of coins.

"There," said he, as he placed a small coin before Sir Hildebrand, "what do you say to that?"

Sir Hildebrand examined it attentively with a glass of great power, and, after a minute or two, said,

"The King Cymbeline of Shakespeare!"

"Even so; C V N O for Cunobelinus, on the reverse C A M V for Camulodunum, or Colchester, which was his capital,"* said Captain Fortescue; "and, once more, I ask what have you to say to that?"

"That you are a most fortunate man," said Sir Hildebrand, with great cordiality, the vexatious occurrences of yesterday forgotten, and his whole heart and soul in the present moment.

* " Coins of England," by Noel Humphreys.

"I believe you, my boy," said Captain Fortescue, rubbing his hands together.

"I congratulate you with all my heart," said Sir Hildebrand; "and pray what else have you added to your already excellent collection?"

"A gold Boadicea, and some few specimens in silver of about the same date," said Captain Fortescue.

"Did you meet with a Richard I.?" said Sir Hildebrand.

"Why, you were right on that subject, as you very generally are on most," said Captain Fortescue, with a smile. "The three coins that were offered to me proved to have been struck on the Continent, and call Richard Duke of Aquitaine, as well as King of England."

"No; Richard did *not* coin money in England; but let me see what you have," said Sir Hildebrand.

"I do not think much of them, for, in addition to my doubts as to the genuineness, they are not in such very good preservation ——"

"I should not lack faith in this," said Sir Hildebrand, after a careful examination of one of the coins. "It is worn a little, but I think it a treasure."

He replaced the coin on the table as he spoke, and took up the other two, of which, after carefully scrutinizing, he said joyously,

"Why, these are in still better preservation!"

"Then do me the favour to add these to your

own collection," said Captain Fortescue, selecting
the two best of the three; "and I have also
duplicates of some others, which I hope you will
accept."

"My dear friend, have you just received your
pay?" said Sir Hildebrand, jocosely. "We know
sailors throw away money so soon as it comes
into their possession, and you are no exception—
eh? But, indeed, I thank you much."

Sir Hildebrand had before this entirely
recovered his good looks, and his customary
happy manner, and Captain Fortescue displayed
his remaining treasures.

When luncheon was announced, Almeric made
his appearance, and gave his arm to Sir Hildebrand; but as Captain Fortescue could not be
prevailed upon to remain, he took leave, and set
off on his return. Soon he overtook Miss
Barrymore in her walk through the Park; she
was on her way to the Vicarage, to lunch with her
friend, Miss Thorn. It was perhaps natural that
she should introduce the subject of coins, and ask
Captain Fortescue what recent additions he had
made; and he, pleased with the interest she
appeared to take, very willingly gave her the
information she required; and he also explained
to her that it was not that his late acquisitions
were in themselves very valuable coins, but that
they were precious to him because they exactly
filled up such and such gaps in such and such
series. And very pleasantly they walked and

talked together, until Miss Barrymore said, somewhat brusquely,

"Grandpapa has had a sad loss."

"A sad loss!—Sir Hildebrand, did you say? What has he had the misfortune to lose?"

"Did he not tell you?"

"No," said Captain Fortescue, in some surprise, and an incipient dread of something unpleasant creeping over him.

"Did not Sarah tell you?" said Miss Barrymore, now in a marked tone of astonishment.

"Sarah!—no, indeed. What has Sir Hildebrand lost?—and what has my daughter to do with it?"

Miss Barrymore now related the conversation Sir Hildebrand had had with the two young ladies, and spoke of his kind offer to show them the two famous coins—the "first gold sovereign of Henry VII.," and the "six-angel piece of Edward VI.;" and she told how the first tray had been upset, and all the coins recovered and replaced, and that the second tray had also fallen, but that the whole of the coins were not replaced, &c. At this point she added, with more vehemence than was natural :

"I really do wonder Sarah did not tell you, for it was my dear grandfather's kind wish to show them to her and to Miss Thorn that was the cause of his loss."

"The cause of his loss!—Sarah the cause?" said Captain Fortescue, in a tone of indignant surprise; and he stopped in his walk, and gazed sternly at his companion as he added, "Then, for heaven's sake, Miss Barrymore, tell me what are the coins that are lost!"—for he had high ideas of the duty of children to parents, and he had believed his own the most good and dutiful child in the whole world, and now, by Miss Barrymore's asseveration, it appeared that Sarah had wilfully concealed what ought to have been mentioned immediately on her return.

"I speak of the loss of the 'six-angel piece,'" said she.

"The 'six-angel!'" said he, in a voice of consternation—"what, the 'six-angel piece' of Edward VI.! Do you mean to tell me Sir Hildebrand once possessed a coin of that value, and that it is now lost?" And then, after a pause of a few seconds, he added, without waiting for a reply: "How on earth could it have been lost? Lost, say you? That is simply impossible! You recovered every coin from the fall of the first tray, and why not of the second? It seems to me absurd," and he now recommenced his walk —"positively absurd, to talk of anything being 'lost' that has fallen upon the carpet in your own library!"

"So it may appear to you, and, indeed, I do not wonder at your opinion. I kept up my spirits and hoped we should find the two coins that were missing—until——"

Captain Fortescue again stood still, for the tone

of Miss Barrymore's voice was not agreeable.
"Until," persisted Miss Barrymore, and speaking very rapidly, "until Miss Thorn came back
from the stile at the bottom of the hill, with the
'first gold sovereign.' She and Miss Fortescue
had walked away together, and the sovereign fell
from—why, we suppose it fell from Sarah's dress!"

And here we must observe, Miss Barrymore says
"she kept up her spirits." This shows us she was
certainly anxious, and perhaps also to some extent
hopeful, that the coins might still be found in
the library; and we may also infer from her conversation that only when the "gold sovereign" was
restored by Miss Thorn did she actually lose all
hope of recovering the " six-angel piece!" In
addition to the loss of this hope, the wrong information given to her, that the coin had fallen from
Miss Fortescue's dress, made her wrathful and
sceptical. She felt convinced a thin muslin, without frill or flounce, could not have harboured two
heavy gold coins at any time unknown to the
wearer! Still less could they had been carried by
such slight means so far as the stile in the wood!
Miss Barrymore's intellect was of the practical
order, and she made her conclusions accordingly.
If Miss Barrymore had asked herself this question,
" Do you think Miss Fortescue pocketed the coins?"
she would not have been prepared to reply in
the affirmative. Unfortunately she did not so
question herself; but she suffered her annoyance
at the loss of "the six-angel piece" to vent itself

in covert inuendo and hard speeches, that were alike unworthy of herself and undeserved by her friend. The real truth, that the first gold sovereign had been caught and retained in the ruched heading to *Miss Thorn's* flounce, never for one moment struck her as possible! And so Miss Barrymore's manner to Captain Fortescue, and her insinuations, were such as at some future period she will recall with regret. But to return:

"Sarah's dress!" repeated Captain Fortescue slowly, and as if he did not understand what Miss Barrymore meant. "How could it fall from Sarah's dress? •What had her dress to do with it? I confess I do not comprehend."

"When the tray fell, the probability is that the coins lodged in some of the trimmings of—" but Miss Barrymore paused with a sensation of choking in her throat, for she knew that the dress was quite plain—"if her dress were trimmed, or——"

"What a strange and unprecedented occurrence!" said Captain Fortescue, "that valuable coins should be accidentally lodged in the flounces and furbelows of a lady's dress—a light summer material, such as is generally worn at this time of the year," continued he, as he turned and scrutinised Miss Barrymore's pretty muslin, "and should actually remain concealed in that trimming during so long a walk, only to fall out at the very spot where they could be instantaneously secured, appears to me a wonderful violation of the laws of chance! For the chances certainly were that the coins would have fallen long before then, and been absolutely lost, beyond recovery, in the long grass in the wood !"

Captain Fortescue was decidedly pleased with this curious fact of the "violation of the laws of chance," and he walked on once more in high good-humour, talking for some little time most learnedly on this law and that, and not being in the least aware that the more he proved the impossibility—or the improbability—of the gold coins being able to travel so far, in so insecure a position, the more he supported Miss Barrymore's theory also—viz., That the coins could *not* have been caught and carried away accidentally in Miss Fortescue's *very plain* muslin dress.

"But only one coin was recovered," said Miss Barrymore, as soon as she could interrupt the torrent of eloquence that had imposed silence upon herself for a time.

"Only one? Ah! I remember," and now the expression of Captain Fortescue's countenance suddenly changed. And in proportion as he had been gratified by the recovery of the "first gold sovereign" under such exceptional circumstances, so was he now startled and grieved at the recollection of the loss of the still more valuable coin !

"And you say the 'six-angel piece' of Edward VI. is missing?"

"Unfortunately, yes," said Miss Barrymore. "But perhaps Miss Fortescue may yet find it, and the good and wonderful chance that has restored to my dear "grandfather one coin, may in time even give him back the other."

Captain Fortescue did not comprehend Miss Barrymore's meaning. Neither was she herself aware of the force of her own words. She had no intention of accusing Miss Fortescue of theft; and yet, carried away by her own annoyance at the loss of the coin, she implied the possibility that her friend might yet find and restore it. Captain Fortescue was mystified by her ungracious manner, and he said rather brusquely,

„It must have fallen in the long grass; what could prevent it? And in that case it is indeed lost!—lost!"

" Why did not the sovereign fall? What prevented that?" said Miss Barrymore. " You have proved beyond a doubt that nothing short of a miracle caused the recovery of the sovereign, why may not another miracle, or even the very same, have prevented the fall of the " six-angel " in the long grass? Perhaps it is even still clinging to some part of—of——"

" To some part of Sarah's dress! Impossible— impossible—or, at all events, very improbable !"

" And Sarah did not tell you of our vexatious loss ?"

" No. I wonder she did not," said he.

" It was wrong not to tell you. But do ask her to look well over her dress," said Miss Barrymore.

" Ask Sarah! I confess I do not understand you. Do you really cling to the hope that 'the

six-angel piece' may yet be found on Sarah's
dress? How can a gold coin stick to a muslin
dress?"

"I have repeatedly asked myself the same question," said Miss Barrymore—"'how can a gold coin
stick to a muslin dress?' and yet by that wondrous
anomaly we recovered the 'first gold sovereign!'
Therefore, though I cannot reply to that query
with any feeling of satisfaction, I can hope that
what has been once may be again." She stopped
in her walk, for they had now reached that part
of the road that branched off to the Vicarage.
And, notwithstanding the very evident frown on
Captain Fortescue's brow, she added, "You have
been very eloquent on the laws of chance, and if
Sarah can but manage to find the coin still stick-
ing to her muslin dress, you and I will have another miracle to discuss. Good morning." She
turned away as she spoke, and walked rapidly
on, leaving Captain Fortescue wrathful and indignant. Her manner almost insinuated the fact
that she thought evil of Miss Fortescue! Incredible as this appeared, Captain Fortescue could
not entirely dismiss the idea, and he hurried home
in an unusually irritable state of mind, determined
to see Sarah immediately, and hear her version of
this very disagreeable affair. We are sorry to add
that the fact that his daughter had concealed from
him the occurrences of the previous day, and had
even allowed him to go to Heraldstowe unconscious of Sir Hildebrand's heavy loss, greatly ex-

asperated him against her. She, whom he so loved and trusted, to so deceive him !

And then again, what would his old friend Sir Hildebrand think ? He had not sympathised, he had not condoled with him on so irreparable a loss ; and a loss—as it had been stated to him —caused by his own child! Captain Fortescue felt he had a right to be angry.

"As for the sin 'of theft,' why, that was impossible—absurdly impossible," said he to himself ; "but it was wrong not to tell me ; it was also wrong to allow me to go to Heraldstowe unprepared ;" and, after a little thought, he added, "and now that I recall the fact, Sarah did look heated and agitated on her return yesterday !"

Captain Fortescue bowed his head as this last recollection arose in his mind ; then he silently breathed a prayer, "that God had kept his child innocent !"

CHAPTER XVIII.

" A GOOD SAILOR MAY MISTAKE IN A DARK NIGHT."

WHEN Captain Fortescue reached home, he found Sarah at the piano, quietly practising a sonata of Beethoven's, unknowing of the doubt cast upon her integrity.

"What is all this about Sir Hildebrand's loss of valuable coins ?" said he, as he stood by her side with his hat in his hand. "Why did you not tell me, Sarah, that something unpleasant had happened yesterday? I feel more out of temper than I like to acknowledge, for circumstances are against you; and until now I had the most perfect trust in and reliance upon you."

"My dear father!" said Sarah in accents of dismay, as she hastily left the piano.

"Since Miss Barrymore left me," resumed he, "I have been recalling the facts of your return from Heraldstowe yesterday. They were these—that you were much later than I expected, that when you did arrive you looked anxious and care-worn, as well as hot and fatigued with your walk. But you allowed me to ride away without giving any explanation of these signs of discomfort or unhappiness, and my entire trust in my only child prevented me from being disturbed by them."

Captain Fortescue unconsciously spoke with more severity than was natural to him; and even the astonishment expressed in Sarah's countenance, and her pleadingly clasped hands and tearful eyes, did not prevent him from adding,

"Have I cause to feel that my love and my confidence are misplaced?"

"Misplaced! My dear father, what can you mean? I have not a thought unknown to you; why are you so extremely severe?"

At Captain Fortescue's desire, Sarah now recounted to him most circumstantially all that had occurred at the stile. He was then convinced that the coins must have been carried away unintentionally by Miss Thorn, and not by Miss Fortescue. He could see no reason why Miss Thorn should try to fix this fact upon her companion, instead of allowing that the coins had fallen from her own robe; but then he was entirely oblivious of the jealousy both Zara Barrymore and Sara Thorn had for the third Sarah, Miss Fortescue.

And after a short silence he resumed,

"You ought to have seen me before I went to Heraldstowe."

"I did not know of your intention. I thought you were to meet Mr. Thorn in the vestry at 'St. Mary's.'"

"And so I did. No, my dear, you were not likely to know that I intended to walk through the Park. Miss Barrymore says Sara Thorn was at a distance from the stile when the coin fell. Now, your version does not agree with this," said Captain Fortescue.

"I assure you Sara Thorn was at the top of the stile when I distinctly——"

"There, that will do; you need not tell me again. Put on your hat," said he, looking at his watch; "we can go to the Vicarage and back before dinner. Thorn is a sensible man; he will see things in their true light, and put down that impudent daughter of his better than anyone. Come—come along."

Captain Fortescue had never until now applied such epithets to Miss Thorn. She was a leading belle in that immediate neighbourhood. A little vain of her personal appearance, perhaps, and a little jealous of the favour shown to Miss Fortescue by Sir Hildebrand. But she was not considered an ill-natured, gossiping young lady, prone to speak evil of her neighbours. She was a little bit scornful in her manner towards Miss Fortescue, whom she looked upon as a plain, rather stupid companion, but that was all. She was not detractive, or otherwise unamiable. It so happened that Captain Fortescue had often noticed this ungracious manner to his daughter, and now that he himself was angry, and more angry than the occasion justified, he remembered Miss Thorn's sins of the past, and indemnified himself for his former provocations by using scornful terms to her now.

Miss Fortescue quickly prepared for a walk, and she and her father set off for the Vicarage. Captain Fortescue was very much excited, and took such lengthy strides, and walked so fast, it was almost as much as Sarah's strength could bear to keep up with him. When they were within sight of the Vicarage gate, Rosa, a younger sister of Miss Thorn, and her governess, were seen coming out into the road. Rosa was a clever but a forward child, a great pet with her father, and, therefore, often unchecked, when perhaps a little restraint would have been the better both for her present behaviour and her future career. In this instance she rushed up to Miss Fortescue, and exclaimed loudly, " Oh ! Miss Fortescue, they are talking about you."

" About me ?—who is doing me so much honour ?"

" Miss Barrymore and Sara ; they are talking about the gold coins you dropped at the stile."

" I did not drop them," said Miss Fortescue, retreating from the child's caresses.

" No—so they say ; they say you only dropped one."

Miss Fortescue made no reply, and the child resumed :

" They say there were two coins lost at the same time, but you only let one fall at the stile. Have you found the other ?　Show it to me, will you ?—I do so want to see it."

The poor child must have been very much astonished at the result of this query, for at this moment Captain Fortescue, who had heard every word, could not longer restrain his indignation ; he caught hold of the child, and giving her a hearty good shake, said, in loud, angry tones,

" What do you mean ?"

Without waiting for a reply to this unexpected question, Captain Fortescue released the child and strode hastily on towards the Vicarage. But now his resentment overpowered his judgment, and when he arrived at the entrance porch he pulled the bell with so sharp a jerk as to make it peal forth a startlingly hasty and discordant summons.　Sarah could not restrain her tears, for she had never before seen her father give way to such passionate bursts of temper, or known him unjust in his reproaches to herself. Her tears only irritated him the more, and with this unwonted exposure of the agitation of both, and in this great excitement of mind, they were shown in to the Rev. Ulric Thorn. Now, Mr. Thorn knew nothing about the loss of the coins, and, therefore, Captain Fortescue's anger and Sarah's tears were alike inexplicable to him. After some discussion, Miss Thorn was sent for, but her presence seemed to make the mystification greater instead of less, when, at length, Captain Fortescue turned to her, and said :

" Will you have the goodness to describe to me your own position, and the position of my daughter, with regard to the stone stile at the bottom of the hill, when you heard the coin fall ?—that coin, whatever its name or value, that you afterwards restored to Sir Hildebrand Barrymore."

" Stone stile !" said the Vicar—" what has this to do with our present discussion ?"

" Everything," said Captain Fortescue, impatiently.

And then followed a long conversation between the two ladies, as to the facts that occurred at the stile. But as Miss Fortescue was agitated, and in dread of what her father, in his present excitement, might do or say next, and as Miss Thorn was full of displeasure at Captain Fortescue's treatment of her darling little sister, and, moreover, very much provoked at this moment with Miss Fortescue, it came to pass that the listeners could neither make head nor tail of all the talk, and it was eventually put an end to by the Vicar; who made a sign to his daughter to prevent her speaking again, and who then said :

"Listen to me—listen to me. It appears—and it has always appeared to me—that these stupid coins—I wish there were no such things on the face of the earth"—it is evident the Vicar has no taste for numismatics—"that these stupid, battered, hammered, defaced, even bent, and certainly worthless coins—for they are worthless, except to feed the vanity of a few—they are worthless, I say, and, therefore, it is the more senseless to hoard them, and harangue learnedly over them. Confound it all !"—even the Vicar was losing the customary equanimity of his temper in the excitement of the subject, and his own position as connected with it—"it has always appeared to me that the less said about them the better ; for it comes to this—it must come to this, even in the very best specimens that can be collected together from one end of the kingdom to the other—ay," added he, waxing eloquent with his subject, " from one end of the whole earth to the other—it must come to this, that either they are, or they are not, genuine. If they are not what they are supposed to be, that is *genuine,* they are not worth a snap of your fingers ! And if they are *genuine,* or have the credit of being

so, they are just worth a little hiding place in a
very shallow drawer!"

Here the Vicar paused, and looked from one to
the other of his listeners—and then resuming, he
said,

"And for this shall we, who have been hearty good
friends ever since our first introduction to each
other, shall we become foes? Nonsense, Captain
Fortescue!—this cannot be."

"But it is not for this or for that, allow me to
say," said Captain Fortescue. "It is not the real
or the reputed value of 'the six-angel piece,' or of
'the first gold sovereign of Henry VII.'—but
that you—you," turning to Miss Thorn, "or any
one, should dare to cast a stain upon the integrity
of my daughter; or even in thought fancy that
she would take a penny reel of cotton knowingly."

And he tossed a half-used reel from Sara's
workbox as he spoke.

"And no one here does dare so black a thought,"
said the Vicar, impulsively, as he arose and offered
his hand to Sarah Fortescue. "Do not weep, my
dear young lady; what have you to weep for?
Dry up your tears, and content yourself with your
position in our estimation."

But Sarah was disturbed by her father's anger.

"But then tell me," said Captain Fortescue,
"how did this unaccountable report get bruited
about?"

He was totally oblivious of the fact that he himself had made all the commotion.

"I do not understand you," said Mr. Thorn; "but I may even say that, in my own private opinion, I should have thought my own Sara more likely to have carried off the coins, in some of the many trammels of her dress, rather than that this plain muslin," touching Miss Fortescue's robe, "should have been able to attract to itself and take away anything so heavy as gold coins!"

"Even as now there is something in your flounce," said Captain Fortescue interrupting, and pointing to Sara Thorn's dress.

"Yes, my dear," said the Vicar stooping.

He tried to extricate a thin slip of paper that seemed to cling to the ruched heading; but as he did not succeed, Captain Fortescue said,

"Let me try?" And in a second or two he had drawn out the paper. "It is written upon," added he, looking up at Sara Thorn with a mischievous smile, "and it is parchment or vellum; certainly not paper. I think I ought to read what is written, for the trouble I have taken to dislodge it."

"Pray do—I have no idea what it is. Something I have caught up from the rubbish in the work-room probably. But parchment, do you say? Oh! then, from the housekeeper's room, she has been re-labelling her keys, in all probability; but it cannot be anything of importance, and it must have been dragged away by the ruche in passing."

"How very eloquent young ladies can become when it suits their purpose," said Captain Fortescue.

"Indeed I have no purpose to suit," said Sara, blushing brightly, but in most perfect good-humour. "I do not think I need much eloquence to shield myself from any discovery that can be made by an old label."

"Well, I do not wish to accuse you," said Captain Fortescue, evidently trying to become less morose in manner, as he apparently took some trouble to smooth out the slip of parchment on the palm of his hand.

"The first gold sovereign coined in England," said he, reading aloud. "In the reign of Henry VII., A.D. 1485—1509."

For a few seconds a dead silence fell on the party, each turning to gaze on another with looks of surprise. Then the stillness was broken by Sara Thorn, who rushed impetuously up to Captain Fortescue, and said,

"You are trying to tease me; let me see the label—it cannot be so."

"It is so," said Captain Fortescue, as he held the label between his thumb and finger high above Sara's head.

"Then I am the thief!" said Sara Thorn, clasping her hands together, as in mockery of her position; while Sarah Fortescue put her hand on her father's arm, and said,

"Is it really the label to the coin found at the stile?"

"Tell us—tell us truly," said the Vicar, as he approached Captain Fortescue; "does that slip of parchment indeed throw any light upon the missing coins?"

"I should say," replied Captain Fortescue, now in firm and pleasant tones—"I should say, unhesitatingly, that this is the label in which 'the first gold sovereign' was folded when it fell from the drawer. Allow me once more to touch your dress," continued he to Sara Thorn, "for it appears that this—this——"

"Ruche," said Sara.

"That this ruche caught the coin in its fall, wrapped in this slip of parchment; and that in process of time the natural weight of the coin worked its way through the slight obstacles that had detained it, and it fell, while the parchment still remained entangled in the ruche."

"Then you really mean deliberately to tell me that I *am* the thief?" said Miss Thorn.

"I do mean to say, if there have been any purloining in the case, that you have been the thief—and a very pretty thief you are, Miss Thorn," said Captain Fortescue with a low bow.

"Spare me!" said Miss Thorn, covering her face with both hands, in an affectation of terror.

"Humph!" said the Vicar, "and so I was right in the main; and my daughter actually did carry off those little bits of mildewed ore! I shall not put myself out of temper for her sake, as you have done for the sake of your daughter; but then I do not pretend to any degree of taste or—" but feeling instinctively that it would not be wise to create a fresh misunderstanding, he turned to his daughter and said laughingly, "but since there can be no doubt of your guilt, pray may I ask what reparation you mean to make to these my very ill-used friends?"

"But, dear sir, it is so plain she could not help it!" said Miss Fortescue appealingly to the Vicar.

"God bless you, my generous darling!" said Captain Fortescue whisperingly in her ear. For he remembered but too well how differently Miss Thorn had acted, in her sarcastic accusation at the stone stile. And then gently putting aside his own daughter, and extending his hand to Miss Thorn, grasping hers, and heartily shaking it, he said,

"Will I not torment you for this! I will have you put in the stocks, set in the pillory, pelted with hard words, black-balled——"

"All for my innocence?" said she.

"Because you are one of those *unconscious* thieves who infest this neighbourhood, and commit terrible depredations on the property of elderly gentlemen, and also on the hearts of——"

"Stop, stop!" said Miss Thorn. "You will black-ball me, put me in the pillory, pelt me with hard words, but—all for my innocence?"

"For your innocence, of course," replied Captain Fortescue; "for, my dear young lady, learn now, from one who has seen a great deal of the world, that the innocent too often suffer for the guilty; and as you are so really, truly, and heartily

innocent of breaking the seventh commandment,
'Thou shalt not steal,' or even the ninth, 'Thou
shalt not bear false witness against thy neighbour,' you must prepare yourself to suffer in the
place of him or her who has committed such crimes.
The law must have its example—crime must have
its victim; and as the innocent·are very heedless
of consequences, the consequence of their innocence, they too often become the prey of more reprobate minds."

In all this Captain Fortescue was very satirical;
and Miss Thorn, though too wise to remark upon
it, felt that he was so.

" Well, I am as thankful as I can be," said the
Vicar heartily, " that we have this proof-positive
of the way in which those worn-out bits of battered coin found their way to their mother earth
once more !" and then he looked round deprecatingly as he continued, " and to fancy a father—a
well-grown father of my unwieldy proportions "—
the Vicar was both tall and stout—" feeling thankful, under the circumstances, for the fact that his
beloved daughter is proved to have carried off a
golden sovereign, the property of his personal
friend !   One of those very valuable, begrimed,
cracked, and worthless bits of metal that very
worthy county gentleman," bowing low to Captain
Fortescue, " put away safely, in a very shallow
tray or drawer, guarded by a patent Bramah, and
most graciously exhibit—but only on ˙very state
occasions—to their very well-beloved friends !"

Everybody laughed. But the Vicar had proved *he* could be as satirical as Captain Fortescue.

"I shall not resign this parchment," said Captain Fortescue, exhibiting it triumphantly. "Indeed, I shall go to Heraldstowe, turn informer, proudly bring forward the witness to the delinquency of a certain lady, and call upon Sir Hildebrand to prosecute her with the utmost rigour of the law."

"Shall you go to Heraldstowe to-day?" said the Vicar.

"Dear father, take me!" said Miss Thorn, "for I foresee you intend to accompany Captain Fortescue."

"You will be afraid to pass the stocks on the village-green," said Captain Fortescue.

"Not with you for my champion," replied she.

"Ah! now you are artfully trying to interest the most chivalrous feelings of my nature," replied he; "you know it is my ardent wish to protect the innocent, and give homage to beauty."

"Let us all go together," said the Vicar.

"And all tell of each other," said Miss Thorn.

"No; we condemn you to tell of yourself," said Captain Captain Fortescue, "and to shew yourself no favour."

"Hard-hearted man! is this your chivalry?—do you thus protect the innocent?—is it thus you give—" but Miss Thorn stopped.

"Pray go on," said the Vicar.

"Give homage to beauty?" continued Miss

Thorn. "Why, on the contrary, you will delight yourself in my terror—you will revel in my despair!"

"If I saw you exhibit a symptom of real terror," replied Captain Fortescue, "I would pity you. If I saw you in despair, I would comfort you; but I do not think you will otherwise draw largely upon my stores of compassion or consolation."

Miss Thorn could not mistake the tone of irony with which Captain Fortescue spoke, and she felt very keenly that her foolish and uncalled-for fit of annoyance at the stone stile on the previous day was the first great cause of his resentment.

"But seriously, we all go to Heraldstowe, and explain the actual facts to Sir Hildebrand," suggested the Vicar.

"By all means," replied Captain Fortescue.

"Suppose you and Sarah stay and dine with us, and then, in the cool of the evening——"

"Thanks—that is impossible," said Captain Fortescue, interrupting the Vicar. "Mrs. Fortescue will wait for us; nevertheless, I agree with you in the opinion that it will be as well to see Sir Hildebrand as soon as possible."

"Yes—I do think, for the sake of all parties, we had better meet at Heraldstowe to-night."

"I will drive Sarah after dinner; there is a charming moon, in addition to the long summer evening twilight—between eight and nine. Will that do?"

" To be at Heraldstowe not later than nine."

CHAPTER XIX.

" TOO MUCH FEAR CUTS ALL THE NERVES ASUNDER."

AT Heraldstowe, the long day that had been so
prolific of vexations to the Fortescues and
Thorns, had quietly jogged on in its customary
routine.

After dinner Sir Hildebrand, as was sometimes
the case, fell asleep in his cosy arm-chair, and
Miss Barrymore proposed to Almeric to stroll out
upon the lawns, among the fountains and flowers,
and enjoy the cool evening air. Soon they
entered the Park.

" We will go to the squirrels," said Almeric.

The moon was sailing high up in the heavens,
casting a shimmering light on the boughs that
were stirred by a gentle breeze. Here and there
stood handsome groups of trees, casting deep
shadows on the earth.

" There is my favourite squirrel," said Almeric,
suddenly stopping in his walk—" do you see him
on that topmost bough ?"

The squirrels were a colony of themselves in a
particular part of the Park.

" Favourite !—why, how can you tell one
squirrel from another ? And what excellent long
sight you must have, Almeric, to see distinctly so

tiny a creature on so large and lofty a tree; it is true, I see him, but not to see any difference between him and any other."

"Come with me under the trees, Zara."

"We are getting too far from the house," said she.

"Oh! nonsense—grandpapa will not miss us; and, besides, Jasper saw us strolling on the lawns; he will look in upon him. Come with me under the trees; the little things congregate round these trees in the cool of the evening, and hold their revels."

Miss Barrymore thought, as she seated herself, and listened to her brother, and his admiration of the squirrels, it was a singular fact that it should be recorded of their ancestor, Almeric Marmaduke Barry-Barrymore, that he also had had a great love for these tiny animals, and that he it was who in his day had made the squirrels in the Park at Heraldstowe tame.

"See how the beautiful creatures leap from bough to bough, from tree to tree," said Almeric. "If you watched nature in all her haunts, as I do, you would know, Zara, that this is their custom in the cool evenings of summer. See how they pursue each other!—how they revel in the fresh air, and enjoy the healthful exercise!"

Suddenly, from the branches of the tree under which they were sitting, one alighted on Almeric's shoulder.

"Here he is," said he, taking hold of the

squirrel, caressing him, and showing him to Miss Barrymore.

"Oh! you beauty!—you darling beauty!" said she, admiringly; "but how shy!—why, he will not let me poke a finger at him without showing symptoms of fear."

"Their nature is timid and retiring, and yet they are very affectionate little creatures when once they become tame," said he, still fondling his pet.

"But how do you know this squirrel from the multitude I see at play now? Is he the only one that is so brave?"

"He is at present the only one who allows me to touch him, but his example will in time give confidence to the remainder of the fraternity," said Almeric. "But now, Zara, look at his large and very handsome tail, really superior to any you see around us. See, again, the rich shade of dark red upon the brown of his soft fur; and then the small amount of white upon the breast. Compare him with any other that comes in your sight for the whole evening, and you will convince yourself he is the largest and the finest of the whole community; he has a fur of the richest in colour, and softest to the touch. Oh! he is easily distinguishable from his brethren."

Miss Barrymore sat silent for a few moments watching her brother play with the squirrel, and again recalling the chronicle of the Sieur Almeric and his love for squirrels, and marvelling in her

own mind if such tastes could be transmitted from
generation to generation; through, as it seemed to
her, countless generations.

"Does he often come to you?" said she at length,
breaking the silence. "And have you a name for
him? I would call him Almeric, after our famous
ancestor."

"I call him 'the Baron,'" said Almeric hastily.

"I suppose whenever you are alone in the Park,
your little friends surround you?"

"Oh! no, no, Zara; they cannot stand the
heat of the day—the sun is too much for them—
they do not disport themselves in the daytime."

"They do not hide themselves, Almeric, for I
often see them as I——"

"Ah! you misunderstand me," said Almeric,
interrupting, "of course you, or any one in passing through the Park, may occasionally see a
squirrel in the daytime. But you never see them
holding their revels, congregated in large numbers
in one place, pursuing each other, leaping from
tree to tree, and thoroughly enjoying their games,
as they do always in the cool of the evening, to
their very heart's content. The day is too hot, the
sun too ardent."

The brother and sister sat some time amusing
themselves by watching the squirrels at play, until
the gradual lengthening of the shadows of evening
arrested Miss Barrymore's attention, and she started up hastily, as she said,

"I am forgetting myself in this charming scene

and enjoyable talk with you, dear Almeric ; grandpapa will awake and want coffee."

" I will follow you presently," said he ; " I cannot toss this little creature too hastily from my
arms ; he has resigned his revels with his own kith
and kin to come to me—I must give him another
sweet nut."

" You must not stay long, dear Almeric—already
the Park begins to look gloomy."

" I will not, dear Zara."

Miss Barrymore walked quickly away from
under the shade of the trees, and Almeric was left
alone with his pet. He was so charmed by the
perfect confidence the squirrel seemed to have
in him, that he, for the moment, forgot he was
at a distance from the house, and without a companion; indeed, he had forgotten that he was
liable to be intruded upon at any minute by his
restless ancestor. He continued to watch the
gambols of the many squirrels holding their revels
there, and to encourage the confidence and affection of the one he still had seated on his arm, when
suddenly he heard the sharp snapping of a bough
somewhere near. He started from his reverie,
remembered his lonely position—seated under the
shade of trees almost in darkness—and determined
to return home immediately. For this purpose he
arose, and turned to place the squirrel on the
trunk of a tree—to his horror and astonishment it
was seized by the hand of some person standing
behind the tree. Almeric peered through the dark-

ness, and saw the Sieur Almeric holding in his mailed hand the handsome squirrel! Suddenly the darkness vanished—it became light as day. Almeric gazed round, and was conscious that the squirrels, in spite of the heat and glare of the day —or of the light that had seemed to turn night into day—were still carrying on their revels; but his pet and favourite struggled in the iron hand of his captor.

It turned its brilliantly sparkling eyes on Almeric, as if it sought his protection, and wished to be set free from its present uncomfortable position. With a hard stern stare Almeric watched his revered ancestor, and saw, to his dismay, that every instant he seemed to press him closer and still closer in his mailed grasp. Almeric saw— but felt himself spell-bound and helpless. With a desperate effort he at length shouted,

" Let him go!—let him go!"

The Baron knocked the little creature's head against the hard trunk of the tree, once, twice, thrice—and then threw him down quivering in his death-throes at Almeric's feet!

" You villainous knight! you——"

Almeric had again shouted loudly, but he stopped in the middle of his speech from sheer astonishment! He saw the squirrels stop their gambols and come nearer and nearer to their dead companion; and as they came one by one within reach of the Baron, he put out his hand and caught them, dashed their tiny heads against the tree, and threw them, struggling, bleeding, and dying, to their so lately living companion!

A heap of squirrels lay close to Almeric! Higher and still higher with dead squirrels did the Baron raise the mound, cutting Almeric himself—as it seemed to him—off from the rest of the world!

Subdued, patient, and speechless as much by the horror of the scene as by the feeling of his own helplessness, he felt himself almost crushed by the dead bodies; for more and more, faster and yet faster, came the tiny animals; and higher, and even yet higher, rose the mound of dead around him!

Involuntarily he put out his hands to push away the carcases, and prevent them from smothering him, when again, with a mighty effort, speech returned.

"You dastardly coward, cease your murders!" and, struggling to disentangle himself, he saw the glare of day abruptly grow dim—become darker, until there was a thick darkness; he breathed hard —he thought he was dying, though he still stretched out his hands, and tried to push away the dead objects that so oppressed him, when suddenly he was startled by the sound of a voice. He listened.

"Miss Barrymore has sent me, sir, to tell you tea is ready." One of the footmen had spoken. "She said I should probably find you under this tree."

"Yes, yes," said Almeric, as he felt himself

breathe easily; and he stepped from under the dark shadow of the trees into the clear moonlight, and gazed anxiously around for some signs of his excellent ancestor. There were none.

" Captain and Miss Fortescue have just arrived, sir, and Mr. and Miss Thorn."

" The Thorns and the Fortescues at this time of night!" said Almeric, hurrying on, and glad of an excuse to hasten away from a scene of so much pain.

But the footman, who had awaked him from a sound sleep, thought he was eager to greet his visitors.

" Did you see the squirrels?" said Almeric. He meant the large mound of dead.

" Only one, sir; it ran up the tree."

" Only *one* remaining!" thought Almeric, but he said no more. "To-morrow I must take assistance, and see what can be done with the poor dead things!" But he did not tell the footman his thoughts.

CHAPTER XX.

" AS A MAN IS FRIENDED, SO THE LAW IS ENDED."

" MAY we come in ?" said Captain Fortescue to Sir Hildebrand, as he and Sarah entered the drawing-room at Heraldstowe, on this same evening—"may we intrude ourselves into your peaceful home, and destroy the comfort of your evening?"

"And here am I," said the Vicar, "and here is my daughter. What do you say to us?—sad intruders at an unusual hour."

"How many more?" said Sir Hildebrand, rising and coming forward to receive his visitors; "the more the merrier, my worthy friends—the more the merrier, and all welcome as the evening dew to the thirsty flowers, or young faces and kind hearts to the old, old man."

Sir Hildebrand was alone. He shook each guest by the hand heartily, and busied himself in little acts of courtesy until Miss Barrymore returned from her walk in the Park. Then the three ladies absented themselves for a short time. When they reappeared, Miss Barrymore walked hastily up to Sir Hildebrand, and said,

"What do you think, dear grandpapa; we know now how the——"

"Stop!" said Captain Fortescue in a loud and authoritative tone; and then, suddenly changing to his habitually subdued and decorous voice, he turned to Miss Barrymore, and said, "I beg your pardon—pray excuse the rough manners of a sailor, and allow me to explain; that we have decreed, as one part of the punishment of our charming young friend," nodding to Miss Thorn, "that she shall herself confess her mighty delinquencies to the honourable gentleman she has so wilfully"—with a strong accent on the word— "wronged!"

Sir Hildebrand had listened in wonder and amazement, but he made no remark. Miss Barrymore smiled as she turned to Miss Thorn, and said,

" Quite right. I will not help her in the least."

The Vicar seated himself in a large easy-chair, and, like Sir Hildebrand, looked on, and remained silent.

And now Miss Thorn placed herself in the centre of the room, and stood in an attitude of deep humility. Her eyes were cast down upon the carpet, as if she feared to look around; her arms drooped listlessly by her side, and the *pose* of her figure was expressive of meekness and resignation to her lot. Her spirits and good-humour rose with the occasion! She felt that Captain Fortescue would shew her no mercy; and she determined that, as far as she could rule events, he should have all his own way, as perhaps the best method of allaying the angry feeling she knew he nursed against her. Therefore, she purposely assumed an attitude of humility, and overcast her features with an expression of hopelessness, the better to meet the occasion, and succumb to circumstances she could not control.

Sir Hildebrand leaned forward in his chair, turning his head inquiringly from one to another, for he did not understand the scene. He, however, beckoned to Sarah Fortescue, and on her replying to his summons, he caused her to seat herself by his side, for he was gradually making

up his mind to the fact that something the reverse
of agreeable was likely to be the subject of the
evening. He had never heard Captain Fortescue
speak in so loud a tone of authority, nor seen Sara
Thorn so submissively unqueened. What could it
all mean? Instinctively he remembered Miss
Barrymore's description of Miss Fortescue's plain
muslin dress, and of its inability to secrete or carry
off coins unknown to the wearer. It was with a
desire to protect her from the consequences of any
rude attack that he had placed her by his side;
and as soon as she was seated, he took her hand,
and said, as he held it caressingly,

"Do not fear, my gracious princess—I will keep
the world in order."

Miss Fortescue did not comprehend what Sir
Hildebrand meant; happily she knew nothing of
the many disagreeable remarks that had been
made at Heraldstowe. She smiled, and blushed,
and remained silent. And Sir Hildebrand
resolved, as he still retained her hand, that he
would rather lose his entire collection of coins
than hear against her one word of disparage-
ment.

"Now," said the Vicar, leaning back in his
chair, and turning to Captain Fortescue—"now it
is time the play should begin, is it not?"

"Yes, yes," replied Captain Fortescue, with an
affectation of sternness in his manner, and speaking to Sara Thorn, he added: "Allow me to
suggest that you make what may be called 'a

clean breast of it.' Confess the enormity of your
iniquity, and—and hope not for mercy; if I am
well supported in my opinion of your conduct,
you will be condemned to—penal servitude for
life!"

Sir Hildebrand was evidently distressed at what
—if he had spoken—he would have called most
inopportune language at such a time, and in such
a presence; but Captain Fortescue felt a positive
pleasure in what he in his own mind called " turning the tables on Miss Thorn," while Miss Barrymore said aloud, in a tone of compassion :

" Poor thing !—poor thing !   But surely she
may be allowed to sit ?   She looks so forlorn, and
so like a—a friendless and—indeed, it pains me
to see her stand so disconsolately.   Do let her sit
down !"

The Vicar laughed, and shook his head, as if he
thought Miss Barrymore's compassion was ill-
timed ; but Captain Fortescue came forward, and
said, in the most courteous tones,

" Your will is law ; the prisoner—we have proof
of her ill-doing, and do not, therefore, misapply
the term—she is our prisoner, and by your wish
she shall be accommodated with a seat."

He then searched round and round the room
for the smallest footstool, and carrying it to Miss
Thorn, and placing it by her side, said :

" For the present, the stool of repentance shall
be your throne."

The Vicar again laughed.   Miss Barrymore

turned away, feeling she had done more harm
than good, and Sir Hildebrand gazed with an
expression of dissatisfaction overspreading his
features. Miss Thorn herself was unmoved by
all the interest she excited, or the trouble she
caused. She did not smile, but as certainly she
did not frown; she still retained her attitude of
humility; but even these outward signs of
patience and resignation were translated in her
disfavour by Captain Fortescue. He saw that
she was standing opposite to a very large mirror,
in which her whole figure was reflected, and he
could not but acknowledge that when she stood
motionless, she looked like a graceful and well-
executed statue of despondency and regret. Sara
had occasionally, but accidentally, raised her eyes
to the mirror—Captain Fortescue thought she was
admiring herself! He did her injustice; she was
thinking only on the best means of disarming his,
to all appearance, vindictive resentment.

Meanwhile, Sir Hildebrand's discontent expressed itself by queries in most gracious and
conciliatory tones.

"My winsome princess!—my winsome princess!
—my beautiful and disconsolate princess, why
does our friend, Captain Fortescue, play the
tyrant over you?—and why are you called by the
opprobrious term of prisoner?"

Miss Thorn slightly raised her head, and as a
statue would turn on a pivot, so she turned to Sir
Hildebrand, as she said, in low and tremulous tones,

" For my misdeeds."

" Misdeeds!" replied Sir Hildebrand, in a voice of astonishment.

"Misdeeds," reiterated Sara; and then, feeling that the ice was broken, and that she was expected to make a full confession, she continued, in rather firmer tones and louder voice : "You, my honoured sir, will easily recall the dilemmas of yesterday."

Sir Hildebrand bowed.

" The fall of the two trays with the coins, the recovery of all that fell from the first tray, the loss of the two valuable coins from the second tray, the consternation at this loss, the strictness of the search, and the time consumed by it. You may remember that every nook and corner of the library possible to reach while the furniture remained in the room, underwent the most rigid examination, and only produced disappointment to all."

Sir Hildebrand leaned forward in his chair, and in an attitude of profound attention he again mutely bowed, while Captain Fortescue said in a positive tone,

" You searched all places but the right one !"

And the Vicar, with a view to support Captain Fortescue, and, like his daughter, wishing to turn aside his anger, added in rather a jocose tone,

" Sir Hildebrand should have searched you, my dear Sara, and then he would have found the coins."

Sara bowed her head the lower, and remained silent.

"Hush, hush!" said Sir Hildebrand, as he leaned back in his chair, with a countenance expressive of much annoyance.

"And also, most honoured sir," resumed Sara, again addressing Sir Hildebrand, "you may remember that my friend Sarah Fortescue and myself, after walking through the wood, eventually arrived at the stone stile——"

"Stop, stop!" said Sir Hildebrand, holding up his finger, and in fear of an attack upon Miss Fortescue; "I am quite sure that——"

"Allow me to proceed, my dear sir," said Miss Thorn, interrupting him, "for I am compelled, by the authority of that gentleman," bowing to Captain Fortescue, "to shew myself no mercy. I am compelled—but not ashamed—to have to confess to you that I am the thief!—I carried off the coin, or coins."

Miss Thorn had used the word "thief" advisedly, thinking it would be acceptable to Captain Fortescue; but Sir Hildebrand was totally unprepared either for so bold an avowal, or—in his opinion—the use of such harsh language. Nevertheless, the courtesy of the gentleman prevailed over all other feelings. It is true the disagreeable sentence, so criminatory of herself, made him start in dismay; but in the next instant he half rose from his chair, extended his hand to Miss Thorn, who said with a smile as she advanced and allowed him to take hers, "But a very unintentional thief!"

"I am sure of that—most sure of that, my winsome princess," said he, shaking her hand heartily.

"Oh! this will not do at all," said Captain Fortescue, rising and approaching them; "we have brought a prisoner to our senior magistrate; we did not commit her to prison, or give her up to punishment, or allow the law of the land to take its course, upon condition that she should herself confess the whole of her wickedness to the kind old friend she had so shamefully injured!"

"She says she is a 'thief,'" said Miss Barrymore; "what more would you have?"

"I would have *all* her wickedness confessed," said he. Now Captain Fortescue thought she ought to confess she had accused another wrongfully; but Miss Thorn never had had any intention of accusing Miss Fortescue, and was almost unable to account for his great umbrage against herself. Miss Thorn thought, if anyone had accused Miss Fortescue, it had been Miss Barrymore. But that lady also felt herself innocent; and yet, strange to say, it seemed as if some one had been very greatly to blame. One thing had entirely slipped Miss Thorn's memory, but it was ever present with Captain Fortescue, viz., that she had been rudely satirical with his daughter at the stone stile.

"Surely that is all!" said Miss Barrymore in reply. "Her own conscience cannot accuse her of more?"

"And may not I protect her, now that she has confessed?" said Sir Hildebrand, still retaining her hand.

"Ah! I see how it will all end," replied Captain Fortescue, shrugging his shoulders. "She will escape—I see it—she will escape. But now listen to me, Sir Hildebrand," continued he. "If she had been innocent she would *not* have escaped —she would have found a foe in every pretended friend, a slanderous tongue under every smiling lip."

Sir Hildebrand did not understand this harsh language. He knew nothing of Captain Fortescue's churlishness at supposed slights to his daughter—he knew nothing of all that had been said and done at the Vicarage on that day; he replied, therefore, in accents of great surprise,

"But she *is* innocent—innocent of intentional wrong. And allow me to say, my dear young lady," turning to Miss Thorn, whose hand he still retained, "my princess—my winsome princess!" becoming more and more earnest with each successive phrase, "I cannot for one moment see the necessity of doubt or difficulty. Am I not your friend?—do I not love and cherish you, trust and honour you as one of my own children? Why, then, on erring as you say—very unintentionally —why mistrust my indulgence?" Sir Hildebrand was now making a serious matter of that that Miss Barrymore had supposed would amuse him, and she felt some anxiety that he should not be further mystified. She was prevented from speaking by Captain Fortescue, who said,

"The guilty always find friends, while the really innocent suffer in their stead."

"The innocent also find friends, my dear," replied Sir Hildebrand, "and I will befriend you and your innocence."

"Then you did not take the coins, Miss Thorn?" said Captain Fortescue. "If you are innocent you did not carry them away? Come, tell us; did you or did you not carry off the two coins?— the 'first gold sovereign of Henry VII.,' and the 'six-angel piece of Edward VI.?'"

"To the best of my belief I did," said Sara in tones of marked decision.

"You did!" said Sir Hildebrand, now relinquishing her hand with a start; for Captain Fortescue had succeeded, by the pertinacity of his accusation of Miss Thorn, in for the moment conveying an impression of wilful secretion.

It was but momentary, however; and then he remained standing and listening to all that was said.

"She did," said Captain Fortescue, coming forward, "the prisoner has confessed;, now gentlemen of the jury," addressing an imaginary audience, "your verdict?"

"Guilty, certainly guilty," said the Vicar, with a slow shake of his head.

"Guilty, certainly guilty," reiterated Captain Fortescue.

"My lord," addressing Sir Hildebrand, "we find the prisoner guilty!"

Sir Hildebrand, who did not at all comprehend what was true, and what was not true, remained silent. And after a pause of a few moments, the Vicar said,

"Now, my lord, pass sentence; what shall be done to this—this——"

He hesitated, between his unwillingness to use an opprobrious epithet, and his desire to say something that should put an end to a scene that was evidently becoming irksome to Sir Hildebrand, when Miss Barrymore came to his assistance, and said,

" Recommend her to mercy."

" No, no—that we shall not do; we think her deserving of the full penalty of the law," said Captain Fortescue.

" That must be because of my innocence," said Miss Thorn.

" But I fear we are fatiguing grandpapa," said Miss Barrymore, in a low voice to Captain Fortescue.

Sir Hildebrand seated himself, and Captain Fortescue offered his hand to Miss Thorn, at the same time saying in playful tones—

" Come, come along, Miss Innocence."

And leading her to Sir Hildebrand, he took from his pocket a small piece of paper, and presented it to him, saying,

" Do you know this label?"

Sir Hildebrand took the paper, and after carefully examining it, replied in a voice of astonishment,

"This is, in truth, the very label, in my own handwriting, in which was folded 'the first gold sovereign!'"

"I thought as much," said Captain Fortescue.

"And it was found here," said Miss Thorn, exhibiting the trimming of her dress.

The pros and cons were all talked over again; the wonderful chance that "the sovereign" had been carried so far before being liberated was once more eloquently dwelt upon—and the absolute certainty of the loss of "the six-angel piece" made matter for much discussion.

Miss Thorn stated that the ruches of her dress had been searched most minutely, since the discovery of this label, in the renewed hope of finding either the still missing "six angels" or the label that had belonged to it.

"There was no label with that unique coin," said Sir Hildebrand.

"Then, my dear old friend, it would the sooner disentangle itself from the slight confinement of the muslin ruche," said the Vicar with a sigh. Not that he cared for the coin; but that he sympathised with Sir Hildebrand.

"I am afraid so."

"Meanwhile shall we adjourn to coffee?" said Miss Barrymore.

Captain Fortescue seated himself by Miss Thorn,

and began to converse with his customary ease and courtesy. While the Vicar looked on as he said to himself,

"I hope he will not harbour an ill-natured feeling against Sara—he has certainly been much more intolerant than the occasion—in my judgment—required."

But then the vicar did *not* know of Miss Thorn's rudeness at the stone stile!—and Captain Fortescue did.

It was at this moment that Almeric entered the drawing-room. Miss Barrymore said to herself as soon as she saw him,

"Ah! I should not have left him! What can be the matter with him? How haggard and pale he looks!"

Almeric went forward and cordially greeted his friends; coming last to Miss Fortescue, who was still seated by Sir Hildebrand, and at a distance from the large table.

"And so we have discovered the real thief at last!" said Sir Hildebrand to him.

When the little drama was concluded by producing the label of the first gold sovereign, Sir Hildebrand understood it had been got up in sport, more for the sake, he supposed, of amusing him, than for any other reason. For Sir Hildebrand was entirely unaware of the real reason of that evening's recreation; namely, Miss Barrymore's and Miss Thorn's supposed ill-behaviour to Miss Fortescue. And though the innate refinement of his mind and habits felt jarred by the use of language to which he was unaccustomed, and which he thought sadly out of place in his own drawing-room, and applied to his personal friends; now that he felt sure the *divertissement* had been got up entirely for his gratification, he thought he could not better show his appreciation of these efforts than by still carrying on the joke. And as we have recorded, he said to Almeric:

" We have discovered the real thief !"

But Almeric had not yet recovered from the scene in the Park, and could not, therefore, comprehend what Sir Hildebrand meant. The loss of the two coins had no abiding-place in his mind, for two reasons. First, that the "gold sovereign" had been found and restored; and second, that he knew exactly where to put his hand on the " six-angel piece !" It would be vain and foolish to say that Almeric's present sufferings were caused by a dream !

Absolute reality was firmly impressed upon him, from the two facts, as in the former case, that the locality was the same as that he occupied, and the subject of the dream was only a continuation of his waking employment, but certainly—as is the case with most dreams—strangely travestied and exaggerated beyond the endurance of any one really awake. And yet this dream was embued with a positiveness and a verity that no power could overturn in Almeric's mind.

" Yes, yes," said the Vicar, coming forward and

giving Almeric a playful tap on the shoulder, " we are all right now. The thief is discovered, and has made a public confession."

" I do not understand," said Almeric wearily.

"My dear boy, it is all a joke," said Sir Hildebrand, as he fancied he saw signs of languor and exhaustion almost overpower him.

" He is not well," said Miss Barrymore in a whisper to Captain Fortescue; " but I say as little as I can, for fear of making dear grandpapa anxious."

" It is all a joke," reiterated Sir Hildebrand, seizing Almeric's hand, and looking earnestly at him.

" A joke!—far too serious for a joke, I fear," said Almeric, thinking of the scene in the Park.

" He is ill," said Miss Barrymore, coming forward. " Sit down, my dear Almeric; you look tired.

Captain Fortescue drew forward a large easy chair; the Vicar busied himself by ringing for restoratives, wine or brandy; Sir Hildebrand tried to explain, and then Sara Thorn came to Almeric, and said,

" I am the thief, Almeric; the label was found in my dress."

Almeric listened, but he could not comprehend. For, as we have said, he had no memory for the two lost coins; and his mind was still painfully full of his cruel ancestor Sir Almeric and of the dead squirrels in the Park.

"Still, I tell you I am in the dark," said he.

Meanwhile, wine had been brought, and Almeric drank eagerly, one, two, three glasses. The exhausting scenes through which he had just passed, in which he had been an unwilling witness to a hecatomb of murdered squirrels, rendered some powerful elixir necessary to restore him in some measure to his ordinary state of mind.

"There, that will do," said Miss Barrymore, when she saw him drain the third glass.

"It cannot harm him," said the Vicar, "in his present plight."

"He has suffered more than any of us from the loss of these coins," said Miss Barrymore.

"Dear boy!" said Sir Hildebrand, as he stood by the side of Almeric's chair, and once again seized his hand, and held it caressingly in his own.

The wine assisted in restoring Almeric, not only to some degree of physical strength and moral courage—both of which had been overpowered for the time being by the supposed presence of his ancestor—but also to some comprehension of his present position, for he began slowly to remember that he must come back to civilized life—forget for the time being the actions of his extraordinary ancestor, and make one in heart and mind of the present party of friends assembled there.

"What is it?—something I have not understood?" said he.

"He always had the kindest heart," said Sir

Hildebrand, "and now he cannot bear to hear this epithet applied to my winsome princess."

"You have a better opinion of me, Almeric; have you not?" said Miss Thorn.

"I confess I do not know to what you allude," said Almeric quietly.

"No, poor dear fellow! how should you?" said Miss Barrymore caressingly. "And, dear grandpapa, you will fatigue yourself; go to your cozy chair."

Sir Hildebrand hesitated, seemingly unwilling to leave Almeric, and Captain Fortescue said,

"I will push Almeric's chair close to yours;" and he suited the action to the word, and the chairs were placed side by side.

"But, you see, Almeric, we were just holding our court when you came in," said Sir Hildebrand, "or it was just over, or—we were——"

"And Almeric was so astounded at the sound of the word 'thief' in so refined a circle as the present," said Captain Fortescue, as he brought a cup of coffee to Sir Hildebrand, "that I, for one, do not wonder he could not understand."

"But suppose we tell Almeric the real circumstances?" said Miss Fortescue.

And then by degrees he understood that Miss Thorn had been convicted of carrying off the coins. That she had lost—or was supposed to have lost—the "six-angel piece" in her walk from Herald-stowe to the stone stile; but that by accidentally dropping "the first gold sovereign" there, it had been recovered and returned to Sir Hildebrand. All this was said to be "proved" by the discovery of the label in the ruche of her muslin dress.

After this the conversation gradually fell off upon other topics. Mr. Thorn said he had heard that Prellsthorpe was preparing for the reception of Lord and Lady Prellsthorpe—and Miss Fortescue had a long talk with Sir Hildebrand on the expected *fête* in the grounds of Prellsthorpe Abbey, which would take place on the following Thursday.

"We shall all meet there, I suppose," said Miss Barrymore.

"Yes," said Miss Thorn, "and I am told by Mrs. Cheetham the *fête* is to be on a grand scale."

"Mrs. Cheetham idolizes Mr. Hamilton," said Miss Fortescue; "for my part I hope he will make himself more agreeable than is usual with him—he is almost too stately to please me."

And the *fête* took place on the appointed day. The details of which have been given in one of the early chapters.

CHAPTER XXI.

"TRUTH AND HONESTY HAVE NO NEED OF LOUD PRO-
TESTATIONS."

A DAY or two after the *fête* at Prellsthorpe Abbey, Lord Danby and the Lady Irene

Stuart talked over at their ease the incidents that had occurred, and the people they had met.

"That Barrymore girl has grown very queenly and handsome since I was here some six years ago," said Lord Danby.

"I did not see much of her, but your friend Almeric is a remarkably handsome man," said the Lady Irene, "with much more of spirit and point in his remarks than I should have expected from your description of him."

"Undoubtedly 'the muff' has grown well-looking, but, oh! Ren—he has touched pitch!" said Lord Danby.

"Touched pitch! Now what do you mean, D.?"

"The youth hath sinned!"

"We all do that."

"But we do not all lament our sins, Ren. Now this excellent youth—one of the Excelsior class—instead of climbing to the top of his high mountain, has somehow or other tumbled over a precipice!—and, my dear Ren, he laments his fall. Either this or the ghosts—it may be the latter—but something has alarmed the mediæval 'muff!' He had the audacity to say a few threatening words to me, but as I know he is a fool who does not mean half he says, I called in the aid of that mild Sir Vicar Stowe, and turned his own tables on himself!"

"Who is Sir Vicar Stowe, D.?"

"That skim-milk Parson; the Vicar of Stowe-in-the-Valley—you must have seen him, Ren."

" Mr. Thorn, I suppose you mean."

" He jogs through the world with the laudable intention of making everybody comfortable."

" A very praiseworthy intention, indeed, D."

" Oh! commend me to such wise-acres! I cannot endure them."

" Did you see much of the Maynooths?"

" Now, why did your serene ladyship make such a fuss with those great staring Maynooths?"

" And now, may I ask, why do you depreciate them? You told me on your return from Prellsthorpe, the last time you were here, that Miss Maynooth was very beautiful, extremely accomplished also, and altogether an acquisition to a very dull neighbourhood. Of her brother—I forget his name——"

" Raymond," said Lord Danby.

" Yes, Raymond, a charming name—and you said of him that he was beyond all praise, or words to that effect."

" No doubt it was my pleasure to mystify you, my dear Sisse; for which sin, then, I humbly crave your pardon now. Listen, Ren—Raymond Maynooth out-Herods Herod! He lies so magnificently, you will absolutely marvel at the greatness of his imagination, and the boldness of his words!"

" He must be very diverting," said Lady Irene, laughing; "but yesterday I heard none of these grand conceptions; he was like all other country gentlemen who——"

"Oh! nonsense, Ren; he is not like any other. Sometimes I confess he *is* amusing; but sometimes one has not the patience to sit and listen," added Lord Danby with a yawn.

"Has he still this great gift, do you think?"

"Still, my dear, this large Maynooth amuses himself, and affects to amuse his hearers by the most arrant lies to which your ears ever listened."

"In what way, D.? Cannot you cheer me now by repeating these extraordinary exaggerations?"

"Impossible," replied he, again yawning; "I could not take the trouble to repeat his tomfooleries—even if I could remember them—no, not for the wealth of the Indies. It is true I put him on at the Abbey, in the very middle of the *fête*, so he attracted a great crowd around us, and he curvetted and pranced, and blew his horn in the old fashion."

While the Lady Irene was indulging in a hearty peal of laughter, the door of the saloon was thrown open, and Mr. and Miss Maynooth were announced.

"Talk of the angels, and they flap their wings," said Lord Danby, as he offered his hand to the lady.

"We had not heard of your arrival," said Mr. Maynooth, "and you may judge of our surprise on meeting you at the Abbey so unexpectedly."

"We left London suddenly. Change of air

was so very necessary for our dear mother," said Lady Irene; "and the air of Prellsthorpe at this particular season of the year is so bracing, that Dr. Campion would not listen to her wish to remain in town."

"Ah! that we who dwell in these remote districts for the greater part of the year, should have to thank the good Countess for her very opportune illness!" replied Mr. Maynooth, with some gallantry of manner.

"But we know you are a great traveller—a great wanderer from these remote places," said Lord Danby.

"I have been away a good deal, but not very recently," replied Mr. Maynooth, in quiet and courteous tones.

"Have been!—yes; but you do not stay at home all the year round? Your brother could not spend his life in so small a place as England, could he?" said Lord Danby to Miss Maynooth.

"I think Raymond prefers England as a residence," said she.

"Triste place for a sojourn of any length of time; but Mr. Maynooth has travelled all over Europe, I think."

"Europe!—oh! yes, over all the world," said she with enthusiasm.

"The world!—bless me," said Lord Danby, "I no longer wonder at the extent of his knowledge, or at the marvels he recounts." And then, turning to his sister, and interrupting her dialogue

with Mr. Maynooth, he said : " Ren, dear, Mr.
Maynooth surpasses all travellers of all centuries ;
he goes—but only occasionally, I suppose—to
another world."

Mr. Maynooth slightly raised his eyebrows, and
looked at his sister, while Lady Irene said :

" Is it possible ?—then let me hope it is to the
higher, not the lower, of the two worlds left to our
choice."

No one replied. Miss Maynooth looked
uneasily, and with an expression of surprise, at
Lord Danby, and after a few moments of silence,
Mr. Maynooth turned to him, and asked, with a
smile,

"To which of those worlds have you travelled?"

" I ?—oh ! bless my heart, do not ask such
intemperate questions. It is all I can possibly do
to continue to live in this world. I assure you I
do not follow your example—I have no fancy for
exploring any other world."

" Indeed, I have no fancy for other worlds,"
said Mr. Maynooth, in a serious tone.

Again a short silence fell on the party. It was
eventually broken by Lord Danby, who said :

" No. You do not fancy another world as you
do this—that is to say, you do not like it so well.
I can understand that. Some of the visions you
are reported to have seen in other worlds quite
bear me out in that idea."

" I have not travelled so far as you have been
led to believe," said Mr. Maynooth at length, and

in a tone that was calculated to disarm irony or misunderstanding, and he turned to Lady Irene as he said: "You spoke of the higher and the lower worlds. If by the second you mean to specify the place of eternal punishment, I do not yet feel myself sufficiently wicked to deserve its thraldom; consequently, I have never seen its dread portal, nor read inscribed there, '*Lasciat ogni speranza.*' And if by the higher world you mean to point out heaven, I confess I have hitherto found my heaven upon earth; and I may add that I do not feel myself good enough for a better 'heaven' yet. If, however, you meant to say I had travelled in more worlds than one, you could not be contradicted with truth."

He was now addressing Lord Danby.

"For assuredly, long after the days of Columbus, America was called the 'New World;' and even in our own day we often speak of Europe as the 'Old World.' "

"Then, was it you or Columbus who saw the spider you told us of the other night?" said Lord Danby.

"I only recount the marvels I have myself seen," replied Mr. Maynooth, with much suavity.

"You saw that spider with your own eyes?" asked Lord Danby, in a tone of strong disbelief.

"If you mean a large spider, of the species *Mygale avicularia*——"

"Oh! it might have been a Mygale, for anything I know to the contrary; not that you spoke of it as Mygale—at least, I cannot remember that. And in the avuncular matter, I am unlearned—I have no uncle living," said Lord Danby.

" Some are born without uncles ; they are not a state necessity, and you may be so situated," said Mr. Maynooth, complacently.

" I am," said Lord Danby. " Did you see that abominable spider ?" continued he to Miss May-nooth.

" I did not travel with my brother," said she, simply.

" That does not impugn the fact of the spider, I suppose ?" said he.

" I do not understand you."

" You mean I mystify you ; it is a peculiar talent—I have it largely given to me. But, Ren, you have not heard of this Uncle Spider, who jumps upon birds, and sucks away their lives ?"

" Never !—never !" said she—" what, a strange creature ! And you have seen this spider actually suck away the life from a lovely bird ?"

" No," replied Mr. Maynooth in a decided tone, and with a shake of his head. " Lord Danby has travelled further, and seen more than I."

" Nonsense," said Lord Danby laughing ; " now do not be so modest. I assure you I have not been to t'other world."

Mr. Maynooth very adroitly changed the topic of conversation, and addressed his remarks to the Lady Irene, and when Lord Danby again attempted to introduce the subject of "another world," the Maynooths arose and took their departure.

"You were rude, D.," said Lady Irene, as soon as their visitors had departed.

"The man would not lie in your presence; did you observe that, Ren?"

"I observed that he was a remarkably handsome man, and courteous as a perfect gentleman! His eyes are most expressive; and I admire that light hair, and that long silken beard!"

"Ah! Ren, Ren! And so you were so serenely charmed with the man, that you would not take my hints, and draw the 'lion' into talk. And talking of 'lions,' Ren, this travelled Maynooth ought to be quite as much of 'a lion' as that grand bookworm, Hamilton. I honour this man for his courage; he tells, or I have heard him tell, such superb lies with the gravest face, they ought to be framed and glazed, and handed down to posterity. But the Hamilton has a smooth sort of taciturnity, that provokes a man of my ardent disposition. I bear with him for your sake, Ren, but I do not like him."

"I like Mr. Maynooth better than Mr. Hamilton, D.; there is something very sterling in his manner—he impressed me with a faith in his sincerity."

"All liars do that, Ren, or where would be the use of lies? They would go out of fashion. But now, Ren, listen to me. You must not admire

this man. These Maynooths are Roman Catholics.
They have been so from Paul downwards—I mean
from the times of Peter and Paul. They keep a
heterogeneous staff of priests about their dwelling-
houses. They are considered by the *elite* of the
county of Z—— as great hobgoblins; they have
chapels attached to their residences, and—oh!
Ren, what shall I do?" added he slowly, as he
yawned and finally stretched himself at full length
on the sofa. "This place bores me to death, and
the people are such intolerable idiots."

"You have just driven away the Maynooths.
They are not idiots, and I am sorry they are gone,"
said she. "I am much pleased with him—so tall, so
handsome, so dignified and well-bred. And Miss
Maynooth is certainly *not* so lovely as you led me
to expect!"

"Your imagination led you to endow her with
a beauty she did not possess. The young creature
is well enough, but"—yawning—"stupid, Ren—
stupid!"

"You made her so by your own rudeness."

"There, Ren, that will do," again yawning.
"I wish somebody else would come—somebody
with——" the next yawn was nipped in the bud.
The saloon door was thrown open, and Dr. Quinn
announced. After the customary greetings, he said,

" I have the pleasure of assuring you her ladyship is decidedly better. She seems to dread the
fatigue of a drive——"

"She is like me—very tired," said Lord Danby.

"But, indeed, she will be all the better for fresh air," said Dr. Quinn, without noticing Lord Danby's interruption.

"She was so shaken by the great stones, when we passed through the village of Prellsthorpe, she has not had courage to leave the house," said Lady Irene.

"Then do not drive that way; avoid the village by all means. Good morning. I am off to Heraldstowe," said he, rising; "Mr. Barrymore is ill."

"No!" said Lord Danby in a tone of surprise. "We met him and Miss Barrymore at the Abbey *fête*." Dr. Quinn shook his head.

"That is no proof that he is in good health," said he with a smile.

"You rather mean, no proof that he does not require your professional skill?" said Lord Danby, also with a smile.

"I certainly mean I must say good morning, and explain about Mr. Barrymore at some future time."

As Mr. and Miss Maynooth drove from Prellsthorpe to Heraldstowe—where they intended to call—they indulged largely in remarks upon the Lady Irene and Lord Danby.

"He certainly intended to be rude, Raymond."

"That is his concern."

"I feel indignant. I did not like him when we met him at the Abbey; he was less agreeable than when he was last in this neighbourhood, and that is very condemnatory, for I did not like him even then."

"Dear Yolande, why fuss yourself for this man's extravagant behaviour? It does not move me."

"Nothing moves you, Raymond!" replied she in a tone of pique, "you take everything quietly. But *I* am vexed that you, Raymond, who are so superior, should be so rudely treated."

Mr. Maynooth smiled. And then, bending his large blue eyes with a kindly look upon his sister, he said,

"But suppose we change the subject—of the two I largely prefer the lady to the lord. Now, what think you, Yolande, of the Lady Irene?"

"She is very charming, Raymond. Her manner is so queenly, and yet—I had almost said loveable."

"It is more queenly than hearty, more condescending than loveable," said he.

"You are so hard to please; I *do* hope you admire her?"

"I hard to please!" said he in a tone of extreme surprise. "There is no greater admirer of the sex than I——"

And he broke into a merry laugh.

"Ah! Raymond!" said his sister with a sigh.

"Come, Yolande, dearest; now do not be foolish, you know I am a great worshipper of ladies," said he still laughing.

"Of what use is that?"

" Use!—why, the greatest possible use ; *I* am pleased with their pretty faces, God bless them all —*all*," he added with an additional laugh, " and *they* are pleased with me!"

" But that is the worst of it, Raymond !"

" Worst of what !" said he again in a tone of surprise.

" Why that ladies always admire you so."

" I am very much obliged to them, my dear ; but what then makes that the ' worst ' of the matter."

" You know you never care—really care—for any one of them—even the prettiest, or the handsomest, or the cleverest, or the——"

" Wisest !" said Mr. Maynooth. " Yolande, love, you are mistaken ; I care for them all."

" Oh! nonsense, Raymond ! that will not do. And then you really must marry some time !"

" I see no ' must' on that subject."

" Then what is to become of our fine property, and our fine old name ?"

" You shall marry, Yolande, and keep the name, and have the estates, and I will roam the world again !"

Miss Maynooth did not reply. And after a few moments of silence, Mr. Maynooth continued in a gentle tone,

" Forgive me, my dear ; I did not mean to touch that sensitive chord. And yet I must say, that for your own sake I wish you would let the past take care of itself—" and after another slight

pause, he said in a cheerful tone—" but now, darling, I will tell you something that will please you
—since you are so thoughtful for my future. I
admire the Lady Irene Stuart more than any lady
I have ever seen in my whole life!"

" Ah!" said she in a glad tone, " now that
is something to tell me; it makes me feel quite
happy, dear Raymond!"

" She is remarkably handsome—and——"

" And what else, Raymond?—do go on."

"It is not necessary to dissect her, by way of
proving how much I really admire her. But what
I mean most to impress upon you, is that she is
the only woman I ever wish to see again!"

" Raymond!"

" I do not explain myself well."

" I think not, indeed."

" I cannot tell how it is, Yolande, but women.
as a rule, have never touched the sensibilities of
my nature to make me care for them."

" You dreadful sinner ! I know all that, and
I believe you to be incorrigible; pray do not
waste your time in the confession of such sins to
me."

" I do not dislike women ; quite the reverse, I
like to have them about me, to see them at table, in
the ball-room, at the banquet, at all times. But then
I cannot care, or wish, or long—as some men do—
to see such or such a face again. I have often
tried, Yolande, to select from a bevy of lovely—
mind, whom I allow to be most exquisitely

lovely girls—to choose one with whom I could spend my life. It would not do. I never could stand it!"

"I know you are such a dreadful reprobate! And then, Raymond, the women do adore you so! oh dear, oh dear!"

"Very kind of them. I beg to present to them my very best compliments and thanks."

"Oh! Raymond!"

"But, Yolande—now listen, I wish to see the Lady Irene again."

"You think you could spend your life with her?"

"Ah! I have not asked myself that question yet—in fact, Lord Danby quite destroyed my pleasure this morning. I admire the Lady Irene so much, I should like to take every opportunity of knowing her better, but if, when I go to see her, I am to be——"

"Rudely treated by him? What did he mean about the spider?"

"When we were at Prellsthorpe Abbey, I saw some curious and rare spiders amongst the foliage in the grounds. This led to a discussion on the subject of spiders, and I happened to speak of the *Mygale avicularia,* and the death of the two finches."*

"Lord Danby evidently mistrusted the truth of the incident, Raymond—and certainly perverted the words you used."

*See Note 9.

"That is his concern; it does not affect the fact. But here we are at Heraldstowe; and tell me, Yolande, shall we drive to Aunt Nuala's after we have seen Sir Hildebrand? I shall not have time for Wolfscraig to-morrow."

"It will be of no use to drive to Wolfscraig to-day."

"I tell you, Yolande, I shall be very much engaged to-morrow."

"Very well, Raymond, I cannot help that. But we have promised Aunt Nuala to take her to Prellsthorpe Abbey when we call there upon Mrs. Hamilton—and it must be clear even to you, we cannot call at the Abbey to-day. But any day this week will do; and Aunt Nuala and I will await your convenience."

CHAPTER XXII.

"A YOUNG TWIG IS EASIER TWISTED THAN AN OLD TREE."

THE families of Barrymore and Maynooth lived within a few miles of each other, and on the most friendly terms. Sir Hildebrand, as we have seen, is a type of a school fast passing away—Mr. Maynooth a representative of the present day. His intellect is of a more practical nature, and his manners are less exclusive than Sir Hildebrand's, but his tastes are very much the same, and especially as regards valuable collections of various kinds, for the long galleries at Mytreberris are filled with magnificent specimens of natural history, and he is thought on the subject of "coins" to be even more enthusiastic than either Captain Fortescue or Sir Hildebrand himself, and the worthy Vicar of Stowe-in-the-Valley has been known to say of him that—

"Maynooth choked himself with learning that was of no use, and his cabinets with specimens of less use still. For the latter were either so minute nobody could see them without straining their eyes, or such worthless bits of battered metal, that even a travelling tinker would not think them worthy of melting down in his kettle."

But then it was well known that the Vicar had a sort of spite against valuables of this kind; and Mr. Maynooth delighted himself by always exhibiting, when the Vicar was present, those coins that had the most worn and lugubrious appearance, and in expatiating upon them in very learned language, and at a very great length.

So that on the announcement at Heraldstowe of "Mr. and Miss Maynooth," Sir Hildebrand's thoughts at once went back to the irreparable loss he had had in "the six-angel piece." And, as a matter of course, as soon as the compliments of greeting were over, and that his friends were comfortably seated, Sir Hildebrand said,

"You have heard, no doubt, of my loss?"

"Indeed, I am here to ask what has happened?

Rumour is at all times so vague and unsatisfac-
tory. But I hope it is nothing very serious?" said
Mr. Maynooth.

"Alas! yes," said Sir Hildebrand, with a lugubrious shake of the head.

"Veitch came to us direct from Heraldstowe,"
said Mr. Maynooth, "and from him we learned
there had been a great fuss, but he could not give
us any particulars."

"And then came Whitworth to tune the piano,"
said Miss Maynooth, "and he said he had had his
news from a very authentic source, and——"

"You see we were expressing our wonder aloud
to each other in Whitworth's presence," chimed in
Mr. Maynooth; "we were marvelling what you
had lost, and how, when the man's countenance
became suddenly expressive of knowing more on
the subject than we ourselves, and then Yolande's
native curiosity led her to question him."

"Whitworth, the music-master from Stowe-in-
the-Valley!" said Sir Hildebrand sternly; "and,
pray, what could he know about me and my doings?"

"In point of fact, it turned out he knew nothing," said Yolande.

"Oh! said Sir Hildebrand, "then he is simply
on a par with all the people who come from Stowe.
He was pricking up his ears to learn all he could
from you, and so astonish the county as he went
his rounds by the accuracy of the news he had to
promulgate! Those Stowe-in-the-Valley people

are the most gossiping and mischief-making in the whole world!"

"He knew something," said Mr. Maynooth laughing, "for he knew there had been a scene of an unusual kind at Heraldstowe. He seemed also to know that something had been stolen, but——"

"Stolen!" said Sir Hildebrand in a tone of displeasure. "What could he mean?"

"His impression was that you had been robbed —but he did not say your loss was in coins."

"I have not been robbed," said Sir Hildebrand in a positive manner.

"Have you not?" said Miss Maynooth. "Our information comes from the wandering minstrels of the county, for Veitch of Landeswold came from you to us. Your servants told him you had let fall a drawer full of coins, and some could not be found."

"If we could have *dumb* servants, as I understand some people have dumb-waiters, we might sometimes find ourselves more comfortably off," said Sir Hildebrand.

"You see, Yolande and I used the word 'coin' in Whitworth's presence, because Veitch had told us that 'coins' were lost. And, as you say, 'he pricked up his ears,' tuned his fifths so falsely as to take away one's breath, and hugely admonish any sensitive person to leave him and his discords to resolve themselves into harmony at their own leisure; but after I left the room, Yolande, having the inborn curiosity of a woman, questioned the man."

"And what did he know, Yolande?" said Miss Barrymore. Miss Maynooth did not reply immediately, and then Sir Hildebrand said,

"But how could such a man as 'Whitworth the tuner' know what had happened in my house?"

"It appears he had to give a lesson to Miss Rosa Thorn, and she was in some trouble, and in some way unhappy about the loss of the coins. Her sister, Miss Thorn, was present when the trays were upset," said Yolande.

"Poor little Rosa Thorn!" said Sir Hildebrand musingly. "And pray how did she get into trouble about my coins? I have not seen the child for some weeks."

"Even Whitworth could not tell us that," said Yolande. "He seemed to know just enough to make him wish to know more, but not by any means enough to carry as 'a good budget' round the county—unless, indeed, he painted highly from his own imagination."

"But how shamefully some seem to meddle with other people's concerns!" said Sir Hildebrand. "Why need the county of Z—— lose their precious time in gossip because I have lost a coin or two? These things annoy me, and I would rather lose all my entire collection of coins than have 'gardeners' and 'tuners' prying into my household concerns! And then—poor little

Rosa Thorn of all people in the world—what had she done to be drawn into the trouble?"

"That reminds me," said Mr. Maynooth, "that we do not know, and that we wish to know, the pros and cons and ins and outs of all this recent fuss."

And then the Maynooths were told all that the reader already knows; and much discussion ensued afterwards between them and the Barrymores.

"You have had the path searched, of course?" said Mr. Maynooth.

"Almeric and Zara occupied much time in examining the path, and peering into the long grass before the boy's illness," said Sir Hildebrand. "Almeric is not well—he is in Dr. Quinn's hands, and our anxiety on his account has, for the time being, put aside our regret for the 'six-angel piece.'"

"Yes, so it would, naturally. But I hope Almeric is not seriously ill?" said Mr. Maynooth.

"Oh! no, Raymond, nothing serious," said Miss Barrymore; "but still, we are just a little anxious."

"Yes, of course you will be apprehensive, Zara; but we must not let this valuable coin slip from our thoughts. How strange that so unique a coin should be the very one to be carried off in that chance way!"

"You are so enthusiastic on this subject, Raymond!"

"But you will recover it, Zara," replied he,

you will—that is, I mean if you are tolerably careful in your search."

"Indeed, Raymond, it is very desirable that I should recover that matchless coin," said Sir Hildebrand. "And though dear Almeric is as wishful as myself, and, if possible, even more so, yet he very greatly objects—and so do I—to cutting up the park, and having workmen about the place. And then again, Raymond, the chances of recovering the coin are very small, as in my conversation with Almeric he proved to me."

And here it must be remarked that Almeric *knew*—though Sir Hildebrand did not—that the comfort and enjoyment of the Park would be destroyed, and *no* adequate result arise, because Baron Almeric had the coin.

"Ah! you and I think so 'differently on such matters," said Mr. Maynooth. "I agree with you in that, the quiet beauty of the Park will be destroyed for the time being. For if you only employ one or two men, to begin from the house, and quietly work their way to the stile, it will occupy a long time, and the nuisance will be ever present; but if you employ large numbers, one day or two at the most, will settle the matter—and, of course, a reward must be offered, over and above his labour, to the man who is fortunate in finding the coin. I should have diggers and delvers at work immediately."

"It would so spoil the Park, Raymond!" said Miss Barrymore.

"Yes, it will spoil the appearance of the Park for the time being, according to your notions, but we must give and take in this world. The Park will eventually be improved, though its aristocratic and classical beauty may be put aside for the time."

Mr. Maynooth knew such sentiments were painful to Sir Hildebrand, but he himself was of too practical a nature to decline a future good for the sake of a present discomfort, or to weigh, as Sir Hildebrand and Miss Barrymore did, the existing appearance of the Park against the result to be expected. He knew, also, the difference between himself and Sir Hildebrand. The latter had lived a long life in one position, and in one locality, with only an occasional visit to the Continent. He had grown old with his trees, made his Park and its belongings part of himself, and felt that the rest of the world should not show much less honour to his lands than to himself! Sir Hildebrand had been educated in these ideas, and he had not "moved on" with the times.

But Mr. Maynooth was of a younger generation; he had not been brought up to expect "worship" from those born in a lower grade of society; and yet he was as fond and as proud of his estates as Sir Hildebrand. Neither had he lived almost entirely in one residence; he had travelled much, and travelled with his eyes open: not as Sir Hildebrand had in the early part of this century, "the grand Milord Anglais" of that

period, in his own carriages, with his own attendants, but on foot, with his knapsack, when it
pleased him, alone, unattended, and to all parts of
the earth. Mr. Maynooth, therefore, never felt
fettered by distinctions of rank—he had made himself familiar with many phases of life, and felt
himself at home in all. And yet we must do him
the justice to add, that though always affable to his
inferiors, and always willing to help, where help
was needed, he had no intimate companions beneath
his own rank in life. He seemed, so to speak, to
be quite as well aware of his own position in the
world as Sir Hildebrand himself ; but this rank
or place was not a means of separating him from
his kind, nor a cause that he should entrench himself and his belongings behind barriers of etiquette
and of present comfort at the expense of future good.

Meanwhile Sir Hildebrand leaned his head upon
his hand and closed his eyes, as if he would willingly shut out unpleasant ideas. He felt that he
valued "the six-angel piece," but he also valued
his Park. He agreed in opinion with Almeric ; he
did not wish to see the Park invaded by myriads
of workmen, whether for a period short or long.
He did not like to have his privacy intruded upon,
or even the present appearance of the Park changed. He himself set great value upon that great
heirloom that had descended to him intact from
generation to generation ; it sounded little less than
sacrilege in the ears of Sir Hildebrand to hear his
Park spoken of thus slightingly.

"The ladies can easily point out exactly the road they took," said Mr. Maynooth ; and it seemed to the Barrymores as if he were almost determined not to let the subject drop—"or rather they can say if they deviated at all from the direct road, and where—and the rest will be all plain sailing. Hire a huge number of workmen—the more the merrier, and the sooner the fuss will be over —turn up the soil, sift it."

"You think, Raymond, that 'a huge number of workmen ' can be employed in the Park and not do it permanent injury," said Miss Barrymore; "remember the birds, they are now so tame and——"

"Zara, again I say we must give and take in this world ; and as for *permanent* injury, no injury whatever will be done. How can the soil upon which we tread be injured?" said he with a smile. "On the contrary it will be improved by being broken up, and by letting in fresh air. If you mean the road will be closed for the time ; it is your own road ; you can do as you please with it. For my part, I think a host of workmen in their rough jackets, or no jackets at all, with their cradles, their tools, their wheelbarrows, and their sieves— their wives and daughters bringing them their dinners, and their children at play under the trees—the merry gambols of children are so amusing—would make a pretty picture—a very pretty picture."

Miss Maynooth strongly suspected her brother

of great exaggeration in all this. She thought if it had been a case for his own Park, he would not have "hired a huge number of workmen," but that he would, perhaps, have employed so many as he could himself superintend, or in some degree watch over.

Miss Barrymore, also, was silent from a feeling of great annoyance. It must be confessed that it was more for the sake of the future career of the future Baronet Almeric, that Mr. Maynooth stood his ground so manfully, than for the sake of the recovery of the coin. Both Almeric and Zara were, in his opinion, too much trammelled by the etiquette of a past age, too much surrounded by that state in which Sir Hildebrand had been brought up. His real desire was to break through these hedges of exclusiveness, and fit the minds of the young people for the work of the present day. Hence it may perhaps be admitted he pressed the subject of sending workmen into the Park in a strong manner.

But to return to Sir Hildebrand. Did he hear aright! Was the classical beauty of the Park, its magnificent trees, in groups, or otherwise, its shady groves, its undulating ground, its charming vistas here and there, its sunny slopes, its lengthy avenues and lofty shade, its placid waters, its herds of deer, either capriciously frisking along in a fast race, as it seemed, or steadily feeding in peaceful content; and the distant view of "St. Mary-on-the-Knoll" standing on its outskirts—were all these to be made "pretty" by groups of ill-mannered and vulgar men and women in the foreground! Eating their dinners while their tatterdemalion and ragamuffin children were at play. At play!—and such play! Climbing the trees, breaking the branches, stealing the bird's nests, terrifying the deer, probably running after them, certainly killing and carrying off the fawns!

There was sacrilege in the very thought!—and Sir Hildebrand remained silent. The lost "six-angel piece" was dear to him, the privacy and stillness of the Park dearer.

Perhaps Sir Hildebrand had never before felt the difference between himself and Mr. Maynooth so strongly. The latter saw this, and partly apologized for having given his opinion so freely—adding in very suave tones,

"You see, my dear Sir Hildebrand, the longer we remain in one place, the better we like it, and the less we wish to see any change around us. I allow you have naturally a great love for this place as it is; and so have I, and so must all who look upon it. I can understand that *you* do not wish for any change, and, therefore, I must ask you to pardon my enthusiasm, because *I* have travelled so far, and seen so much, that I, unlike you, enjoy change. This opinion, however, need not influence you; only somehow, as the piece is unique, it will be a great loss, and prevent any perfect collection of English coins for the future."

"The coin may have fallen on the turf, Raymond," said Miss Barrymore.

"That would not prove any obstacle; it could be found on the turf as well as in the path."

It was evident Mr. Maynooth would not yield a hair's breadth; his conviction was that the coin could be found, and he persisted in saying so.

"Raymond, you are right," said Sir Hildebrand, with a deep sigh, as he now raised his head from his long reverie. "I cannot, for the sake of the stillness and beauty of my own Park—I cannot allow this unique coin to remain buried on my lands."

"I rejoice to hear you say so. And if you will allow me, my dear Sir Hildebrand, to be of use, I think we can manage with very little fuss—very little fuss indeed."

"Fewer workmen, Raymond?" suggested Miss Maynooth.

"We will think the matter over," said Sir Hildebrand, and the party separated.

CHAPTER XXIII.

"BEAR AND FORBEAR IS GOOD PHILOSOPHY."

MR. and Mrs. Cheetham were seated at breakfast at the Rectory, when Lord Danby was announced.

"Mrs. Cheetham, you are mine for the day—is

she not, my lord?" said he to Mr. Cheetham, whom he sometimes mockingly addressed as if he were a bishop.

"No, my lord," said Mr. Cheetham, with a good-natured smile—"I cannot spare her; she must stay at home. She seems to me to spend her life in chaperoning young ladies hither and thither, to.the no small discomfort of her stay-at-home husband."

"I have always said it *is* a great shame to take wives from their husbands, merely to shut their eyes while we converse with our enchantresses—eh, Miss Brenda? Ah! I know you, you little Queen of the Rectory—do I not, my lord? However, what are we to do?—just remark the state of this neighbourhood. There is Irene, a poor, motherless thing, or to be so considered, for you all know my lady Countess cannot dissipate; Grel in a like plight—at least, no mother; the Barrymore girl in the same predicament—I suppose the Catholic Maynooth is considered to be sufficiently protected by her hirsute brother; and, I may add, the Thorn and the Pine have their worthy fathers, for the most part, looking on."

By the "Thorn," Lord Danby meant Miss Thorn, and by the "Pine," he meant Miss Fortescue, because Captain Fortescue's residence was called the "Pines."

"Only Miss Brenda—charming Miss Brenda," said Lord Danby, bowing to her, "has a mother to keep her out of harm's way. *You* are

extremely well off, Miss Brenda; if you do
wrong, your lady mother will bear the blame; and
so you may run away with me, if you like, or with
anyone else who pleases you better, and *you* will
bear no blame—it will fall on your mother. Now
if Irene, or Grel, or the Thorn, or the Pine, or the
queenly Barrymore go wrong, each must bear the
blame for herself. See how truthful I am!—
listen to my words—think of what I have said—
lay this flattering unction to your soul, Miss
Brenda—attractive Miss Brenda! And so, then,
none of these charming young women can see the
grand Poultry Show at Landeswold, because *they*
are motherless, and your lordship hard-hearted?
Why, a score or so of us meant to ride, and
Hamilton has promised to horse the break for the
ladies. Fancy that sage Hamilton driving such a
lot of beauties in his own break!—Grel, and
Irene, and Brenda, and then the Thorn; but I
object to thorns, even on the stem of the rose. I
think it one of Nature's mistakes to have given
thorns to the lovely rose. But to return: the
Pine and the Thorn are with Irene by this time.
Their wise fathers have consented to put them
under her queenly care till to-morrow, because she
is supposed to be under your care for to-day,
Mistress Cheetham the amiable."

"But, I tell you, Mrs. Cheetham cannot go,
and Grel is ill in bed," said Mr. Cheetham.

"Never mind these opinions of yours, my lord
—or, rather, I mean in spite of them—the break

will be at the Rectory at twelve of the clock ; and as we expect to see his lordship, the Bishop of Prellsthorpe, join the riding party, we feel pretty sure that——"

Mr. Cheetham laughed, and shook his head, but Brenda jumped up, and put her arms round him coaxingly, as she whispered,

"Dear papa, how can you refuse?"

"But, my love, you forget Lady Grel is ill in bed ; she cannot go."

"If you will promise not to teaze her, I feel sure the drive would do her good," said Brenda to Lord Danby ; "and I will use my influence with her, for, of course, if Grel remains at home, neither mamma nor I can go."

"If you, Brenda, will promise to ride on the box with Hamilton," replied Lord Danby, with a mischievous smile, "I will agree not to speak to Grel for the whole day."

"I!—I sit by Mr. Hamilton's side? Thanks— a very pleasant day I should have!" said Brenda, with the habitual sneer, so often seen on her handsome face.

"Just as you please, Brenda, only the break will be here by twelve o'clock," and Lord Danby went away.

A silence of some minutes fell upon the trio at breakfast after Lord Danby's departure. Mr. Cheetham looked serious, Brenda pouting, and Mrs. Cheetham anxious.

"I do not like this Danby coming and going in

my house as he does. I have said this before, but
as I am not supported, he still seems to do pretty
much as he pleases. I acknowledge, conisdering
Grel's residence here, and the intimacy there always has been between Prellsthorpe Park and the
Rectory, it is sometimes difficult to know where to
draw the line. But again, I think, when I put
forth a plain refusal to a jaunt of this kind, you,
Brenda, should support me, instead of using your
influence in a contrary direction."

Brenda's pouting did not lessen by this reproach,
and Mr. Cheetham continued,

"I know you will shelter yourself—as you have
done before—under my laughter at lord Danby's
idle words. But it is wiser to laugh at follies you
cannot correct than rebuke them in the presence
of others. There is no reliance to be placed on
his words at any time. He eternally wears this
mask of folly. He may be better than he really seems
—he does not want intellect; but I would see as
little of him, and hear also as little from him, as
possible."

Mr. Cheetham ceased speaking, but no one replied. He then resumed:

"I should wonder at so quiet a person as Hamilton horsing his break to take ladies twenty
miles to a poultry show, only that I suppose the
Lady Irene is the getter up of the party, and the
tempter and reward to him! But I must say I
am sorry we are so eternally interrupted; quiet
seems to be gone from our home since the party

arrived at Prellsthorpe Park. Neither, my love, do I like, as I have before said, always to lose you," continued he to Mrs. Cheetham. "I know your tastes too well to suppose you would willingly jaunt off here, or get up a *fête* there, except as a matter of duty. I know you go for Brenda's sake; but believe me, though I thank you, I am sorry for the necessity."

" I quite agree with you as to the idle life Lord Danby's intimacy brings upon us, and I have no more pleasure in such a life than you," replied Mrs. Cheetham; "and yet, indeed, I never know how to evade a party of this sort. Lord Danby is right, this immediate neighbourhood is strangely short of matrons. Often and often have I felt that to refuse is to break up a party. This I am at all times sorry to do; and again, I cannot help having some pleasure and interest in young people."

" You are right, my love, though I confess to a certain degree of annoyance at this constant up-setting of one's plans. However, I suppose you must go to-day. Brenda is gone to carry the news to Grel, and they will both be eager to enjoy the drive, and see the show.

" And you will ride?—you really require a good gallop."

" Not to-day. There is a good deal in Prells-thorpe awaiting my time and attention, and this is one of the days I can best spare from—even higher duties—therefore, my love, I can only hope

that you will return for dinner, for not the least
of our troubles, as it seems to me, is, that when we
once set off with Danby, we never know when we
shall return."

"True, but Mr. Hamilton is coachman to-day;
I fancy, therefore, we are in better hands."

Mrs. Cheetham was, as we have before said, the
second wife of the good Rector, and Brenda, his
only daughter—his only child, indeed, and by his
former wife. Brenda had gained great power
over her father's affectionate heart before his second marriage, and retained it even after that
event. Mrs. Cheetham had early seen the wilfulness inherent in Brenda, but, finding no good result from her own interference, had very wisely
ceased to interfere.

A stepmother is always in a false position between the daughters of the first wife and her own
husband. Brenda had the will, and she certainly
exercised her power, to make her stepmother uncomfortable. Mrs. Cheetham gave up this un-
seemly struggle, contented herself with the Rector's esteem and regard, and avoided as much as
possible at all times putting herself in opposition to
his loved daughter Brenda.

And, we need hardly add, fostered by her
father, not interfered with by her mother, Brenda
Cheetham's wilfulness increased, and eventually
became a prolific source of discomfort to all
three.

Just as Mr. Cheetham had foreseen, Brenda

had sought the Lady Grel, and entreated her to rise and try to join the party.

At first Grel gave a positive refusal, and added,

" Brenda, I am so unhappy in the presence of D., that I am turning through my brain all available friends, or relatives, or places, with a view to leaving this neighbourhood, and so escaping from the sort of thraldom in which I feel myself held."

" Would you make me believe you do not value his attentions, Grel? You know he got up the *fête* at Martindale on purpose for you; he drove you to the dale-head and pointed out to you all the more remarkable beauties, and——"

" There Brenda, that will do. I went to Martindale entirely to please you, and now you want me to go to Landeswold! What is 'a grand poultry show' to me, who so much want rest and peace. Brenda, you do not know, and," she added with a sigh, "I cannot tell you." Lady Grel meant, she could not explain to Brenda, that Lord Danby paid her great homage in the presence of others, and tyrannised over her when they were alone.

" You are very *unselfish*, Grel—very," said Brenda with her habitual sneer. " You know very well, if you remain at home, neither mamma nor I can go. Indeed *I* cannot," continued she in reply to Grel's look of astonishment. " Mamma cannot go if you are ill in bed, I cannot go without mamma, and, for that matter, nor can any of us. Mamma only goes to take care of us—what

Lady Irene calls 'play propriety;' what Lord Danby calls 'look stupid!' And so this charming party must be put aside, Mr. Hamilton may drive an empty break to Landeswold, the county of Z——may stare at the poultry-show, minus the Prellsthorpe party—and all because the Lady Grel Stuart has a headache!"

Grel felt very indignant; but she did not reply. She knew Brenda had put the case thus strongly on purpose to act upon her want of selfishness, and cause her to consent to go.

"Now there is mamma," recommenced Brenda. "She wishes to see you, Grel. She does not wish to go to Landeswold, but *I* think, and do not you also, that it is rather selfish to keep Lady Irene and all the rest of us at home because *she* does not wish to go?"

The door opened and Mrs. Cheetham entered, unseen by Grel.

"To say nothing of the untimely headache of the Lady Grel Stuart," said Grel, with more vexation in her tone than was often heard.

"It will do her good, mamma," said Brenda, trying to distract Mrs. Cheetham's attention; "you know it will, mamma, it is only a nervous fit, she says, brought on by Lord Danby's wild ways. But she will be safe with Mr. Hamilton, will she not?"

Grel hid her face on the pillow and smiled.

"I should like to go with Mr. Hamilton," thought she.

She had forgotten he was her cousin Irene's devoted admirer.

"Mr. Hamilton is quiet enough, and silent enough, and stupid enough," resumed Brenda, though she had not seen Grel's satisfaction at the sound of Mr. Hamilton's name.

"And so Grel, love, you have a sad headache," said Mrs. Cheetham.

"But I do not wish to be a cause of breaking up the party," said she.

"You give up all idea of making one? You will not go with us?"

Grel smiled, and evidently was shaken in her resolution.

A name had done a great deal—almost removed her headache. Grel longed to know more of Mr. Hamilton; to watch him, unknown to himself, to listen to him, and judge for herself if he were really worthy the high opinion the Cheethams had of him.

"Do not so trouble yourself about Lord Danby; there will be more to attract his notice to-day, certainly Miss Thorn and Miss Fortescue. And then we shall meet all the world at Landeswold."

"As Brenda says, the county of Z—— would not be complete on these public occasions without the 'Prellsthorpe party,' I suppose I must go," said the Lady Grel.

"Believe me, my love, I think it very necessary to sacrifice largely at the shrine of duty. I would stay at home willingly, most willingly; but then if by my presence I create the happiness of others, I am contented to go."

"Yes—I will soon be ready," said Grel, as she rang for her maid.

CHAPTER XXIV.

" FRIENDSHIP THAT FLAMES, GOES OUT IN A FLASH."

WHEN the break arrived the Lady Irene, Miss Thorn and Miss Fortescue were there, the former on the box by Mr. Hamilton's side. Lord Danby, Captain Fortescue, and others were on horseback, and grooms were in attendance on the party.

When Mrs. Cheetham, Lady Grel, and Brenda made their appearance, Mr. Hamilton said,

"Where is the Rector? Of course 1 depend upon him."

"No," said Mrs. Cheetham, " he cannot spare the time."

"Entreat him to give me this day—this one day."

Mr. Hamilton called to his attendants—

"Here, hold the horses, I must try my skill," and he alighted from the break. " Why, my dear madam, we shall not reach home until three or four o'clock in the morning. A moonlight drive! I have pledged my word!"

"Indeed he has, Mrs. Cheetham," said Lady Irene.

"Ho, ho! Grel, ho! why need you look so intensely handsome? Have I not told you I acknowledge your power? Quite right, love, always drop your veil when the men stare," added Lord Danby in a whisper, as he handed her into the carriage.

"Grel, love, do not mind D.," said Lady Irene, "he will leave off plaguing you when he sees you do not care."

"She is handsomer to-day with her pale cheeks, than beforetime with her roses, Ren," said Lord Danby.

"Oh! yes, certainly," said Lady Irene, "and so is Mrs. Cheetham also. What makes you two look so pale?"

"Brenda has stolen the roses from both," said Lord Danby.

"But you look so very serious, my dear Mrs. Cheetham," said Lady Irene, laughing. "Are you meditating flight? What shall we do for a *chaperon*? Shall I take off my hat and tie a large shawl round my head, and pretend to be a very old lady keeping the young ladies in order?"

"We had no intention of remaining away beyond the morning. I have ordered dinner at eight, an hour later than usual, to give time for our return. Mr. Cheetham will be uncomfortable; I was thinking—and that accounts for my serious face—I was thinking I wished I had not altered the hour—for fear——"

Mr. Hamilton returned at this moment, and said to the Lady Irene,

" What will you say if I ask you to resign the box and join the ladies ?"

" I shall say I have lost the favour of our coachman, and so 1 will not wear his colours," said she, throwing into the body of the break a bouquet she had in her hand.

" Ah ! but hear me—and pray accept my apologies. Our friend Cheetham has consented to go with us. I explained our plans for the day, and the utter impossibility of getting away early. But he does not wish to ride. Now, 1 thought perhaps you would allow me to offer the box to him, just as a fit bribe for the occasion ; of course I entirely deprive myself of the——"

" Pleasure of my smiles—certainly. And so pray help me to alight," said Lady Irene.

" Pallid Cousin Grel, allow me to present to you the 'cast offs' of your Cousin Irene," said Lord Danby, offering the bouquet that had been discarded by the Lady Irene.

" It is a pity to waste or destroy such lovely flowers," said Grel ; " thanks, D."

" Well, upon my word, you do amaze me !—you are a humble cousin, indeed ! And so you will even take up with Ren's leavings !"

Mr. Hamilton had again mounted the box, and as he stood there, with the reins in his hand, he

turned to speak to the ladies. After Lord Danby
ceased speaking, he said, with a smile:

"You are kind to notice the fallen Lady Grel,
but *you* are fond of flowers, I see. With your
permission I will send some to the Rectory
to-morrow."

"There, Grel—first hand—yes, you may well
smile, and plume yourself," said Lord Danby.
"But do not let your little head be turned by
admiration and dainty words from others; you are
mine—promised to me. And I do not mean to
worry and terrify you to-day—I mean to——"

"I mean to lay my whip over your shoulders, if
you do not move from your position," said Mr.
Hamilton, affecting to suit the action to the word,
for Lord Danby was leaning on the side of the
break, and thus preventing the start.

The ladies were all comfortably placed, and Mr.
Cheetham by Mr. Hamilton's side on the box.

"That Thorn is a monstrously lovely girl!"
said Lord Danby to himself.

And then, turning to speak to Captain Fortescue as he mounted his horse, and as the cavalcade
began to move on, he added, with a laugh:

"I have half a mind to teaze that Thorn for
my own especial pleasure to-day. There is something irresistibly ludicrous in a woman's despair,
when she finds herself in a fix. You should have
seen Grel the other day, when I drove her away
from the Abbey!"

"But it is hard upon the lady to what you call

'put her in a fix,'" said Captain Fortescue, "and then leave her to struggle in her chains."

"Women, by their struggles, increase their beauty for the time being," replied Lord Danby.

"Have we twenty miles to ride?" asked Captain Fortescue, with a laudable desire to change the subject of conversation.

"Circa twenty," said Lord Danby.

The day was fine, the drive enjoyable. Mr. Hamilton drove at a steady pace, up hill and down, the same even trotting on, let the valley be ever so level, or the hills even ever so steep. On arriving in Landeswold, the party prepared to go immediately to the show. There they met other "county people," but only two families of whom it will be necessary to speak—the Barrymores and the Maynooths. Mr. Maynooth was a great admirer of the beautiful birds, spending much more time over them, and expatiating much more learnedly upon them, than some of the ladies of the party thought necessary.

Almeric Barrymore looked very pale, and he was unusually silent. He had, too, an air of discontent, and an appearance of languor that was not customary. Miss Barrymore looked anxious, and did not enjoy the show or the company; her thoughts were full of her brother, and the recent change in his health. Dinner had been ordered at the Landeswold Hotel, and they all congregated there at a given hour. Lord

Danby had taken Miss Thorn to dinner, and placed himself by her side.

"What is the matter with your neighbour, the mediæval Baron?"

"Do you mean Mr. Barrymore?" said Miss Thorn.

"I mean the white youth with the mournful visage," said Lord Danby.

"He has never recovered from the vexatious loss of the ' six angels,' " replied she.

" Six angels!—Miss Rose, what can you mean?"

"I am not christened Rose," said she.

"You are misnamed Thorn," said Lord Danby, with a smile.

"That is not my fault, and I really cannot call it a misfortune," replied she.

"You have no fault, and I am sure I hope misfortune will always keep a long distance from you."

Miss Thorn felt flattered by Lord Danby's attentions.

"But tell me," resumed he, "did the mediæval youth possess ' six angels ' at one time?—not fair —certainly not fair."

"No; he has not the ' six angels ' now; the piece—the ' six-angel piece'—it is lost, and Mr. Barrymore is much vexed."

"I am sure I should vex myself for the loss of *one angel*—I cannot longer marvel, therefore, that upon so heavy a loss he has so absurd a visage.

It is curious," added he, as he gazed slowly round
the table—" it is curious, on such occasions as
these, to note the anxiety of each one to creep into
the wrong place."

" I do not know what you mean," replied Miss
Thorn, in her turn looking round ; but she saw no
incongruity.

" Ah ! you do not feel in the wrong place—
good !" said he, with a little laugh, which sounded
unpleasant in the ears of his companion.

Up to this time Miss Thorn had felt. very
comfortable in her place by Lord Danby's side,
but now she began to fear he was only amusing
himself at her expense.

" Look round, and I will explain. You see
Hamilton has Irene by his side, and he is very silent
and very solemn. The mediæval has Grel—he too
is silent, and very solemn. Maynooth has the
Barrymore, and though *she* is ever so handsome,
he does not care one straw; he has seen larger
spiders ! The Bishop holds the Roman Catholic
in pious conversation ; he is very tired, and she
very sleepy."

" Do you mean Mr. Cheetham, when you say
the ' Bishop?'—and is Miss Maynooth the ' Roman
Catholic ?' "

" I mean what I have said; then, you see,
Captain Fortescue has that curious little piece of
young ' Maidenhood,' Brenda Cheet-them—all on
the dexter side, and the village mother on the
sinister—not that she is sinister ; and Brenda does

not care for the posted Captain—how should she?
—he is married. As for the 'Pine,' in my
judgment she is too modest to live; she will melt
away before she comes to maturity, because she is
so afraid of everything and everybody."

" I do not understand half you have said to me."

" Then *I* am indeed mistaken; I thought you,
Miss Rose, were wiser than you admit. I should
have thought, to look at you, that you were not at
all dull; quite the reverse—rather sharp. But
since you confess your own short-comings, why, I
will give in. I also will become silent, which is a
difficulty, solemn, which is out of my line, and
dull, for the first time in my life. Miss Rose, you
ought to become very unhappy."

Lord Danby ceased his remarks, and Miss
Thorn reflected that when it suited him to talk
"nonsense" she should accept it only for its value,
and not assume that he really meant her to credit
his actual words. It was a species of conversation
to which she was entirely unaccustomed; but she
determined to improve herself if the occasion again
offered.

Soon afterwards Lord Danby said,

" You know we go to the theatre?"

" Yes; Lady Irene told me the arrangements
for the day. It will be late before we can turn
our faces homewards."

" Circa twelve of the clock; and then, Miss
Thorn, at what hour, think you, shall we arrive at
Prellsthorpe?"

"Circa three, ante-meridian—but there is a moon!" said she.

"Charming!—charming, Miss Rose!" said he now, with so broad a stare of admiration at his companion as to bring the colour vividly into her cheeks. "I knew you could not be dull—you are, in truth, most agreeable and piquante! Those few moments of silence so refreshed you—you dug deep down among the depths of your intellect, and discovered the word 'circa'—keep it. I intend to introduce it into private life—why should it be applied to dates only?—utter nonsense!"

And this was the beginning of Miss Thorn's intimacy with Lord Danby.

CHAPTER XXV.

"LOVE SEES NO FAULTS."

AS Lord Danby had said to Miss Thorn, it was curious that several had contrived to be seated exactly where he or she did not wish. The facts were that—

Mr. Hamilton wished to have the Lady Grel by his side. But he could not without rudeness leave the Lady Irene—with whom he happened to be conversing when dinner was announced—to cross the room for Grel. Mr. Maynooth had riveted his attention upon the Lady Irene ever after leav-

ing the poultry-show. No other face had made
even so small an impression upon him as to make
him conscious of its presence, although he spoke
to and shook hands with all, and apparently behaved as if he were as much present in mind as
he was in body. He was the tallest, and, for that
style of beauty, the handsomest gentleman of the
party; well made, on a large scale, and without any
superabundance of flesh. Erect in carriage, and
courteous and affable in manner, rather than dignified, he had many more admirers from this very
affability than Mr. Hamilton. His complexion,
originally fair, was now bronzed by exposure under
a tropical sun, but his hair still retained its light
colour, and its great luxuriance. His beard was
a marvel, even in these days of beards—very long
and silky, and wavy. Mr. Maynooth was a strong
contrast to the other handsome gentlemen of the
party, for they were all dark, with dark hair, or nearly
so. It happened that Mr. Maynooth took Miss Barrymore, and placed her by his side at dinner. She
was an old friend, and would not be offended at
his neglect, for he had set his heart upon watching "the lovely Lady Irene." Almeric Barrymore conducted Lady Grel—not for any particular reason, it so happened; and, indeed, he was
now too much out of health, and too low-spirited
to care to make himself agreeable, and Lady Grel
did not notice this, for she was watching Mr.
Hamilton !

The Lady Grel is only just seventeen and a

few months. She has seen no society but that of
Prellsthorpe Rectory—a society of the dullest and
most confined circle. That she had raised her
hopes in the future very high, on the arrival of
her relatives at the Park, is certain. That these
had died a natural death, through the persecution
she underwent from her cousin Lord Danby, is
also certain. The Lady Grel Stuart is naturally
of a thoughtful turn of mind, a great but indis-
criminate reader, and, as the phrase goes, an accomplished young lady. But she is inexperienced
in the society of gentlemen, and has a little inclination in her own mind to deify, to herself, handsome, clever, and those whom she supposes to be—
good men. Mr. Hamilton stood so high in the
estimation of her friends the Cheethams that, unconsciously, she had formed her own opinion upon
theirs. And because she had this high appreciation of him, it was a pleasure to her to sit silent, and,
amid the hubbub of the dinner, to watch him—
Mr. Hamilton!—to listen to every word he uttered, to note the musical inflections of his voice,
and mark his courtesy and polished manners. The
Lady Grel was glad that Mr. Barrymore was so
silent and inattentive, because she could the more
easily exercise her own will, and watch Mr. Hamilton unknown to any one but herself.

This is not an uncommon trait in "Maidenhood." The Lady Grel had by no means given
her heart—unasked as it would have been—to
Mr. Hamilton. She had only set up a shrine,

as " Maidenhood " will, for her own secret admiration and worship !

Now, it so happened that Almeric and the Lady Grel were seated exactly opposite to Miss Barrymore and Mr. Maynooth, and when the dinner was nearly over, by a mere accident, the Lady Grel bowed her head in acknowledgment of some trifling, and almost unconscious, courtesy from Mr. Maynooth, and their eyes met. Mindful of the Lady Irene alone, as he had been up to this time, for the moment he allowed his eyes to rest upon a face like that very one, already so powerful an attraction.

Wonderingly he returned again and again to this second face, and then a new charm was added, and the large man felt his chest heave and his cheeks tingle with a sudden glow, as he heard the dulcet tones of her voice in conversation, for a few minutes only, with Almeric Barrymore. Another sense had been touched. Always sensitive to melodious sounds, Mr. Maynooth listened for the rise and fall of that voice that had so powerfully, combined with the face, attracted him.

Well might Lord Danby say, " Though the Barrymore was ever so handsome, the traveller had seen larger spiders in his day." Mr. Maynooth was utterly unconscious of Miss Barrymore's presence, for while he watched the Lady Grel, and listened to her gentle and most musically-toned voice, he was powerfully aware of a certain witchery over his senses, and thraldom

over his will, he had never before experienced.
The quiet hum of the dinner proceeded ; the large
man raised his head, and gazed round the room,
as he said to himself,

" This will never do—I declare I cannot tell
what *is* the matter with me."

He felt as if he should like—nay, as if it were
necessary to conceal these new emotions from the
penetrating eyes of lookers-on. He pulled his
coat tightly round him, and began to button it, as
if to button his coat would necessarily shut out his
inexplicable sensations from those that were
present.

" Are you cold, Raymond ?" said Miss Barrymore, with a smile.

" I beg your pardon," said he, stooping from his
erect position.

" Are you cold ?" said she again, " for I see you
have buttoned up your coat."

" Ah ! I beg your pardon once more," said he,
now thoroughly aroused from his reverie. " You
may well ask if I am cold," added he, rapidly
unbuttoning his coat. " No, Zara, I certainly have
not a *cold* fit at this moment. I may have been
' absent,' for which I pray your compassion."

He then exerted himself to converse with Miss
Barrymore, but more for the purpose, as he
acknowledged to himself, of hiding his unprecedented sensitiveness from her, than for any other
reason. And then again, his desire to watch
those lovely *sisters*, as he concluded the *cousins*

were, made him—much to Zara's amusement, though she knew not the cause—give unexpected and out-of-the-way replies, as well as ask startling questions.

Only the Barrymores drove home immediately after dinner. The remainder of the party were to appear at the theatre—places had been taken. Lord Danby contrived that the Lady Irene should be under Mr. Hamilton's care; he himself secured the Lady Grel, in spite of his delight in the companionship of Miss Thorn. The rest of the party were seated as they pleased, excepting only Mr. Maynooth, who deliberately left them to enjoy the spectacle as much as they pleased, and walked away. Later in the evening, he entered an opposite box, and with his *lorgnette*, contrived to gaze on " those exquisitely lovely sisters."

When the festivities of the evening were over in Landeswold, the break came round, and the party set off for the moonlight drive to Prellsthorpe. But Mr. and Miss Maynooth took leave of their friends, and drove home in their own carriage.

" Dear Raymond, though I am so tired, I must tell you how much pleased I am with the Lady Irene; and it is my happy conviction that you admire her as much now as you did when you saw her at Prellsthorpe."

" I think, Yolande, I admire her sister more."

" Her sister!—oh ! if you change about in this

way, no good can ever come ; but what sister do you mean ?"

" Why, that very lovely Lady Grel."

" Lady Grel!—she is only a cousin of the Prellsthorpes."

" I do not care if she be a cousin, or only a quarter cousin—I say I admire her more than the Lady Irene."

" How strange you are, Raymond !—I quite despair of any woman ever fixing your wayward fancy."

" I marvel we did not see this lovely cousin when we called at Prellsthorpe."

" Nonsense, Raymond ; she lives at the Rectory."

" How can that be, Yolande ?"

Miss Maynooth then explained to her brother the reason for the Lady Grel's former and continued residence at the Rectory.

" Then why have not we known her before this, Yolande?   By-the-bye, why do we not call at Prellsthorpe Rectory ?"

" The Cheethams do not profess to visit, and they are a terribly long way from us," said Yolande.

" Then why do they act contrary to their profession ?—they do visit, for we have met them several times lately."

" While the Earl and Countess are at the Park, the Cheethams are necessarily there a good deal, and are thus drawn into more visiting than is usual with them."

"But why do not *we* visit them?" asked he, still thinking of the Lady Grel.

"We never have done, Raymond; they are out of our line."

"Oh! nonsense; no one is out of my line—no one who is respectable; and now, if it be only for the sake of the Lady Irene's lovely sister, I must call."

"Well, Raymond, you are more than ever *outré*. For all your whole life, you say, you have never seen a woman worth caring for, and now you suddenly fall in love with every woman you meet! Lady Grel is no handsomer than Lady Irene, only you perversely fancy so."

"Fall in love with every woman!—*I*, Yolande? —God help the women, then; but good night. There is something new and peculiar about me; perhaps I shall have come to my senses by to-morrow; and so, good night."

Once in his own apartment, Mr. Maynooth threw open the glass doors and seated himself in an easy-chair. Mytreberris—the name of Mr. Maynooth's residence—was beautifully situated, and equally distant from three small towns, Thorny-dyke, Stowe-in-the-Valley, and Prells-thorpe; it crowned the summit of a hill, looking down upon Stowe, lying like a gem in the valley beneath. The room Mr. Maynooth had entered was on the ground-floor, the windows opened upon

a flowery lawn, adorned—in the prevailing tastes
—by statues and fountains, with which the moon
now made merry by travesties of all kinds, as she
partially lighted up the scene here and there, the
better to bring out the contrast with the stern
dark shadows. Apparently Mr. Maynooth sat
listening to the splash of the fountains, and watching the vagaries caused by the moon ; but suddenly
he spoke,

"It comes to this; that I am a fool! After
wandering over hundreds of thousands of miles, and
gazing on all the women in all the near and all
the remote parts of the earth, to come home and
suddenly be struck all of a heap by two lovely
sisters—cousins I mean, can savour of nothing but
folly—egregious folly!"

We have recorded Mr. Maynooth's delight in
natural history. On this occasion the night birds
held their revels, the grasshopper-warbler continued its sibilous note—the *sylvia locustella* of
Latham ; the quail called *perdrix coturnix*, the
corn-crake, the night-jar or fern owl—there was a
considerable hooting also from the white owl. All
these broke on the stillness of the early part of
the night ; but, unlike Almeric Barrymore, whose
vigil we have described, Mr. Maynooth heard
them not. It must be admitted Mr. Barrymore
was *not* in love.

"When a man is a fool it is all up," resumed
he ; "I declare I have never once had that face
and those eyes out of my foolish head since I heard

the sound of her mellifluous voice! It went
through me like a shot! I do not wonder that I
took to buttoning up my coat, to hide my sensations
from the assembled throng. I am ashamed of them
at this moment, when I sit here alone—positively
blushing at nothing, like a girl in her teens.
If my beard is not ashamed of me, it ought to be,"
and then he stroked it down with much gentleness.
"Fancy a great big fellow like me, six feet four, if
he is an inch, with a beard eighteen inches long
from the root to the point—fancy me, sitting
mooning for a woman!"

"I suppose there never was on the face of the
earth, since Adam, a fellow in such a fix! Now
Adam had some reason to feel in a 'fix,' because
there was but *one* woman then; and if she would
not have him, he was pretty well 'fixed' for the
rest of his life. But here, on this blessed earth of
ours, I suppose if there is one woman there are
millions—millions of women! That there should
be millions of women from whom a man may
pick and choose, and be as dainty as he pleases ;
and that I should seat myself here, and make a
fool of myself for the sake of *one* only, seems
strange! I have read somewhere of a 'wise fool.'
Did he then get out of the scrape? When I can
recall his name and station, I will look him up ;
his example may be of use to me in this dilemma.
I declare I deserve to be painted and exhibited by
the Royal Academy, as 'the man with the woman
in his head!' I wonder how I look!" Mr. May-

nooth arose, and took a deliberate survey of himself in a large mirror; walking up and down the room, and returning again and again to the glass. "Sleep," resumed he, "oh, it is all a humbug, how can a man sleep with a woman in his head!" He reseated himself, and crossing one leg over the other, sat musing. "I know what I will do," said he, at length starting up eagerly, "I will smoke her out." He took a meerschaum and began to fill it as he went on with his talk, "I never knew a woman yet who could stand smoke, if you only give her enough of it! I will give her enough— I will get rid of her. But, bless her sweet angel looking face, and her thrilling and dulcet-toned voice—I do not like to part with her," and he placed the pipe on a table. "She is so unlike all others—a man would put his finger upon her, and pick her out from millions of other women. But what am I to do? I cannot waste my days in mooning. Ah! I see—I must smoke her out to-night, and then go and see her to-morrow, as a reward for my manliness." He then seated himself comfortably in his easy-chair, and lighted his pipe. "Not gone yet," said he, as he knocked the ashes out of his pipe and re-filled it. And so he went on throughout the night, smoking pipe after pipe without getting rid of the image of his fair tormentor. The morning broke, the night-birds vanished, the singing birds awoke, insect life hummed through the air, rural sounds were added to those of the birds and insects; but still Mr.

Maynooth smoked on. At six A.M. his dressing-room, which adjoined, was intruded upon by his servant, who prepared his bath, &c., and then he put aside the meershaum, as he said, " It is no go, she is such a charming creature, smoke has no effect ; in this, too, she differs from all other women! I have smoked out some thousands in my day—but *she* is too wise to permit such a liberty. I admire her the more for the stand she makes ; women ought to stand up for themselves until they are married. I wonder now if she is one of those whom Yolande said adored me, or does she differ from all other women in this also ? I must hope not ; or what is to become of me! I will ask Yolande while I think of it."

Mr. Maynooth went rapidly from his own room to the drawing-room, where he had left his sister on the previous evening ; but, to his surprise, he only stumbled on the housemaids at work. He stood for a second or two staring at them, and they ceased their work, and made their curtsies to him. He was going to say, " What on earth are you doing here ?" but. he suddenly recollected himself, and said :

" I want Miss Maynooth."

" She has not left her room yet, sir."

" Oh ! never mind," said he ; and he went back to his own apartments.

" I said I was a fool," said he, seating himself, and leaning his head upon his hand. " But I had no idea of the extent of my folly. If Almeric

Barrymore had done this, it would have been nothing to marvel at, for *he* is always in the clouds; but I, Raymond Maynooth, deliberately to sit up a whole night thinking only of this one charming woman, and forget that others are wise, and retire to their beds and sleep. I must dress first, and examine myself after."

When his morning toilette was completed, he resumed his soliloquy.

" I must ask Yolande if these lovely sisters— cousins, I mean—admired or adored me; she says all the girls admire me. God help them!" added he, stroking his beard—"if to fall in love, or to ' adore,' be to feel as I feel. Heigho!—I shall split the ceiling with my stentorian sighs."

Mr. Maynooth went to breakfast at the usual hour, and after the customary greetings of the morning, he said :

" It is no go, Yolande; she stands smoke like a chimney—the more you smoke her, the warmer she grows."

Miss Maynooth smiled, and shook her head, but made no reply.

" Was she one of that large lot you said ' adored me?' "

" You keep me quite in the dark, Raymond," said she.

" You told me yesterday ' all the women adored me.' "

" So they do—that is the misfortune," said Yolande.

"Never mind the misfortune. What I want more particularly to know is—do the two lovely sisters—that is, cousins, adore me?"

"Oh! the two ladies Stuart? I never heard either of them speak of you in any way," replied she.

"Of course not; I concluded *she* would be the exception. Give me some coffee."

CHAPTER XXVI.

"NO RAILLERY IS WORSE THAN THAT THAT IS TRUE."

YOLANDE had said but the truth to her brother—"the women adored him." Before retiring to rest after the long day at Landeswold, the Lady Irene had communed with herself, and acknowledged that she preferred Mr. Maynooth to Mr. Hamilton. She knew that by her own family the latter would be considered the more eligible match for her, and, therefore, she determined that she would keep her own counsel, and not betray her incipient liking for the Master of Mitreberris, and owner of Wolfscrag to any one. She had observed his patient watching of herself in the early part of the day, but she had *not* noticed the transfer of his allegiance to her cousin, Lady Grel. She knew it was in her own power to become upon very intimate terms with all these

houses—Prellsthorpe Abbey, Mitreberris, and
Wolfscrag—this latter, for the present, in the
occupation of Mistress Nuala Maynooth. She
determined that while she would never put a
slight upon Mr. Hamilton, nor let him see his
attentions were not valued, she would, by every
means in her power, increase her intercourse with
the Maynooths. She acknowledged Mr. Hamilton
was a remarkably handsome, and very gentlemanly man—one whom she must on no account put
aside. It is true, he had much more reserve of
manner than Mr. Maynooth, and she was by no
means so sure of his devotion to herself as the
neighbourhood had given him credit for. Ladies
generally had some slight awe of Mr. Hamilton,
and this gave him a greater value still in the eyes
of any lady he was supposed to prefer. This
enviable position the Lady Irene had now, and
she felt it would be unwise to resign it. But with
Mr. Maynooth the case was different. No one
stood in awe of him, and all ladies admired him.
His manners were affable, but at present he was
fancy free, unless she herself had been the
fortunate lady to touch his hitherto insensate
heart, as his constant, though quiet watchings in
the morning led her to infer. Most ladies talked
of *him* very unreservedly to his sister, and
declared their admiration. Yolande said they
were thus open-hearted, because she had so
sincerely made known " Raymond's infirmity "—
viz., " that he admired all the women under the

sun, that he loved them all, but that he could never dare to single out *one*, in the fear of offending all the others, and so he made much of his beard, and meant to live a bachelor."

It is true, he had a large number of "little sweethearts" up and down, and here and there in the county of Z——, from the ages of four to ten; but year by year, as these grew *into* "Maidenhood," they *grew out* of the notice of Raymond Maynooth.

" It would be something to attract such a man," said the Lady Irene, as she placed her head on her pillow; and as for his being a Roman Catholic, I determine *that* shall not stand in my way!" and the lady slept.

Miss Thorn and Miss Fortescue had returned in the break with the Lady Irene to Prellsthorpe; and it had been arranged that on the morrow Mr. Thorn and Captain Fortescue should lunch at Prellsthorpe, and take their daughters home. Lord Danby had made very good use of his time, and greatly increased his intimacy with Miss Thorn —many lookers-on would have said that the Lady Grel Stuart had now a powerful rival. He called Miss Thorn by many different names, but never Sara, and amused himself and her by his peculiar style of conversation, which at times—and with a laudable wish not to appear stupid in his eyes— she encouraged by adopting. It happened that Miss Thorn had complained in the course of the morning of a slight headache, and when they were all seated at luncheon, Lord Danby said to Mr. Thorn,

"The 'York and Lancaster' does not flourish at Prellsthorpe. Our air is not suited to such delicate plants. Stowe-in-the-Valley is very mild."

"Milder, certainly, than the air of Prellsthorpe," said the Vicar.

"I should think so, upon the principle that all valleys are more temperate than hills, and the inhabitants of lowlands slightly given to mildness of temperament also!"

There was a little satire in Lord Danby's tone, but the good Vicar heard nothing wrong, and immediately asked,

"But what do you mean by the 'York and Lancaster?' The old rose of that name? I thought it was gone, even from the gardens of our cottagers!"

"The rose, of course," said Lord Danby.

"Indeed, that will bloom anywhere," said the Vicar; "it is a hardy flower. I never cared much for it. Do you?"

"I admire the 'York and Lancaster,'" said Lord Danby adroitly, bowing to Miss Thorn, who blushed brilliantly; but again the Vicar saw nothing.

"Now, Miss Rose," resumed Lord Danby, "is there nothing here to suit your taste? We have no squirrel's eggs, I am sorry to say."

"Squirrel's eggs!" said the Vicar in a tone of surprise.

"The egg of a lady bantam is far too large for Miss Rose's delicate appetite."

"Her name is Sara," said the matter-of-fact Vicar with a smile; "my daughter Rosa is at home with her governess."

Lord Danby bowed, and then said to Mr. Thorn,

"But the reason I would get squirrels' eggs if I could for Miss—this daughter—is, that they might chance to be of a suitable size, and might sufficiently appease her small inclination to eat."

"But squirrels do not lay eggs," said the Vicar.

"That is a vulgar error, as you will find recorded by Mr. W. H. Edwards in his voyage up the River Amazon."

"Impossible!" said the Vicar in a tone of much surprise.

"D. read us the passage this morning," said the Lady Irene. "Miss Thorn and I were alike incredulous, until——"

"Until I gave them chapter and verse," interrupted Lord Danby; "and here it is again. Will you allow me to read it to you?"

"Do, pray do, D.," said the Lady Irene; and, accordingly, Lord Danby read aloud a part of the passage referred to.*

"I remember the passage well," said Captain Fortescue, "and I have always thought that

* See Note 10

writer's account of the River Amazon very interesting."

" Yes, it is interesting," said Lord Danby; "but
then it beats Maynooth hollow ! Does it not ?"

The Vicar was mystified, and did not reply.

" This must be true," said the Lady Irene.

" True !" said the Vicar ; " impossible !"

" You look at the book as if you thought I had
printed it !" said Lord Danby, offering it to the
Vicar, who, upon taking it, said courteously,

" No, indeed ! I should never suspect you of
anything so tedious, and altogether out of your
line, as to print a book. I thought, it is true, that
you had misread the passage," said the straightforward and honest old Vicar.

" You did !" said Lord Danby.

" Yes. I should not have wondered at—but—I
beg your pardon," added he heartily ; " I see the
passage is literally——"

" Word for word," interrupted Lord Danby.

" Exactly as you read it," said the Vicar, returning the book.

" Now, that beats Maynooth hollow," said Lord
Danby.

" Because it is true," said the Lady Irene. "But
Mr. Maynooth is a great favourite of mine, and I
will not hear a word against him."

" He is always a favourite with ladies," said the
Vicar.

" Except the ' York and Lancaster ;' she prefers
me," said Lord Danby. Sara Thorn blushed,

Captain Fortescue smiled and bowed to her, but the Vicar looked puzzled.

"D. has such strange ways of expressing himself, no wonder you do not understand him," said Lady Irene.

"It is all my own fault," said the humble-minded Vicar.

"No, indeed, it is all D.'s fault; is it not, Miss Thorn?"

"Lord Danby says I am misnamed Thorn, papa," said Sara.

"Does he, my dear? I make no doubt you will have plenty of opportunities to mend that accident," replied the Vicar, with a gratified laugh at his own wit.

"Yes, he says she is misnamed Thorn, and so he calls her Rose," said the Lady Irene.

"Ay, indeed," said the Vicar, "very good; but I though he meant her name was Rose."

"And it is not; it is Sara, which makes her a princess. Rose is only a flower," said Captain Fortescue, laughing. "But now tell us about the York and Lancaster?"

"He further deduces 'York and Lancaster' from her pink and white complexion," said Lady Irene.

"For the complexion," said the Vicar.

"Papa is always so matter-of-fact," said Miss Thorn.

"I understood you to say," said the Vicar, but Lord Danby interrupted him.

"Yes, you are right. I deduce 'York and Lancaster' from the complexion."

"From the complexion! Allow me to say I do not understand—what has the old rose to do with the complexion?" said the Vicar.

"Do you not see how it blooms on the Thorn?" said Lord Danby, pointing to Sara.

"Ah! my Lord, you are much too clever for me," said the Vicar, with a shake of the head.

"Do you believe in Maynooth?" said Lord Danby.

Now, if the good Vicar had answered impulsively, he would have said, "I believe in God," &c.,—but fortunately he drew in a long breath, and said,

"I like Mr. Maynooth very much. He is a neighbour—I mean not a very distant neighbour, and——"

"And he is very hospitable and very charitable," interrupted Lord Danby.

"He is, he is," said the Vicar in a glad tone, as if it were a relief to say something that really pleased him; "but as he is a Roman Catholic, we should naturally expect——"

"That he would speak the truth," added Lord Danby.

"The truth! of course. That was *not* what I meant to say," said Mr. Thorn.

"Your meaning to 'say' and mine may differ," said Lord Danby with a smile.

"But has he told you of any of the wonderful

sights he has seen in his travels?" said Lady Irene.

"I do not remember just at this moment," replied the Vicar in an attitude of thought.

"Mild—very," said Lord Danby to Captain Fortescue, who, if he heard, took no notice.

"But, Sir Vicar Stowe," said Lord Danby, "have you ever heard of the *Sipo Matador?*"*

The Vicar paused as if calling upon his memory, and then said,

"Do you mean the Spanish Picadors at the bull-fights? Of course, we have all heard of them."

"Ah! Sir Vicar, that will not do."

"My name is Ulric—rather a singular name," said the Vicar laughing; "and I have no lay title, I am neither Knight nor Baronet."

"Nor Knight Banneret made on the field of battle, I dare swear!" said Lord Danby.

"No," said the Vicar, stretching himself up, "only a plain parson."

"You misjudge yourself; you are handsome," replied Lord Danby, "only that has nothing to do with Maynooth."

"He is very handsome," said the Vicar,

"When Maynooth was travelling somewhere, he says, he saw a parasite grow up by the side of a tree and kill it."

"Kill it," said the Vicar. "How was that?"

"Yes, kill it. He described it to us when we

* See Note 11.

were at the Abbey *fête*, or at Landeswold—or somewhere."

"He has been a great traveller," said Captain Fortescue.

"Yes, his spiders are very large," said Lord Danby.

"And I assure you he saw one tree deliberately kill another. Now do you believe in Maynooth?"

"I never heard him recount such marvels," said the Vicar, "and I did not know he had seen such sights."

"Oh! yes, indeed he has," said Lady Irene, determined in her own mind to defend him against Lord Danby's attacks.

"Now do you believe in Maynooth?" persisted Lord Danby.

"You mean do I believe the story?" said the Vicar.

"No, indeed! I should not expect you to believe a lie—if you knew it—but do you not think this sounds more like invention than reality," said Lord Danby.

"I think travellers see wonderful things, and tell wonderful tales," said the Vicar; "think of Bruce, and Irby, and Mangles, and—"

"Thanks I do not wish," said Lord Danby.

"Mr. Maynooth has certainly been a great traveller," added the Vicar. "Will you allow me to ring for my carriage?"

And thus he tried to put an end to the conversation that had been more painful than pleasant, from first to last; for he did not understand one half Lord Danby said.

The Thorns and the Fortescues drove away at the same time. And Lord Danby declared to Lady Irene that the "Pine girl" was a fool, or deaf, or dumb, or, in all probability, all these. (The real truth was that she was shy!) That the Thorn was a beauty, a belle, a charming specimen of "Maidenhood," who amused him immensely, and who had more real talent than the better half of the county of Z——. That her excellent father was "too mild" to be endured, and that for the future the intimacy between Prellsthorpe and the Vicarage of Stowe-in-the-Valley must all be confined to the luxuriantly budding and gracious female Thorn! and that the "Pines," father, mother, and stupid daughter, might all become "coffins" as soon as they pleased for what he cared about them.

CHAPTER XXVII.

"POSSESSION IS ELEVEN POINTS IN THE LAW, AND THEY SAY THERE ARE BUT TWELVE"

AND now we must return to Heraldstowe, and chronicle all that has taken place there from the time of the Abbey *fête*. For though Almeric and Zara were present at the grand Poultry Show at Landeswold, they were both shown to be out of spirits, and unable to enjoy the day. One thing had occurred there that was favourable to Almeric's peculiar state of health, and this was that he came to an understanding with Lord Danby, to the purport that he had not played off any practical joke at Heraldstowe, nor in any way been a party to any such ill-behaviour in others. It may seem strange that this was a source of great comfort to Almeric; he had the greatest dread of being an object of ridicule to the county in general, and he was glad to be relieved from this dread. But then, if he was not the victim of a joke, what was the matter? He literally wanted time to think over all that had happened to him, and in the presence of his friends at Landeswold, as Lord Danby had said to Miss Thorn, " he sat silent, solemn, and sad."

After the scene with his great ancestor in Heraldstowe Park, Almeric became puzzled. But this took place before the poultry show—even before the Abbey *fête*. He was totally unconscious that he had slept, and he treated his dream as a terrible reality. He still persisted to himself that he did not believe in ghosts, in spite of all that was said of Heraldstowe, and of the presence there of such beings. He still continued to light up his rooms in the evening, and through the night; sometimes he watched till a late hour; sometimes he threw himself on a sofa in a train of thought, and afterwards dropped off to sleep unconsciously, and slept many hours. Miss Barrymore observed that he continued this practice of lighting up his rooms through the night, and at Dr. Quinn's request, attempted to ascertain from her brother the reason for so extraordinary a proceeding.

"Has he been dabbling in German metaphysics?" said Dr. Quinn. "Do you think he has been studying too hard, and so touched the nervous system? This attempt 'to throw light on the subject' in the hours of darkness, savours of nocturnal visitors. I rather mean, as if he were preparing himself at all points for some unusual, or, if not unusual, at least, not very desirable visitor."

"I have not heard him say," said Miss Barrymore.

"Of course you have not," said Dr. Quinn, with a smile. "If our patients would condescend to give us any clue to their vagaries, we might have a chance of soon bringing them round. At present his general health is but little altered— perhaps the pulse a little quicker, showing a little excitement in the system; otherwise—— But pray, my dear Miss Barrymore," said he, extending his hand as he rose to go, "do not let your usual spirits desert you. I must confess your brother *is* a little out of sorts—just a little. But we will soon put that right, I assure you—a mere nothing to me, though it does seem so formidable

to you. Sir Hildebrand, he is a wonder—a
perfect wonder, at his age, in the enjoyment of
such excellent health. Good morning—keep up
your spirits—good morning."

But this conversation, though in part so
hopeful, was not satisfactory to Miss Barrymore.
She determined to be very watchful over her
brother, and for this purpose she gave immediate
orders for the dismantling of her own apartments,
and for the arrangement for her use of those
rooms that joined her brother's, the dressing-room
of which opened into a small sitting-room, fitted
up for Almeric's use, and, indeed, *en suite* with
the rooms he occupied. Miss Barrymore did not
make known to her brother this contemplated
change in her locality until she had entirely
completed her arrangements. She took the
opportunity of their continued absence at the
Abbey *fête* for many consecutive hours, to have
all finally arranged to her satisfaction.

On their return home from this *fête*, Almeric
was particularly talkative, and for him, who was
usually quiet in manner, very imperious, and very
irritable. He thought he had now discovered a
solution to all that had puzzled him.

"If I had known that we should meet Lord
Danby at Prellsthorpe Abbey, I would have
remained at home."

"You and Lord Danby were formerly such
good friends," replied Miss Barrymore.

"Yes; but if there is one thing I hate more

than another, it is a practical joke ; and if there is one thing D. likes more than another, it is a hard practical joke. All is made clear to me now— clear as the sun at noonday. If I had only known of D.'s presence in the neighbourhood, I should have understood the matter long before this."

" What has puzzled you, Almeric?"

" He is very clever, and very lazy," replied he, following out his own thoughts, rather than replying to his sister's query ; " and because he has nothing to do himself, he tries to make others lazy also. How very angry and discomfited I should have been if I had fallen into his trap!"

" What has he done, Almeric?" said Miss Barrymore.

" Oh ! never mind, my dear sisse ; I spoke rather sharply to him, and perhaps he will· feel 'he has gone far enough."

And then, with a view to change the subject, he added,

" We must call at Prellsthorpe as soon as we can. I told Lady Irene that though our father did not fuss himself with the duties of morning calls, that I felt sure he would call at the Park !"

" Indeed he will not, Almeric ; he has quite for- gotten the Lady Irene, and he does not like Lord Danby. And as he never knew this Earl Prells- thorpe, I do not think dear father likely to make a call at the Park."

" Well, never mind all that; you and I must

call soon. And, Zara, Raymond Maynooth admires the Lady Irene."

"I am glad he admires somebody. Hitherto he has been a cold, insensate sort of—very handsome man."

And then, when Almeric and his sister alighted from their carriage—for all this talk had been as they drove home from the Abbey *fête*—and went up the stairs, and through the long corridors of Heraldstowe together, Miss Barrymore made known to her brother, "that her rooms were in an unusual state of decay, and that it was necessary to dismantle them entirely, and have them attended to. And that, meanwhile, she should take up her residence in the wing that he occupied, and in apartments contiguous to his, and Almeric was very much pleased with this arrangement.

By meeting with Lord Danby at Prellsthorpe Abbey the idea of a practical joke had been assured, and Almeric then felt certain that he had been the victim of a joke of this nature.

But yet, in spite of the warning he had given Lord Danby, viz., "that he would shoot him if he again intruded into the grounds at Heraldstowe," and also, in spite of his sister's presence in the same wing that he was accustomed to occupy, Almeric did not feel inclined to retire to rest without lighting up his apartments as has been before described. Miss Barrymore wisely made no remark, and this night also passed without any molestation from the Sieur Almeric.

Almeric arose the next morning in better health and in excellent spirits. We have omitted to make known that in passing through the hall, as he did several times a day—if he were alone—he invariably went up to his renowned ancestor and examined him, to try and discover if he had been in any way tampered with, and to prove to his own satisfaction that the coin still remained in the rerebrace.

He always found the statue in the same attitude, and if he touched the cloth sleeve that filled up the hollow in the rerebrace, he heard something rub or grate against the metal that convinced him the coin was still there.

On this day, that is, a few days after the Abbey *fête*, Sir Hildebrand had again mooted the question of sifting the soil in the Park, prompted, as we have seen, by Mr. Maynooth, to try to recover the coin; and Almeric, as he listened to his grandfather's remarks, determined to walk to Stowe-in-the-Valley and bring back a smith, who should take off the gauntlet, and thus, in all probability, set "the six-angel piece" at liberty, which, to preserve the Park from being broken up and intruded upon by workmen, he determined to take at once to Sir Hildebrand.

With this determination came a fresh temptation.

The well-known fact that the "first gold sovereign of Henry VII." had been carried off in the trimming of Miss Thorn's dress suggested the hope of recovering "the six-angel piece" by disturbing and sifting the soil in the Park. The supposed loss of the "six-angels," and the probable search through the Park, had already, as Almeric said to himself, "raised a hubbub in the County of Z—". On this account he felt unwilling to explain that he had all along had the "six-angels" in his own possession! We must do him the justice to acknowledge he wished most heartily to state the real circumstances exactly and truthfully to his sister and to Sir Hildebrand. But he felt an uneasy sense of ridicule creep over him, as he fancied himself questioned and bantered by the whole county. He wished to escape this ordeal if possible. And yet he did not feel equal to the making up of a lie! So contemptible a practice was opposed to his habits and principles. And yet, to state to his grandfather the actual facts of the case, would be to make them known to the county of Z——. Sir Hildebrand was so straightforward by nature, as well as so simple-minded, that if he promised, for Almeric's sake, never to repeat the history of the supposed loss of the coin, he would certainly be caught, on some occasion or other, telling somebody all about it. These considerations tempted Almeric at this moment to keep the "six angels," and not restore the coin to his grandfather.

As Almeric passed through the hall, with an intention of walking to Stowe-in-the-Valley, he made one more attempt to remove the gauntlet,

and save himself the journey. He did not succeed, and then he went his way to fetch a smith,
musing to himself how he could best give back
the coin if he decided to do so, but totally unob-
servant that he had so far disturbed the gauntlet
as to allow its own weight gradually to drag it
lower, and that it would eventually fall off!

"If I walk in with the coin in my hand, Zara
and grandpapa may probably assume I have found
it in the Park. I could not confirm them in this,
indeed I should not know what to say. I wish I
had never seen the coin—never touched it—never
troubled myself about it! If I do *not* return it,
the Park will be molested—if I *do* give it back, I
myself shall become a martyr to the queries of the
neighbourhood! If I were to repeat the history
of this coin, from the moment I took it from the
tray until this present moment, only my own near
and dear relatives would really credit my words.
It slipped into the rearbrace and I could not recover it. Yet I *saw* the Sieur Almeric throw it
down on the carpet in the library! Only the
clouds passing over the moon prevented me from
seeing where it lay, and seizing it at once. Who
would credit this? But it was so, of that I am
morally certain."

On his return with the smith, the man set to
work, and soon took off the gauntlet. It was
easy then to push anything out at the wrist that
had slipped in at the elbow joint; but strangely
enough the coin could not be found. Almeric

began to feel extremely annoyed and impatient; but he directed the man to remove the rearbrace from the elbow piece. This was done, and the rearbrace drawn off. There was no coin to be seen—none inside the piece of armour just removed, none about the cloth sleeve, or to be seen anywhere about the armour!

The smith stood looking on, while Almeric, forgetting the man's presence, became angry with his ancestor, with "the six-angel piece," with himself, and even with the poor smith standing there so humbly. At length, after some little lapse of time, and much ill-temper, and many hard words, Almeric felt that it would not do to keep the man waiting in the hall at Heraldstowe if he could be of no use, neither would it be wise to leave the statue without its arm!

He then explained to the man that some time previously he had dropped a coin into the arm through the joint at the elbow, and that it was for the purpose of recovering this coin, he had had the gauntlet and rearbrace removed.

The smith, like most of his fraternity, was a clever, clear-headed man, and after examining the statue and the padded arm, and the pieces of armour he had taken off, he assured Almeric there was no space nor interstice anywhere to conceal a coin, even so large as a sixpence! Reluctantly Almeric had the pieces of armour replaced and the statue put into his customary attitude. Then he allowed the smith to return to Stowe-in-the-Valley.

Left alone, Almeric walked up and down the hall in a strange perturbation of spirit. Now he returned strongly to his former supposition—he was the victim of a practical joke! What else could it be? He had seen Lord Danby at Prellsthorpe Abbey, and felt convinced then that *he* it was who was amusing himself at Almeric's expense!

But these were the real facts—hardly had Almeric passed out of sight, on his journey to Stowe to fetch a smith, before Palmer, the butler at Heraldstowe, happened to cross the hall, and saw the gauntlet fall from the hand of the Sieur Almeric. He took it up with an intention of replacing it, and then saw the edge of " the six-angel piece " protruding from the armour at the wrist !

" Now what coin can this be?" said he, as he drew it forth. " I do think the 'old witch' has dropped her glove * on the roof as she passed over Heraldstowe on her broom ; and that she must have had an especial dislike to ancient coins is clear; for all her ill-will falls upon that department of the arts." He stood closely examining the coin while he spoke. " A very wonderful coin, indeed ; I dare say Sir Hildebrand will be glad to see it, perhaps it has been in that statue ever since the old gentleman came from the Crusading Wars! I should not much wonder ; indeed, if one is to believe all one hears of these worthy barons in armour, one need not strain much to credit so small a thing as that——"

* See Note 12.

A bell rang at this moment.

"I must replace this gauntlet temporarily, for Sir Hildebrand cannot bear to see anything out of order."

In his hasty attempts to draw on the gauntlet he dropped the coin ; the bell rang again, and he put down the gauntlet and followed the coin with his eye, as he turned to leave the hall, but it rolled away from his sight, and he hastened to reply to the summons. On his return he thought it better to replace the gauntlet first. He did so, leaving it in a safe position ; then he turned to pick up the coin ; it was nowhere visible! He had seen it roll across the hall, and thought he should surely be able to find it as soon as he had time to look for it. But no—it was not to be seen!

"The house is ' bewitched ' in the matter of coins, as I have before said—the old lady has a spite against them. Humph ! perhaps it has rolled under some one of these statues, or at the back of some shield or other piece of armour." He fetched a long stick, and for some length of time poked under all the likely and unlikely places, but without any result. He never saw the coin again. Because he could not find the coin he never mentioned the fact that he had liberated it from the statue at the time the gauntlet fell off. Indeed he did not mention that the gauntlet had fallen ; he kept his own counsel in the fear of the consequences, and Almeric lost the coin.

The day after was the day of the grand Poultry

Show at Landeswold. As we have before recorded, Almeric and Zara met their friends there, and Lord Danby then convinced the former he had had no hand in the strange things that occurred at Heraldstowe.

The moment he met Almeric under the tent at the poultry show he grasped his hand heartily, and held him fast, in spite of his very reserved looks. He told him he must be labouring under some mistake.

"No, old friend, I will not resign your hand," said Lord Danby; "and though this is no place for explanations, I must insist that you will allow me to tell you you misjudge me in some way or other."

"I suspect you of a practical joke," said Almeric, even in his resentment too honest to conceal the truth.

"I see you suspect something; but you have hit upon an innocent person this time. I have not been near Heraldstowe, except once with Irene, to leave cards, for even the good Sir Hildebrand was not at home. And as we were absent when you and Miss Barrymore called at Prellsthorpe, I have had no opportunity until now of disabusing your mind of some wrong idea."

Almeric was easily appeased, and, besides, he had no reason to suspect Lord Danby of a deliberate falsehood; and, oddly enough, the fact that he was *not* the victim of a practical joke—for he could not reasonably suspect any other person—

and, therefore, *not* likely to become a laughing-stock to the county, was, for the time being, a positive relief. He left the poultry show almost immediately after this conversation with Lord Danby. He wanted to be alone, to reflect on all the peculiar circumstances that had happened to him. If, then, he was *not* the victim of a practical joke, what was the matter with him? The armour in the hall could not move of its own accord! Ghosts he must put out of the question —he never would be brought to believe in such myths. Optical delusions were possible, but hardly practicable at Heraldstowe, and certainly not without apparatus of some kind—at least, not such as had troubled him. And then he recalled the morning on which he had first seen the form of his ancestor in his own room; he remembered how very little this appearance had disturbed him —indeed, he suffered his mind to dwell upon it as a curious illusion, probably to be accounted for by the vividness of his own imagination. The scene in the library arose before him with such startling clearness, he impulsively looked round, and almost expected to see his ancestor walking by his side. On his recollection of the scene in the Park, he shuddered, though he acknowledged that the squirrels were as plentiful as before he had seen them so unsparingly murdered, and he was quite sure he had seen his pet as he drove through the Park.

All these occurrences were wonderful, and he

felt he could not account for them. If he had spoken at the time, they could have been explained, but Almeric always said to himself,

"Who but my father and my sister will credit me if I recount such very strange events?"

And, besides, he had no thought that there could be any explanation given that could prove these incidents to be only ordinary accidents, capable of a very simple solution.

And then, what had become of the coin?—that was more extraordinary than all the rest, because he himself had let it slip into the armour, and he himself had seen the Baron Almeric throw it down on the carpet! Had he, the Baron, then thought better on that subject! He had pocketed the snuff-box, and then changed his mind, and replaced it on the table. He had thrown down the coin on the carpet—had he then taken it back, and put it into his pocket! But the suit of armour had not a pocket! And as these thoughts and many others went through his brain as he sat at dinner at Landeswold, it is no marvel that Lord Danby pointed him out to Miss Thorn as "solemn, silent, and gloomy." But as they drove home, Miss Barrymore, who had not noticed him so much in Landeswold, discovered that her brother had quite lost his usual buoyant spirits. He was almost too much absorbed in his own thoughts to converse at all. Nevertheless, she made many attempts to draw him out of himself.

"He has been reading some strange German

books, I feel sure," said she to herself; "he has
filled his mind with the tricks of some Mephisto-
pheles, and now half dreads being carried off like
some second Faust."

Almeric at length, out of pure good-nature to
his sister, made an attempt at cheerfulness; but
he did not succeed in blinding his amiable relative
to the fact that he was suffering from some severe
depression of mind. For some days after the
grand Poultry Show this depression appeared to
increase. Even Sir Hildebrand at length took
alarm at the strangeness in Almeric's appearance.
But Almeric himself always declared he was
perfectly well. He was indignant at being placed
in the hands of Dr. Quinn, and that excellent
gentleman was therefore requested by Miss
Barrymore to discontinue his visits until she could
fix a day to receive him at dinner. Then, strange
to say, in the course of only a day or two afterwards, and before Dr. Quinn dined at Heraldstowe, Almeric recovered his spirits entirely, and
his good looks in part. The reason for this
change lay in the following facts:—

Miss Barrymore had given him a new purse,
and he stood in the hall admiring it, as he was
passing through to the Park.

"I might as well transfer my money at once,"
said he.

He placed his hat and cane on the table, and
took out his old purse. He removed the gold
from one end, and placed it in the new purse.

Then, in attempting to transfer the silver from one purse to the other, he dropped a florin, and he saw it slowly roll round one of the famous ancestral suits of armour standing there. Almeric stooped, and with his cane tried to poke out the florin. He was fortunate, out it came, glittering in the sunshine. He stooped to take it up—lo! the " six-angel piece !"

If Almeric did rub his eyes, and gaze upon it with some degree of astonishment, it is no marvel. He stood for a second or two silent, examining the coin. Then he put it into his waistcoat pocket, and walked up to the renowned Sieur Almeric, and scanned the suit of armour from top to toe, as if he thought that, by some species of legerdemain unknown to himself, the Baron had put his hand into the pocket he had used on a former occasion, fetched out the coin, and deliberately chucked it behind the statue of his brother baron, on purpose to give Almeric a chance of recovering it.

" I shall begin to believe in ghosts soon," said Almeric, with a smile, as he finished his survey of the Baron.

He took the coin from his pocket and scrutinized it once more. Yes, it was undoubtedly the " six-angel piece of Edward VI." By what a wonderful chance he had again recovered the coin ! He replaced it in his waistcoat pocket, and then stood some minutes silently rapt in thought. He decided that the circumstances that restored it to him were so peculiar, that it would be unadvisable to speak of them to any one, satisfied as he felt in his own mind that to state what had really happened, with the most exact truth, would only be to cause a doubt of his word in the minds of those who did not know him as Sir Hildebrand and Zara did; and to tell these two all that had happened would be to bring them, in all probability, into the same focus of strange events as those that surrounded himself. He decided to place the coin in his own cabinet, but he recovered his spirits almost immediately after.

CHAPTER XXVIII.

" PHYSICIAN'S FAULTS ARE COVERED WITH EARTH, AND
RICH MEN'S WITH MONEY."

NEVERTHELESS, as had been pre-arranged, Dr. Quinn came to dine at Heraldstowe. The dinner proceeded much as all dinners do, and the conversation was unchecked in its easy flow, until a message was delivered to Miss Barrymore by one of the domestics, and as Almeric heard only a part, and that part excited his curiosity, he questioned his sister as to the meaning of it.

"Lee cannot come till Monday; he is engaged at the waterworks near Stowe," said she.

"What do you want with Lee?" asked Almeric.

" To overlook the men, and keep them from committing depredations," replied she.

"Overlook what men ?" said Almeric in a voice of astonishment.

" Dear Almeric, do not question me so," said Miss Barrymore, as she turned to converse with Dr. Quinn.

Sir Hildebrand and Miss Barrymore had agreed that now that Almeric's health seemed in a fair way of recovery, that—if the Park must be disturbed—it had better be immediately. But they had not taken Almeric into their counsels, from a wish to keep him as free from anxiety as possible. Unfortunately, he had now gathered enough to excite his suspicions, and make himself very uncomfortable.

He sat moody and silent, annoyed that Zara would not explain, and marvelling what set of workmen were to come to Heraldstowe, and for what kind of employment they had been engaged. But now, as on all occasions of discomfort since the loss of " the six-angel piece," his mind at once reverted to the coin, and again he began to run over in his thoughts how he could best restore it without explaining all the strange incidents connected with it. He feared the " workmen " were meant to be employed in the Park. This made him feel very angry, for though he had not been present when the Maynooths called, he had very strongly dissuaded Sir Hildebrand from this plan, and thought he had succeeded. As soon as an opportunity offered, he spoke again to Miss Barry-more.

" What men are coming, Zara ?—and what are they to do ?"

For one second Miss Barrymore hesitated as to whether she should again try to divert his atten-tion from the subject, or tell him the truth at once. she decided on the latter.

" They are to dig up the path through the Park, and search for the missing " six-angel piece."

" It shall not be !—it must not be ! Who has ordered this ?" said he in louder and more angry tones than usual with him, and entirely forgetting the halo of the dinner, and the presence of Dr. Quinn.

Sir Hildebrand and his guest were both for the moment dumb, through the effects of that well-bred surprise, incited by so extraordinary an in-fringement of the manners usual at dinner. This was succeeded in the former by alarm for the state of Almeric's health, and in the latter by a professional satisfaction but little comprehended by Sir Hildebrand and Miss Barrymore.

It will now be necessary to explain the words " professional satisfaction," which may otherwise be misunderstood. There are several kinds of " professional satisfaction," one of which belongs to members at the fag end of the host, whose " professional satisfaction " is gratified by a case of any kind, and any nature—so it do but " put money in their pockets." Such " professional satisfaction" is often tempted to keep a case in hand, to suit its own purpose. That is *not* what is meant.

Then there is the "professional satisfaction" of the able and experienced surgeon, when he is called to attend to a compound fracture of this or that, and who knows he must exert his utmost skill to save a limb, or perhaps even life itself to a patient. It is not an exaggeration to say that such a man has a " professional satisfaction " in the case itself, independant entirely of any feeling of compassion for the sufferer ; in his estimation it is an extraordinary case—there was a marvellous escape from this or that, and he has as much enjoyment in all the horrid detail of his work as an architect in the exquisite finish of this croquet or the wonderful sharpness of such finials. This is *not* what is meant. Dr. Quinn stood high in the profession, and he was also a man of a kind heart and sympathising mind. He saw Almeric's sudden change of temper with that kind of " professional satisfaction " that is ever on the watch for traits of manner, that more or less betray to the professional eye those hidden springs of human nature that are the exciting cause of many diseases.

" Hush ! Almeric, dear," said Miss Barrymore, as the blush of well-bred astonishment mantled in her cheeks.

" It is of no use, dear Sir, to dig up the Park !" said Almeric to Sir Hildebrand, and still speaking loudly. " The coin is not there !—it is not there, I assure you !"

Almeric spoke from his positive knowledge that the coin was safely placed in his own cabinet. But Dr. Quinn said to himself with that "professional satisfaction" and professional sagacity we have before mentioned,

"Here is the mischief—here is strong annoyance on some particular subject; hallucination perhaps."

And then, though it might appear to lookers-on that Dr. Quinn gave the best part of his time and attention to the excellent viands offered to him, it is, nevertheless, certain that no word or look from Almeric escaped his "professional penetration."

"Indeed, my dear boy," said Sir Hildebrand deprecatingly, "it is quite against my wish. I declare I have the most decided objection to have my Park so destroyed, and made no better, for the time being, than a Village green, where village children play. But then Raymond Maynooth put the case so strongly and so wisely, I saw the necessity of yielding; and if I must yield, let me do it graciously, and let the men have a chance to do their work well."

Dr. Quinn had not heard of the accident to the "six-angel piece." He was at a loss, therefore, for the moment, to account for the anxiety expressed on the countenances of the three, Sir Hildebrand, Miss Barrymore, and Almeric.

"I wish Raymond Maynooth would attend to his own park, and leave Heraldstowe to its own master. I shall tell him I dislike this interference and turning everything wrong. You, my dear grandfather, object to having the Park cut up—I have the strongest dislike to the plan, and Zara agrees with us—why then are we to be annoyed for the sake of Raymond Maynooth's opinion?"

Miss Barrymore turned to Dr. Quinn, and explained that they had been vexed by the loss of a valuable coin.

"It will indeed be a great pity to destroy the superb appearance of Heraldstowe Park, even temporarily," said Dr. Quinn, in a tone of sympathy.

"And for no purpose!" said Almeric, "that is what so discomposes me; that they will do this thing when I tell them the coin is not there."

In his anxiety to prevent what he called the desecration of the Park, he did not see he was on the very verge of calumniating himself.

"No purpose whatever!" said Dr Quinn, with "professional tact" coinciding with Almeric's views.

"Exactly so," replied Almeric, "the coin is not there."

"You see, my dear boy," said Sir Hildebrand again in a deprecating tone, "Maynooth thinks I owe it to the world at large, to the world of science and art, to leave no stone unturned in my efforts to recover 'the six-angel piece;' I appear to myself selfish, when I refuse to stir in this matter."

"And so he persuaded you 'to turn over the stones' in your Park," said Dr. Quinn, laughing;

"but since, as my friend Almeric says, the coin is not to be found there, it seems a pity—a great pity."

"It cannot be found there," said Almeric in a positive tone, "it is not there."

"My dear Almeric, why should you give so decisive an opinion!" said Miss Barrymore. "Each one who has heard the story agrees that the probability is, it fell from Miss Thorn's dress as she traversed the Park. And though I object as much as you or dear grandpapa can possibly—yet I also agree with Raymond Maynooth that the Park is the place to search; and that, if we search well, we may have a good chance of finding the coin."

"True, true," said Dr. Quinn, "there is certainly a chance."

"Why do you persist in saying it is not there?" said Miss Barrymore to Almeric.

He did not reply; and here again Dr. Quinn's "professional sagacity" was called into play. He observed that Miss Barrymore's abrupt question had caused his patient to change countenance, that he lost immediately that animated and almost angry decision of manner that had been prominent but just before; he bowed his head, half turned away, and looked almost as if some inward thought had deprived him of the power to reply.

Miss Barrymore looked from Almeric to Sir Hildebrand, who sat evidently awaiting Almeric's reply, and from Sir Hildebrand to Dr. Quinn. who adroitly turned to Sir Hildebrand, and improvised with "professional tact" an anecdote of a similar loss that had happened to a friend of his. This led the subject into a different channel. Almeric recovered from the shock of his own surprise at his own, as he said to himself, folly.

But Dr. Quinn's "professional wisdom" pointed out to him that there was a something on Almeric's mind that ought to be removed—that is, that *must* be removed before his health could be re-established.

"His mind has received a shock that, for the time being, has upset it—he has some *false* idea of the whereabouts of the coin, but the freaks of derangement of intellect are numberless. I am satisfied in my own mind that something connected with this coin is the cause of his illness— nothing extraordinary!" concluded professional nonchalance to itself.

Before Dr. Quinn took his departure from Heraldstowe, he had a private conversation with Miss Barrymore. He then ascertained positively that Almeric's illness commenced with the loss of the coins, and that he had always been an enthusiastic numismatist.

"We must humour him," said Dr. Quinn; "the shock has been too great for his strength; the disappointment of not recovering a coin dropped on your own carpet seems to have filled his mind with a strange sort of dismay. It was so simple a thing —none could doubt that the coins would all be recovered in a few minutes. And yet, you see, even weeks have passed, and one—and that, I am told, the most valuable—is still missing. It is this exceptional occurrence that has so upset him; it is the having seen the coins fall in the library— on the carpet in your own library, mark you—that makes him steadily set aside the supposition that it can be anywhere else. He is sure it is there on the carpet and *not* in the Park—we must humour him !"

But when he has had positive proof that one coin was carried away in the trimming of a lady's dress, can he not infer from that the possibility also of a second taking a like trip ?"

Dr. Quinn did not reply immediately; he was unwilling to acknowledge the extent of the mischief he thought he saw in Almeric's wilful tenacity to "one idea," in spite of the proof that had been offered to his intellect by the finding of "the first gold sovereign" at the stile. "Monomania" is a disagreeable word to use, and Dr. Quinn did not wish to distress Miss Barrymore needlessly.

" I should rather advise that, for the present at least, you defer to his opinion. If *he* says 'the coin is not there,' affect to rely upon his statement. Humour his vagaries ; do not argue with and excite him."

" Would you, then, advise us, for the sake of Almeric's health, to put aside the search in the Park ?"

Dr. Quinn smiled his "professional smile," and spoke in his habitually low-toned voice, as he said,

x 2

"It is not my wish to dictate to Sir Hildebrand what he shall or shall not do with his own property, or even to attempt to curb his efforts for the recovery of the coin in any way; my business is with my patient, and whatever I think likely to disturb the quiet of his mind I feel it a duty to point out. Therefore, if the search in the Park could be delayed for a week or ten days, and you could by that time make arrangements for Mr. Barrymore to change the scene, to travel about, see the world, enjoy himself, I think his health would have a better chance of re-establishment, and also he would escape the annoyance of seeing the Park in an uncomfortable state. Sir Hildebrand could then, after Mr. Barrymore's departure, proceed with his own plans, and my patient would be free from the danger of a resistance to his will."

Miss Barrymore did not reply. Dr. Quinn had hinted to her before this interview that it might be necessary to send Almeric away from home. She felt the responsibility, in his present state of health, of allowing him to go alone, and she knew Sir Hildebrand himself was not able to leave Heraldstowe and the comforts which had now become necessities to him.

"I can see into your difficulty," said Dr. Quinn with "professional penetration;" "you cannot be in two places at once, and you are necessary to the comfort both of your brother and Sir Hildebrand. But allow me to suggest that Mr. Barrymore may very well be permitted to travel with his personal attendant. He is by no means so ill as to require your care, though that may be considered an uncourteous opinion, for I freely admit we of the masculine gender are but in a desolate state when we are left to ourselves. But undoubtedly the grand desideratum for my young friend is to leave Heraldstowe—to leave the scene of his misadventure. The nervous system is shaken, no doubt by the continued absence of this one coin, that ought to have been found in one moment after its fall. You see he must have been annoyed with the sight of the treasures rolling over the carpet ; then he was worried by the long search ; then much startled, I make no doubt, by the recovery of one from an unlooked for or unthought of locality ; and then he finally settles down with the conviction that the most valuable coin is lodged in some place either out of reach or out of sight."

Was Dr. Quinn's " professional penetration " at fault, or did Miss Barrymore really change colour ? The learned physician paused in his long and recapitulatory speech, to treasure up in his memory these new signs. Miss Barrymore's distress increased rather than diminished. She did not speak, but the troubled state of her mind was expressed on her countenance.

" Have you any clue to this idea of mine ?— that your brother has the notion the coin is lodged in some unattainable place ?—or, perhaps, only attainable by some great discomfort, or destruction of some——"

Miss Barrymore prevented more suggestions from the learned and amiable physician by at once confessing her own carelessness on the morning that the coins were lost. And though she assured Dr. Quinn it would have been quite impossible that any person could have entered the library and stolen that particular coin, and remain undiscovered, he put up his finger deprecatingly, as he said, in a voice of satisfaction that astonished his listener,

"Excuse me, excuse me—I have it now ;" and then he added, in more gentle tones : "I thank you very much, my dear Miss Barrymore, for this revelation. Undoubtedly, your brother has from the first held to that 'one idea'—undoubtedly, he has all along felt convinced that the coin *was stolen* during the time the cabinet was left open."

Miss Barrymore clasped her hands together in mute distress of mind.

"Nothing at all unusual, I assure you," said Dr. Quinn ; "but it is of much importance to me to know these facts. Has he never hinted to you that he has this opinion ?"

"Yes ; on several occasions he has given me to understand *he* thought the coin had been stolen, but I have always explained to him it could not have been stolen."

"All wrong—quite wrong," replied Dr. Quinn, with a lugubrious shake of the head. "Humour him, agree with him ; he has 'a fixed idea'—let him tell you all about it. For, indeed, you might as well attempt to change the course of a hurricane by opposition, as to alter his opinion on this subject. We call it monomania. Ah! do not be disheartened with the word; there is nothing at all uncommon—indeed, monomania is much more frequent than the community at large suppose."

Dr. Quinn ceased speaking, but Miss Barrymore could not prevent the expression of her own sorrow from being visible; her eyes filled with tears, though she courageously restrained them from overflowing their boundaries.

"My dear young lady, you distress yourself unnecessarily. Mr. Barrymore, I make no doubt, will soon recover. For the time being, his mind is unequal to the daily demand; change of scene will restore him. New countries will fill his thoughts with new subjects; his physical strength will increase as this wear and tear of mind is done away with. And when we have him again in robust health of body, you will see this 'one idea' will have been pushed aside amid the crowd of new notions that he has seized upon in his travels."

"But Almeric has already seen so much of the world," suggested Miss Barrymore; "few young men have travelled more—that is in Europe."

"Humph! Has he been to Siberia?"

This was "professional irritability" at the continued opposition made to his decrees, and yet Dr. Quinn repented almost as soon as he had spoken. He resumed, therefore, in his ordinary tone, and with his usual courtesy,

"My meaning is this, to be quite plain and intelligible to you—my meaning is this: if Mr. Barrymore does not leave home, he may grow worse instead of better."

And thus "professional wisdom" spoke, at last, the absolute truth.

"If your brother has been all over the world, he must still leave Heraldstowe. I trust you now comprehend me, my dear young lady," added he, rising to depart.

And Dr. Quinn grasped Miss Barrymore's hand warmly as he took leave, and said:

"I have detained you too long already, but you will think over my words."

CHAPTER XXIX.

"CRAFT, COUNTING ALL THINGS, BRINGS NOTHING HOME."

ON the morning after the grand Poultry Show at Landeswold, Prellsthorpe Rectory was in an unusual state of repose. The inmates had not reached their home until nearly three o'clock, and then they were so exhausted by the long drive and the night air, as to render some kind of restorative necessary before retiring to rest. One consequence of these late hours was that the Lady Irene Stuart called at the Rectory and found Grel still in bed at four P.M.!

Strange times these for the Lady Grel, and a strange way, she thought, of spending her time. Accustomed all her life to rise early, these long mornings spent in bed could not be otherwise than destructive to her health. But Grel was unhappy, and, moreover, peculiarly situated. She could not open her heart to Brenda Cheetham, for Brenda was unamiable and satirical, and matters were not mended when they were submitted to Brenda. She could not make a confidante of her cousin Irene, for though she was not spiteful or malicious, like Brenda—at least, so Grel thought— there was a something in the character of each of the cousins that prevented harmony of thought or opinion between them.

She could not intrude her troubles upon Mrs. Cheetham because they were of a nature to cause a feeling of shyness in sensitive "Maidenhood," and, of course, to hold converse with her guardian, Mr. Cheetham, on such subjects was out of the question. Poor Grel! She envied her cousin, who was on friendly terms with Miss Barrymore, Miss Thorn, Miss Fortescue, and many others. In such cases—that is where companionship could be had—sensitive "Maidenhood" could whisper its troubles to a sister-maiden, and probably receive in return both counsel and advice.

Grel's great trouble was her cousin Danby. She had enjoyed the early part of the day at Landeswold, because she had been allowed to follow the bent of her own inclination. She had—as we have before said—secretly watched Mr. Hamilton. It is true he had not spoken to her, oftener than two or three times throughout the whole day. But she had caught his eye once or twice during dinner, and been satisfied with the expression she read there. Grel was not conscious of Mr. Maynooth's admiration of her cousin in the early part of the day as Irene herself was; but Irene was conscious of Mr. Hamilton's occasional glances at Grel. At the time, Irene cared not to fix Mr. Hamilton's attention upon herself, because *she* was satisfied she had attracted another, and in her estimation a greater prize. Meanwhile, as we have seen, Grel proved a more perfect magnet to Mr. Maynooth than Irene. Of this the cousins were both unconscious.

At the theatre—as we have stated—Lord Danby monopolized his cousin Grel, and in his peculiar way charged her with having attempted to make herself agreeable to Mr. Hamilton, though she had been so positively told he and Irene were very likely to become affianced. Grel winced at these words, and Lord Danby saw it; he charged her with, as he termed it, " that vilest conduct of Maidenhood," the loving a man *before* he had proposed to her. Grel was covered with burning blushes of shame—partly that Lord Danby should dare to take such liberties with her, and partly from a sort of wonder and almost awe—for she could not entirely deny even to herself—that she had "thought much of Mr. Hamilton." It is true she did not understand her own sensations, she had never attempted to analize them. But thus probed to the quick as she was by Lord Danby, Grel's position increased in misery the longer she remained in the theatre. Lord Danby had also upbraided her for taking the flowers Irene had thrown down in her pettishness before they drove off in the morning. Altogether Grel's innocent worship of Mr. Hamilton had been the cause of much uneasiness to herself; she was too honest to deny that her thoughts had wandered very much to Mr. Hamilton, and her cousin unfeelingly made the most of his penetration.

And before she slept, Grel wept at the memory of all the miseries the day in Landeswold had brought upon her; and when she awoke after her sleep, she wept again; as she remembered her own isolated position, her little knowledge of the world, and the few chances she had of increasing that knowledge. But she would not arise, and show her troubled face and tearful eyes to the Cheethams, and also to the domestics at the Rectory. Grel was too sensitive to exhibit herself thus.

But Irene came, and found her in bed at four P.M.! Poor Grel! how much she would have to explain to Irene that she would like to keep concealed! At least, as soon as she saw her cousin standing by the bed the dread that she should be *forced* into some kind of uncongenial explanation was rife within her.

Now Irene was *not* in the most amiable mood

when she thus intruded herself upon Grel. If truth must be told—and, at least, we may hope these chronicles are truthful—though Irene had not noticed the change in Mr. Maynooth's admiration of herself to her cousin Lady Grel, Miss Thorn had —and this had given rise to a conversation between the two ladies that greatly angered Irene. She then recalled to herself the facts of the previous day—Mr. Hamilton had been silent and inattentive during dinner, which she had allowed to pass un- noticed, because she had seen she was an attraction to Mr. Maynooth ; but then she had not supposed Grel was an absolute "loadstar" to Mr. Hamilton —neither had she for one moment suspected her new admirer, Mr. Maynooth, of transfering his allegiance !

But when Miss Thorn made clear to her—first, that Mr. Hamilton's glances had been directed towards Grel during the *greater* part of the time occupied by the dinner, and that Mr. Maynooth's were "actually rivetted" upon her at the close of the dinner, the Lady Irene became intensely ill- tempered. " Was that child Grel, so much less well- educated than herself, and in so much a more humble position—that very child, so much younger than herself "—she was four-and-twenty—" was she—this child—to attract the great prizes of the neighbourhood from her, so much more worthy the regard and the notice of worthy men ?" Irene was angry, she felt powerfully within herself—not without great cause.

But here she is at the Rectory, apparently trying to smother her displeasure, for Grel does not see it.

"I blush for my laziness," said Grel, hiding her face.

"What can be the matter, Grel? Are you really ill?"

The Lady Irene asked this in a tone that was not pleasant to Grel, she felt instantaneously that she was in the hands of her cousin Irene, as she always was with her cousin Danby; that however great her wish to conceal her thoughts and intentions, it was utterly impossible; by some sort of freemasonry entirely unknown to Grel her two cousins could always by their worldly lore probe her heart through and through.

"Irene, I am tired of my life."

This was real and truthful in Grel, and acknowledged from the conviction that Irene would know even if she, Grel, did not confess. But Irene did not so consider it.

"We are very sentimental after our great conquests!" said Irene with a sneer, for she thought Grel knew she had been an attraction to Mr. Maynooth and to Mr. Hamilton. But Grel did not know this. "And I see you have preserved the flowers," added she, as she alluded to the bouquet she herself had thrown away in the break, and that Grel had rescued from being trampled upon. "Tired of your life, Grel?—what has tired you?"

" D.," said Grel, again hiding her face.

" Why, D. adores you, Grel," said Irene with a
sinister smile, to try how far Grel credited this.

" It is not fair that D. should treat me so, Irene.
You know it is not fair. He means nothing himself ; but, then, if he makes this display of admiration or—or what he calls worship, in the
presence of others, what others, pray, will worship
me ?"

In this also the Lady Grel was truthful, according to her own knowledge, and in accordance with
her own aspirations in the future. She had reflected on the subject, and she felt sure, as long as
her cousin D. professed this worship to herself, no
other gentleman would come forward. If this was
a little precocious on the part of " Maidenhood," it
had arisen from the peculiar circumstances in
which the maiden was placed. But yet, truthfully
to chronicle, Grel had felt that this was her position at the present time.

Irene thought that surely Grel had seen Mr.
Hamilton's glances during dinner, and seen also
that transfer of the worship Mr. Maynooth had
certainly given to herself in the early part of the
day. She thought then that Grel was deeply
deceitful, to know all this, and to conceal it from
her kindhearted cousin !

But Grel did not know.

" Ah ! Grel," she at length said, " then I am to
understand that D.'s love and worship of yourself
prevent others more welcome to you from coming

forward. Mr. Hamilton, perhaps!" and she laughed a little laugh; "Mr. Maynooth it may be! Oh! no, I am mistaken there, Grel; *he* is a Roman Catholic, and so you would not think of him—at least I, kindly thinking of you, hope not. For your guardian would not allow you to marry a Roman Catholic, and——"

"Irene," interrupted Grel, "do you mean to point out to me that very tall gentleman with such a magnificent beard?"

"Yes, Grel. Mr. Maynooth."

"And is he a Roman Catholic? What a pity!"

"And why, pray, a pity?" said Irene pettishly, and suspecting Grel of a liking for Mr. Maynooth.

"Why a pity?" said Grel wonderingly. "Oh! I am sure I do not know, only he is so handsome and courteous, I think it is a great pity he is a Roman Catholic."

"Then you are not affianced to him, Grel?" said Irene.

"Irene, you know I have no admirer. Nor am I likely to have while D. bars—prevents——"

"Oh! yes. Then Mr. Hamilton, Grel?" said Irene, determined to dive into her cousin's thoughts.

"Mr. Hamilton is engaged to you, Irene. I do not know why you should insult me by that query," and Grel sighed.

"Dear me! how sentimental we are with our sighs and our denials. But now, Grel, will you be Lady Grel Barrymore?—tell me that."

"Irene, leave me. I am unhappy—I am tired of my life."

"Grel, love," said Irene, now coaxingly, and wishing to have her cousin under her own eye, and so make her of no account to the gentlemen of the neighbourhood by the strong contrast with her much more elegant and much better educated self—"Grel, love, dear papa sent me expressly this morning to ask you to stay at the Park. I should have been here earlier, but Mr. Thorn and Captain Fortescue came to luncheon, and I could not leave home until after they had taken their departure. But about D., Grel. Papa says, if you live in the same house with him for a few weeks you will become accustomed to his manner, which, really, is only playful, though you, I know, think differently. You cannot refuse my father, Grel; it would be so rude."

"I will tell my uncle I cannot come. I mean, Irene, I do not wish to be under the same roof with D. You look surprised, but you ought to know how very much he troubles me."

Irene suppressed the hasty words that arose to her lips, and said in gentler tones,

"If you come to Prellsthorpe and see D. as we see him, you will see his really good and amiable qualities, as well as the better understand those fits of playfulness that ought not to distress *you*, any more than Miss Thorn, or Brenda, or any of us. D. does not alarm his relatives by the practice of vices to which some of his age and rank are prone; call his actions 'follies' if you will, but then we laugh at folly. Why will you lay it so to heart?"

"I am glad to hear he has really resigned certain vices to which he succumbed a year or two since."

"Now, who could have told you this scandal of D.?" said Irene in a harsh tone, and then she added with a sneer, "Of course, these very excellent Cheethams!"

"Aunt Juliana wrote to me from Paris," said Grel, already lamenting her own honesty.

"Aunt Juliana might have employed her time better than by telling you such nonsense; and her heart might have been considered the kinder if she had refused her own belief in such levity, instead of adding to her own hardness by creating yours."

"Then I have been misinformed, Irene?—is it so?" said Grel.

"Oh! Grel, Grel," said Irene, shaking her head, "you know you credit the accusation!—you cannot deceive me. But pray why do you not accuse me as well as D.?"

Lady Grel, who had been sitting up in bed, now changed colour so perceptibly, as to arouse the Lady Irene's suspicions.

"Indeed!—indeed!" said she, as she arose from her chair, and approached Grel; "then Aunt Juliana said ill of me also? Oh! fie upon her, for her shameful gossips, and for you, Grel, for you to listen to such things, and credit them, is beyond my powers of——"

"You are wrong, Irene. Aunt Juliana did not say anything to me against you—pray calm yourself, and at least believe——"

"Oh! yes—I understand," said Irene, impatiently—"believe you are nervous and alarmed when D. attempts to amuse you with a little play. You hate him, Grel—my dear and only brother, full of life, and love, and kindness—real kindness of heart; you hate him, and affect to fear his nonsense. You may well blush, Grel—you ought to feel ashamed. You hate me also—I often see it in your face."

Impulsively Grel covered her face with her hands.

"But why do I stay here?—I will go—I will leave you to the repose you must certainly require," added Irene, in tones of strange mockery. "I will go to my dear father, and tell him of your hate towards your nearest relatives, and of your love for these very worthy Cheethams, who think it so right to allow your mind to be thus warped from its allegiance to its own kith and kin."

"Oh! stay, Irene—stay!" said Grel, stretching out her arms beseechingly; but the Lady Irene left the room with an angry toss of her head, and soon afterwards Grel heard her carriage drive away.

"Now what am I to do?" said Grel, springing

out of bed. "It is of no use to lie here to rid myself of my troubles by that means—I suppose, after all, I shall have to face them, and fight them."

This resolution was so unlike Grel's naturally amiable and pacific character, that at first she started at her own words.

"I sit and weep, because I do not know what to do. I feel as if I were in a net from which I could never escape. Why should Irene be so discomposed?—she knows I have only said the truth with regard to D.'s behaviour in past years. And it was Mrs. Cheetham, and not Aunt Juliana, who told me about Irene—that she, when she was in Paris, played as high as D. And then again, by some means unknown to me, both Irene and D. have the power of reading my very thoughts—I cannot conceal the most trifling thing from either of them. Not that I feel there is anything in myself or my thoughts that requires concealment; but that somehow, what I think, and what I do, seem to jar with their preconceived ideas of right and wrong. I have no one to advise me—I have no wish to do wrong; but, I am afraid, I must confess I do *not* like either Irene or D. And though I have so carefully tried always to be kind and amiable to them, and so to hide my want of affection, yet they see through all my poor attempts, and know that I do not love them. What shall I do? This will cause such quarrels, and torments, and troubles—

Y 2

this unpleasant conversation with Irene this morning."

But we must leave Grel to finish her toilette, and follow the Lady Irene as she drove away from Prellsthorpe Rectory.

"These Cheethams are the most abominable people under the sun," said she to herself, as soon as she was seated in the carriage. "Undoubtedly they support Grel in those stupid opinions of hers as to the proprieties of this life, that quite excite my resentment. What business has Grel to comment on D.'s behaviour here and there? I suppose he may do as he pleases without her consent—a little, puny-faced, foolish girl, as she is. And then, too, to bring me into the scrape! And who but these Cheethams can have told her, if Aunt Juliana have not? Grel affects great modesty as to her powers of attraction—it is all affectation; she knows she attracts. As for my friend, Mr. Hamilton, I am highly displeased with him. How well for me that Miss Thorn saw, though I did not, all that was going on. The glances of the Abbot"—Lord Danby and his sister, when alone together, spoke of Mr. Hamilton as the Abbot—"the desertion of the Spider" —Mr. Maynooth is indicated by the Spider— "and the clear, sharp eyes of Brenda Cheetham fixed upon dear D. Yes, as D. says, there *is* something in the 'Thorn,' and on that account I will befriend and make much of her; and the 'Pine' *is* a little stupid fool, as he also says, and

I am sure *I* do not care how soon she becomes ' a coffin '—so clever of dear D. !" and the Lady Irene laughed at the recollection of the conversation they had had at luncheon on that day. " It was a foolish, thoughtless slip of the hand, to throw away the Abbot's bouquet. He is a proud man, and proud men do not like to have their favours scorned. True, he ought not to have dethroned me—I rather mean, I *felt* that at the time, and I was wrong to show that I felt it. Grel might have done it, and looked the prettier for her waywardness. But *I* betrayed myself—betrayed my momentary annoyance, and opened the Abbot's eyes needlessly to that small imperfection in temper. The Abbot is a thoughtful man ; he will turn me over in his sagacious mind, and perhaps not like me the better for my discourtesy ; but he certainly thanked Grel in his heart for rescuing his flowers from—they were valuable and beautiful flowers—death. I have only myself to thank for having given Grel that advantage over me. She, I make no doubt, thinks more than she says on these matters ; but I will probe her to the very quick, and dear D. shall help me. But I am vexed about the flowers, because the conservatory at the Park is not yet in good bearing order, and the Abbot has all such things in perfection. I might as well—indeed, I must recover my false move—have profited by his stores until our own are in better order. But I must not allow this very proud and very wise Abbot to drive away from my mind the very large, and very handsome 'Spider.' The 'Thorn,' says Grel, was a perfect 'loadstar' to him for a few minutes. It might be so, and the 'Thorn' was right to tell me—right, because it is either a proof of her great simplicity of character, or of her greater comprehension of the ways of the world, and of what it will be proper for me to do to keep the 'Spider' and the 'Pearl' apart"—Grel means pearl, and the Lady Grel was sometimes called "Pearl" by her cousin Danby. "But who comes here?—we shall meet at the turn in the road. It is he—Mr. May-nooth."

With a feeling of gladness that quite sent away the vexations she had had in the course of the morning, Lady Irene smiled, and acknowledged the gentleman's bow.

NOTES.

NOTE 1.—" Biorn was sitting all alone at a huge table, with many flagons and glasses before him. It was his daily custom, by way of company, to have the armour of his ancestors, with closed vizors, placed all round the table at which he sat."—" *Sintram and his Companions*," *from the German of De la Motte Fouqué.*

NOTE 2.—" The six-angel piece is of beautiful workmanship; the figure of the angel is quite in the high Italian school, and might almost be termed Raffaelesque. The reverse—instead of an old ship or galley of the time of Edward III., accurately copied on some gold pieces up to this period, with a man whose scale reduces the ship to about the dimensions of a slipper-bath—has a fine ship of the sixteenth century, the grand original type of our three-deckers of the present day. It has a shield with the royal arms, on the side, behind which is a figure approaching to a proper proportion, and other figures are seen in the rigging, giving due effect to the dimensions of the vessel. This is, perhaps, the finest piece in the annals of English coinage, prior to the reform and introduction of the mill and screw under the government of Cromwell; it is, however, only a pattern, and, as coin, was never issued."—" *The Coins of England*," *fifth edition, 1848, by Henry Noel Humphreys.*

NOTE 3.—" There is not a suit in the Tower older than the time of Henry VII."—" *Critical Inquiry into Ancient Armour*," *by Sir S. Meyrick.*

Quoting from memory. we should say, the same writer

records, " 'That there is not in England a complete suit of armour before the time of Henry VII." But we have not the " Critical Inquiry" to refer to.

NOTE 4.—" It was the Emperor Charles V. who, with all the ideas of parade that had distinguished Maximilian, first collected armour for the purpose of show, and this he placed in the Castle of Ambras in the Tyrol, Ferdinand, his brother and successor, adding to its extent. Previously the arsenals contained weapons and munitions of war for actual service, and the suits were kept in closets, thence termed armouries. This new mode, however, being commenced by an Emperor whose renown not only made him envied but imitated through a spirit of rivalship, was speedily adopted by the sovereigns his neighbours and the petty princes of his own empire. But few specimens earlier than the time of his father were in existence, but it was easy to use contemporary ones either as they were, or with some fanciful alterations suggested by the pageants of the time, and assign to them names of antiquity. This idea, instead of being censured, was as readily copied as had been the spirit of collecting, and the more sedulously, as other parts of Europe do not appear to have possessed suits of armour of so old a date as those in Germany."—"*Ancient Arms and Armour at Goodrich Court, Herefordshire," from the Preface.*

NOTE 5.—" It is well known, for instance, that in certain states of the brain or nerves images of objects not present are perceived by the mind with a distinctness equal to reality. Now, when a person in the full exercise of his faculties perceives a figure which has no tangible existence, such an illusion requires for its production not only an impression to be made on the mind sufficiently strong to excite the idea of an apparition, but also of sufficient power to efface the impressions conveyed to the retina by the rays of light issuing from the objects that the apparition seems to conceal from sight. For suppose the figure appeared to be standing near a wall, then as every ray of light from the wall that previously produced an impression on the retina continues to act with a force equal to that imparted before the figure was seen, those rays which proceed from the points apparently covered by the apparition must, in some manner, be prevented from producing their accustomed impressions on the mind. Were this not the case, as really there is no object between the eye and the wall, the perfect vision of every point sending forth rays of light would preclude the possibility of the perception of any illusion. It must be evident, therefore, that in all spectral illusions visible in conjunction with real objects, the mind must possess the power of seeing not only images which have no tangible existence, but of seeing them also in opposition to the direct impressions of the perceptive organs."—"*Argument from Probability.*" *by Frederick C. Bakewell.*

NOTE 6.—" The great feature of the gold coins of this reign is, that Henry VII. first coined the double real (or royal). Twenty-two and a half such pieces to be coined out of the pound weight tower. On this piece the king is represented in the royal robes, as on the rials of France, and it thus might receive the name more legitimately than those of Edward IV.; but to distinguish it from the previous rial it was determined to call it a ' sovereign,' a term which disappeared after a few reigns, not to be again adopted till the great new coinage of 1817. Specimen 105, is the gold sovereign of this reign—the first coin bearing that name ; the legend is ' Henricus Dei Gracia rex Anglie et France, Dns Ibar.' "—"*The Coins of England.*"

NOTE 8.—" A vision may take place in the course of a lively dream, in which the patient, except in respect to the single subject of one strong impression, is or seems sensible of the real particulars of the scene around him, a state of slumber which often occurs—if he is so far conscious, for example, as to know that he is lying on his own bed, and surrounded by his own familiar furniture, at the time when the supposed apparition is manifested—it becomes almost in vain to argue with the visionary against the reality of his dream, since the spectre, though itself purely fanciful, is inserted amidst so many circumstances which he feels to be true beyond all doubt or question. That which is undeniably real becomes in a manner the warrant for the reality of the appearance to which doubt would otherwise be attached."—" *The Living and the Dead*," *by Sir Walter Scott.*

NOTE 9.—" Species *Mygale Avicularia*—a large spider. Two inches in length of body, but the legs expanded several inches, and the entire body and legs were covered with coarse grey and reddish hairs. I was attracted by a movement of the monster on a tree trunk, it was close beneath a deep crevice in a tree, across which was stretched a dense white web. The lower part of the web was broken, and two small birds, finches, were entangled in the pieces ; they were about the size of the English siskin, and I judged the two to be male and female. One was quite dead, the other lay under the body of the spider not quite dead, and was smeared with the filthy liquor or saliva exuded by the monster. I drove away the spider and took the birds, but the second soon died. The fact of Mygale sallying forth at night, mounting trees, and sucking the eggs and young of humming birds, was recorded long ago by Madame Merian and Pallissot de Beauvois, but, in the absence of confirmation, has come to be discredited."—" *Naturalist on the River Amazon*," *by Henry Walter Bates.*

NOTE 10.—" A letter from Senhor Godinho to his wife requested her to send us a singular pet animal, which the Senhor described as small, having a broad tail, with which, umbrella-like, it shielded itself from the rain, and a lightning-like capacity for moving among the trees, now at the bottom, and quicker than thought at the top. But most curious of all, and most positively certain, this little quadruped was hatched from an egg. We suggested to the

Senhor various animals, but our description of none answered. Of course curiosity was at boiling point. We had heard of furred animals with ducks bills, and hairy fish that chewed the cud; of other fishes that went on shore and climbed trees; of two-headed calves, and Siamese twins; but here at last was something unique—an animal hatched from an egg—more wonderful than Hydrargoses, and a speculation to make the fortunes of young men of enterprise. All day we waited and nothing came: the next morning dawned, the noon bell tolled, and we at last concluded that the Senhora had been loth to part with so singular a pet, and that the instructions of her honoured lord were to be unheeded. Dinner came, soup was on our plates, spoons were in our hands, and curiosity had expended itself by its own lashings, when a strange footstep was heard at the doorway, and a well-dressed, dusky Rachel appeared, bearing a carefully covered cuija intuitively to A——. Here was the wonder. What is it?—what can it be?—what is it like? Down went soup-spoons; suspense was painful. First unrolled a clean little white sheet, second another of the same, the slightest possible end of a tail protruded from under a third, a little round nose and a whisker peeped from the remaining cotton, and up leaped one of the prettiest little squirrels in the world. The little darling! Everybody wanted him—everybody played with him; and for a long time he was the pet of the family, running about the house as he listed."—*A Voyage up the River Amazon," by William H. Edwards.*

NOTE 11.—" *Sipó Matador*, or the murderer of Lima. It belongs to the fig order, and has been described and figured by Von Martius in the Atlas to Spix and Martius's Travels. It is obliged to support itself on a tree of another species. The way it sets about claiming support is peculiar and unlike other plants, and produces a certain disagreeable impression. It springs up close to the tree on which it intends to fix itself like a plastic mould over one side of the trunk of its supporter. It then puts forth from each side an arm-like branch, which grows rapidly, and looks as though a stream of sap were flowing and hardening as it went. This adheres closely to the trunk of the victim and the two arms meet on the opposite side and blend together. These arms are put forth at some regular intervals in mounting upwards, and the victim, when its stranger is full grown, becomes tightly clasped by a number of inflexible rings. These rings gradually grow larger as the murderer flourishes, rearing its crown of foliage to the sky mingled with that of its neighbour, and in course of time they kill it by stopping the flow of its sap. The strange spectacle then remains of the selfish parasite clasping in its arms the lifeless and decaying body of its victim which had been a help to its own growth. Its ends have been served—it has flowered and fruited, reproduced and disseminated its kind; and now when the dead trunk moulders away, its own end approaches; its support is gone, and itself also falls.

"The murderer Sipò exhibits in a more conspicuous manner than usual the struggle which necessarily exists amongst vegetable forms in these crowded forests, where individual is competing with individual and species with species, all striving to reach light and air in order to unfold their leaves and perfect their organs of fructification. All species entail in their successful struggles the injury or destruction of many of their neighbours or supporters, but the process in others is not so speaking to the eye as it is in the case of the Matador. The efforts to spread their roots are as strenuous in some plants and trees as the struggle to mount upwards is in others."—"*Naturalist on the River Amazon.*"

NOTE 12.—In the Northern and Midland Counties, when things happen untowardly, the common people say, "The old witch has dropped her glove on the roof."

ESD OF THE FIRST VOLUME.

www.ingramcontent.com/pod-product-compliance
Lightning Source LLC
Chambersburg PA
CBHW020931030726

47496CB00005B/1137